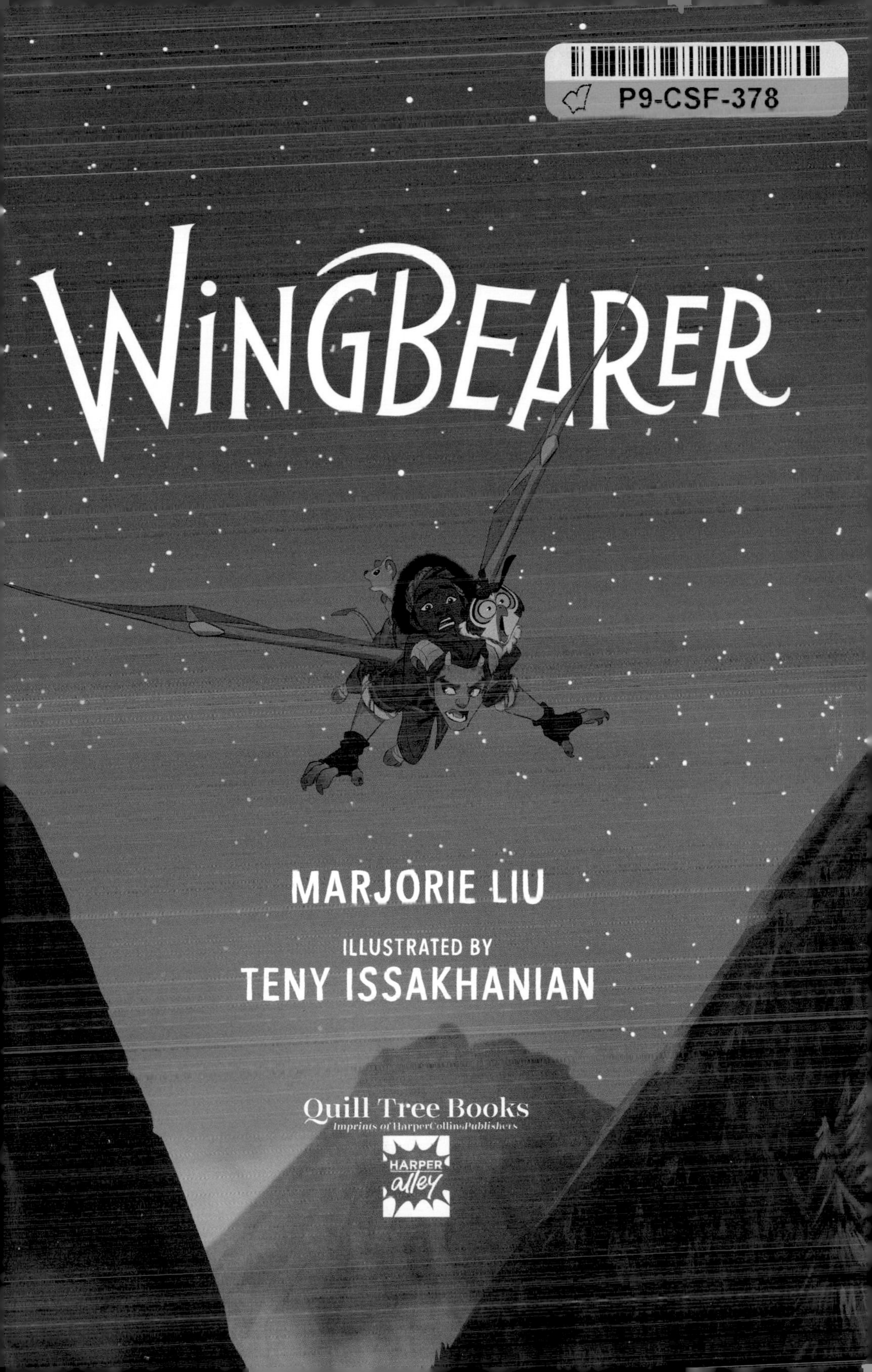

WINGBEARER

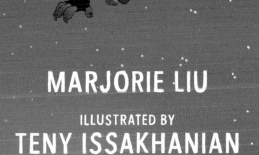

MARJORIE LIU

ILLUSTRATED BY
TENY ISSAKHANIAN

Quill Tree Books
Imprints of HarperCollins Publishers

HARPER
alley

Quill Tree Books is an imprint of HarperCollins Publishers.
HarperAlley is an imprint of HarperCollins Publishers.

Wingbearer
 For information address HarperCollins Children's Books, a division of HarperCollins Publishers, 195 Broadway, New York, NY 10007.
www.harperalley.com
Library of Congress Control Number: 2021942269

ISBN 978-0-06-274116-5 — ISBN 978-0-06-274115-8 (pbk.)

The artist used Adobe Photoshop to create the illustrations for this book.
Typography by Catherine San Juan
22 23 24 25 TC 10 9 8 7 6 5 4 3
First Edition

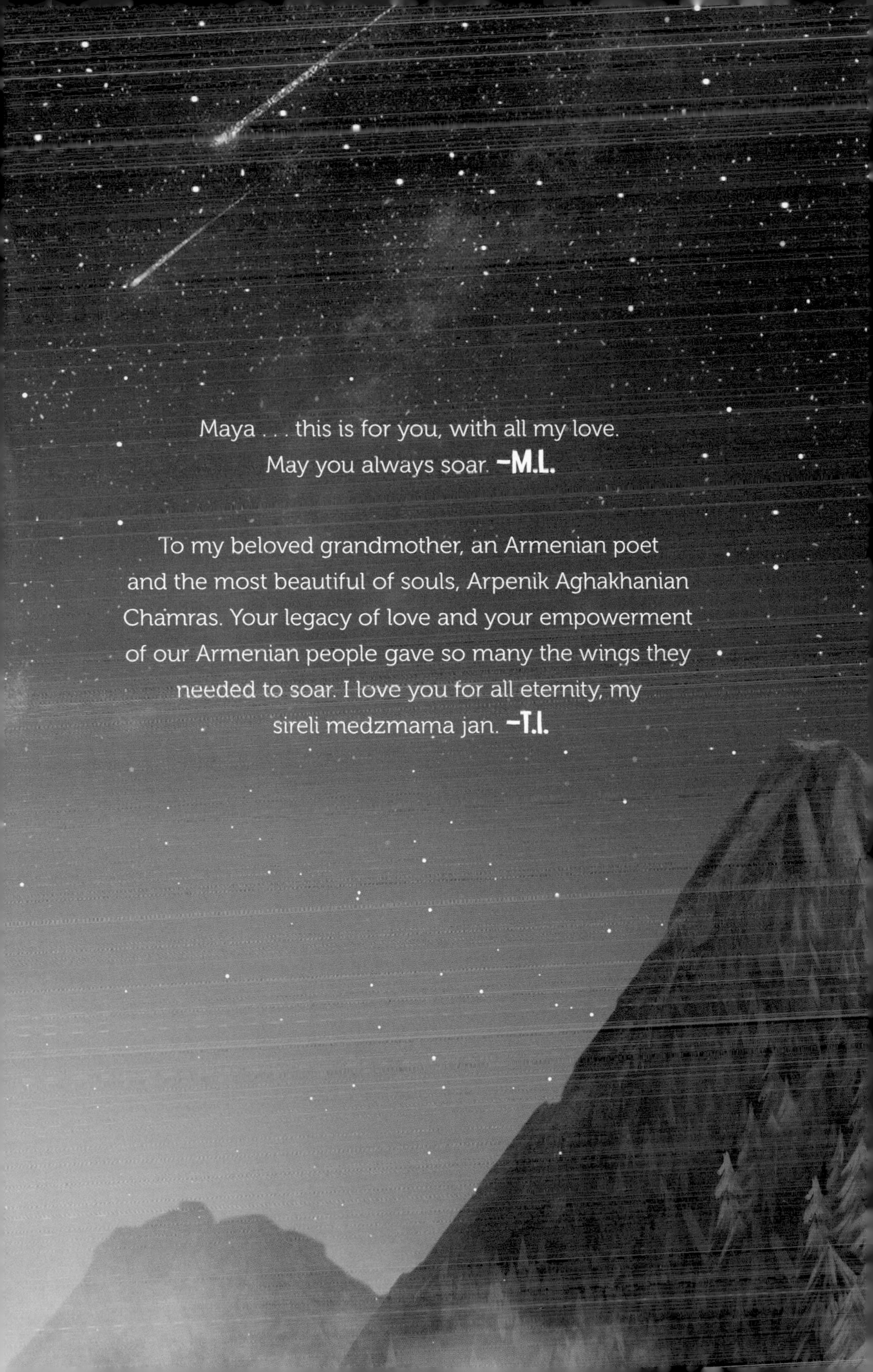

Maya . . . this is for you, with all my love.
May you always soar. **—M.L.**

To my beloved grandmother, an Armenian poet and the most beautiful of souls, Arpenik Aghakhanian Chamras. Your legacy of love and your empowerment of our Armenian people gave so many the wings they needed to soar. I love you for all eternity, my sireli medzmama jan. **—T.I.**

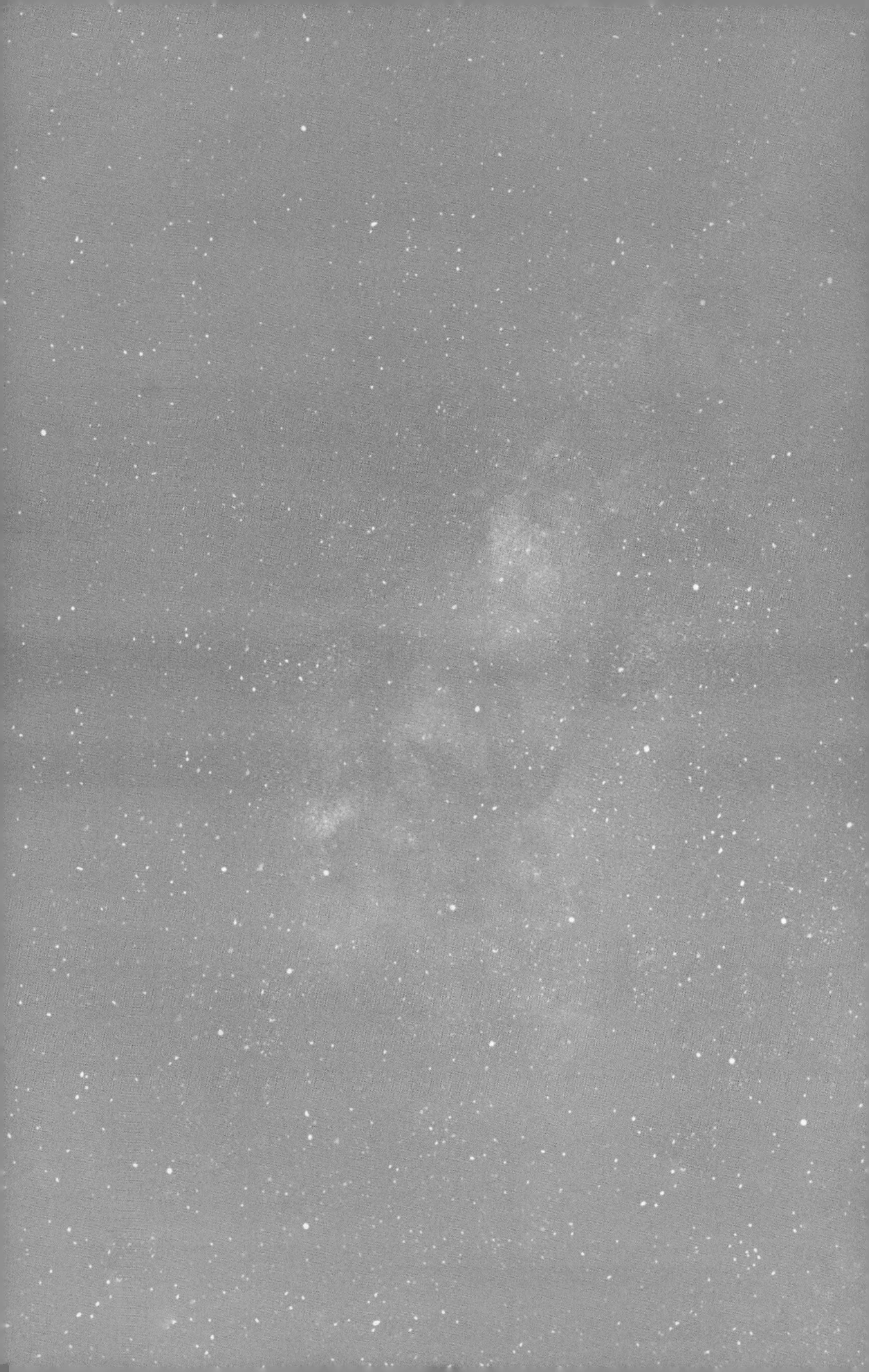

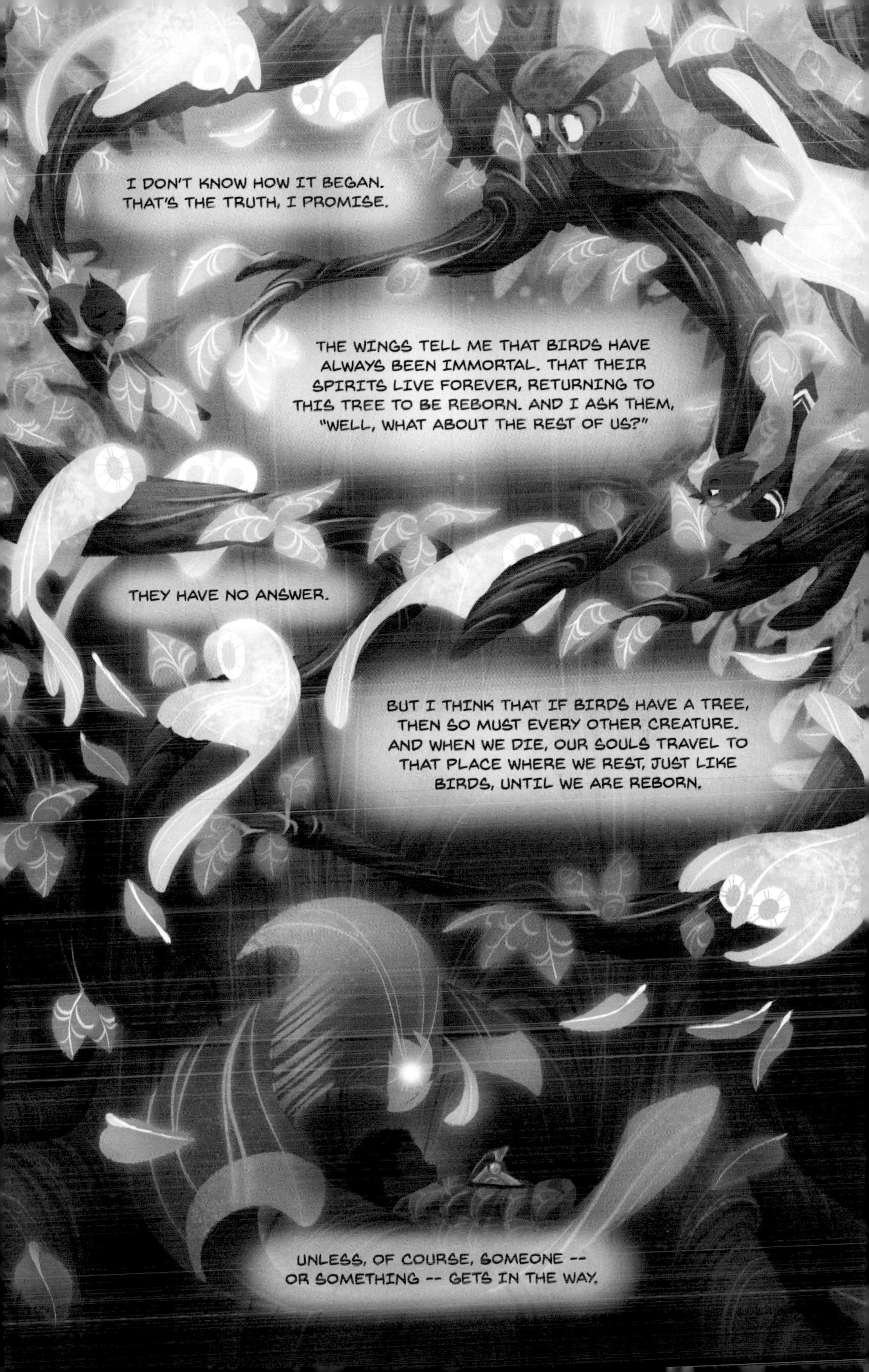
I DON'T KNOW HOW IT BEGAN. THAT'S THE TRUTH, I PROMISE.
THE WINGS TELL ME THAT BIRDS HAVE ALWAYS BEEN IMMORTAL. THAT THEIR SPIRITS LIVE FOREVER, RETURNING TO THIS TREE TO BE REBORN. AND I ASK THEM, "WELL, WHAT ABOUT THE REST OF US?"
THEY HAVE NO ANSWER.
BUT I THINK THAT IF BIRDS HAVE A TREE, THEN SO MUST EVERY OTHER CREATURE. AND WHEN WE DIE, OUR SOULS TRAVEL TO THAT PLACE WHERE WE REST, JUST LIKE BIRDS, UNTIL WE ARE REBORN.
UNLESS, OF COURSE, SOMEONE -- OR SOMETHING -- GETS IN THE WAY.

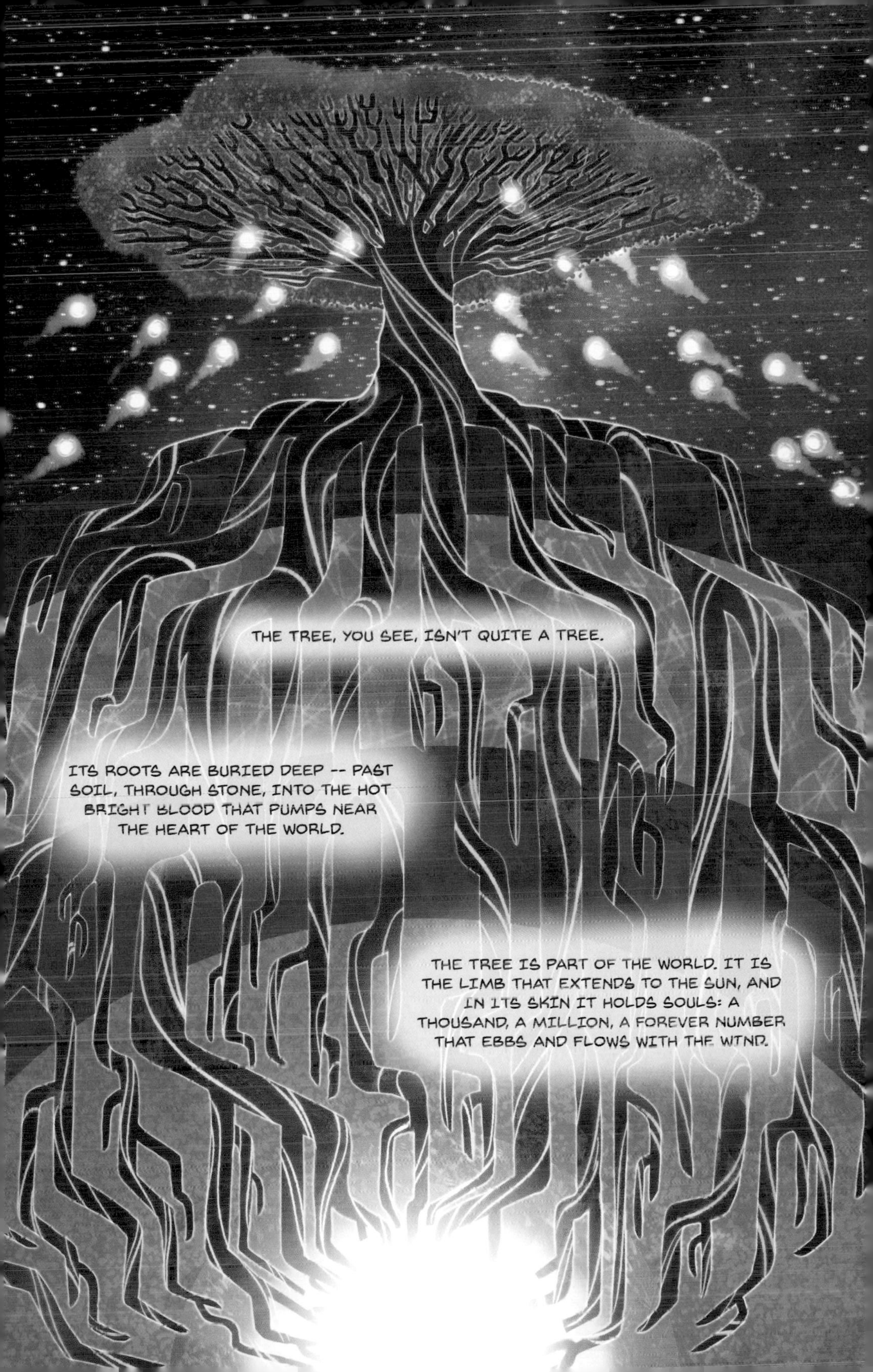
THE TREE, YOU SEE, ISN'T QUITE A TREE.
ITS ROOTS ARE BURIED DEEP -- PAST SOIL, THROUGH STONE, INTO THE HOT BRIGHT BLOOD THAT PUMPS NEAR THE HEART OF THE WORLD.
THE TREE IS PART OF THE WORLD. IT IS THE LIMB THAT EXTENDS TO THE SUN, AND IN ITS SKIN IT HOLDS SOULS: A THOUSAND, A MILLION, A FOREVER NUMBER THAT EBBS AND FLOWS WITH THE WIND.

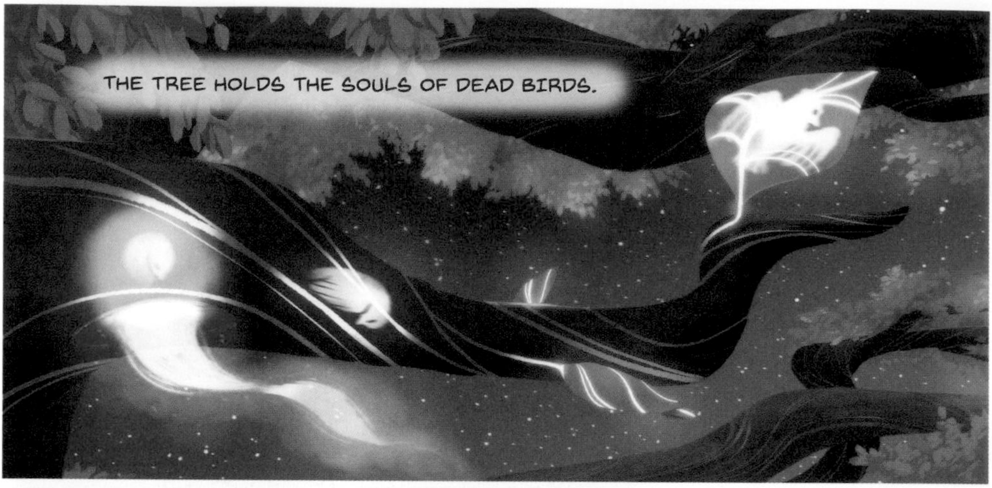
THE TREE HOLDS THE SOULS OF DEAD BIRDS.

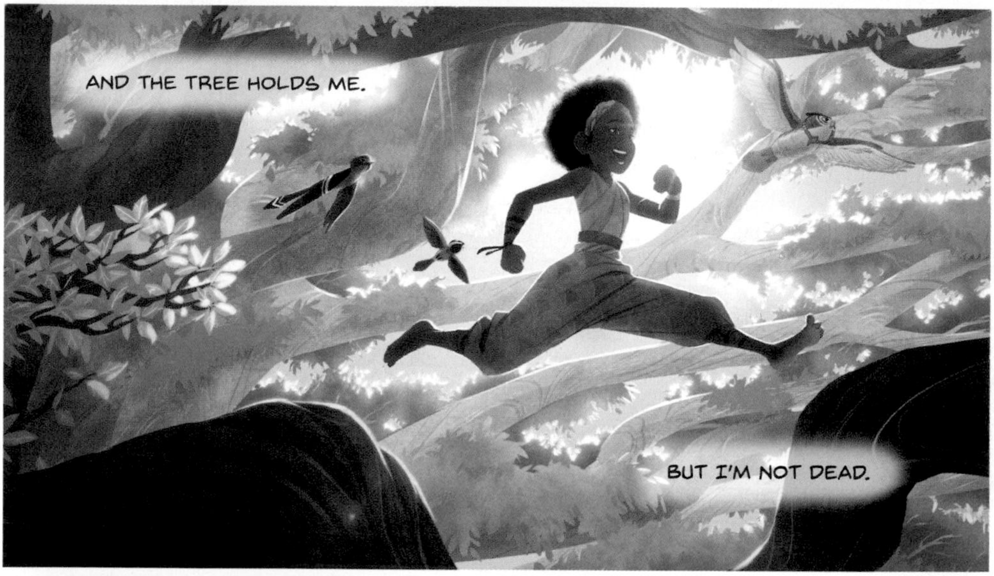
AND THE TREE HOLDS ME.
BUT I'M NOT DEAD.

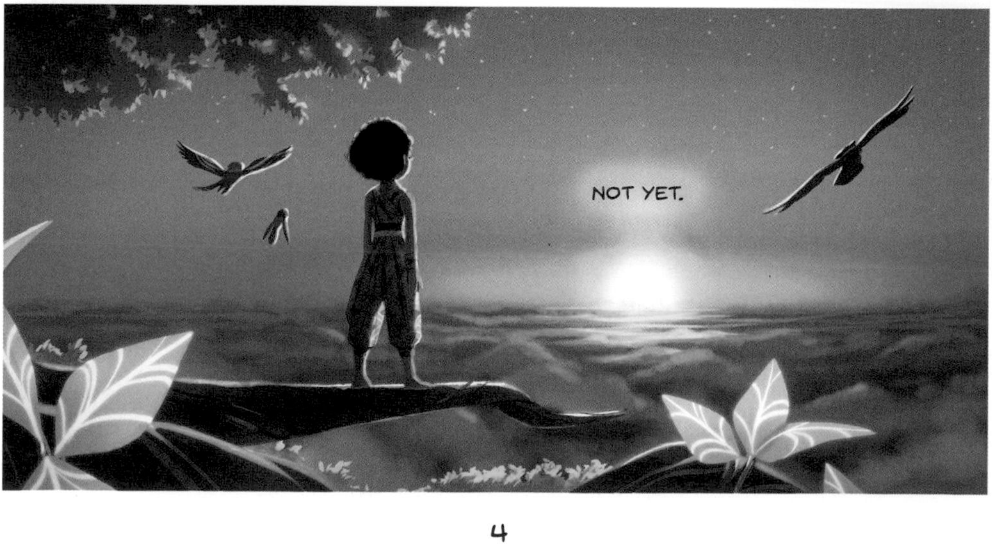
NOT YET.

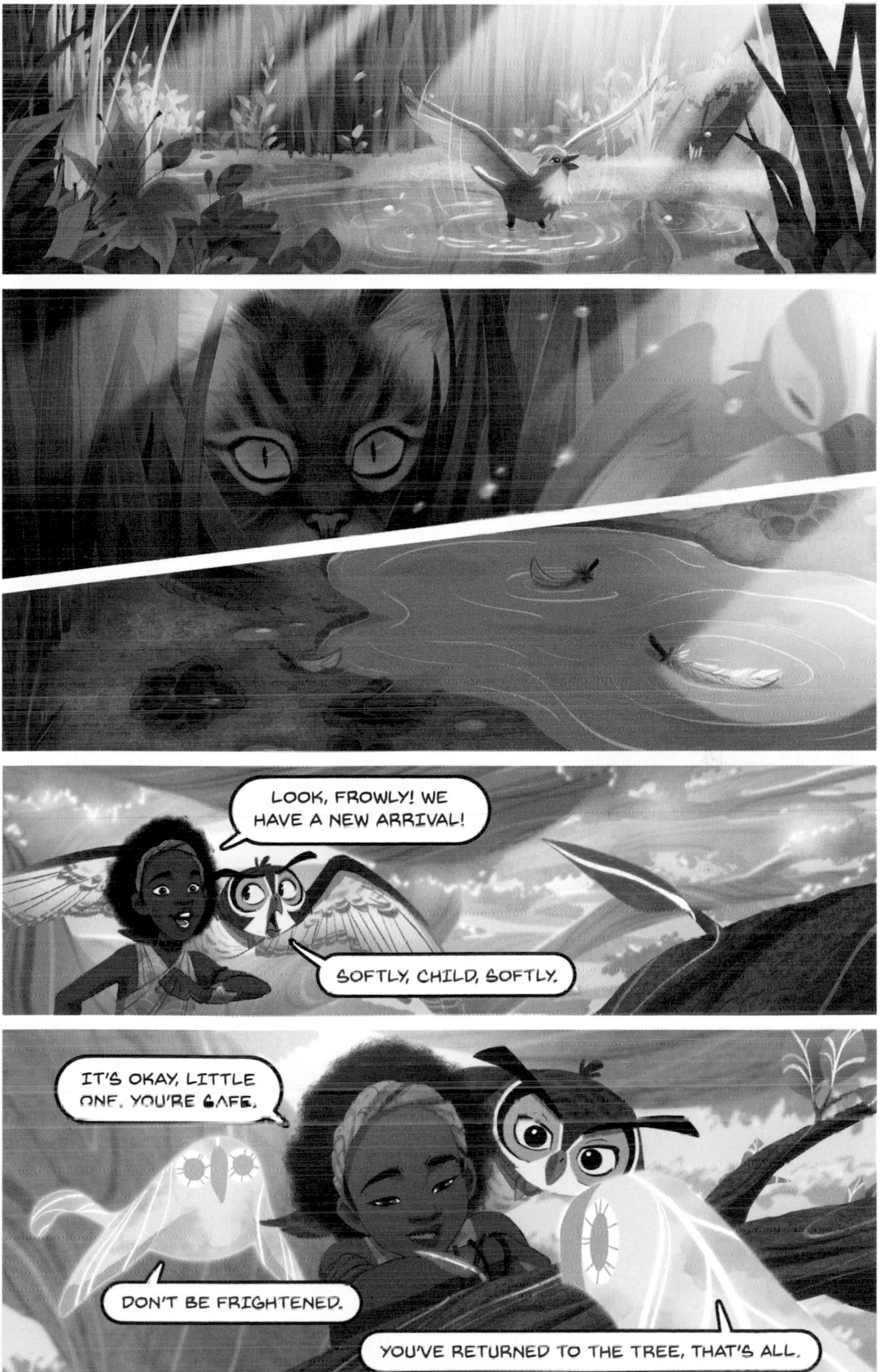
LOOK, FROWLY! WE HAVE A NEW ARRIVAL!
SOFTLY, CHILD, SOFTLY.
IT'S OKAY, LITTLE ONE. YOU'RE SAFE.
DON'T BE FRIGHTENED.
YOU'VE RETURNED TO THE TREE, THAT'S ALL.

8

ONE DAY THERE'LL BE A WHISPER.

THERE CAN'T BE JUST ONE OF ME. RIGHT, FROWLY?

IT'S NOT LIKELY. BUT ONE SHOULD NOT RUSH TO ASSUME.

THERE'S NOT JUST ONE OF ANYTHING. I KNOW THAT MUCH. WHERE I'M FROM MUST BE...VERY FAR AWAY, THAT'S ALL.

FAR FROM BIRDSONG.

NOTHING IS FAR FROM BIRDSONG, LITTLE ONE.

ESPECIALLY YOU.

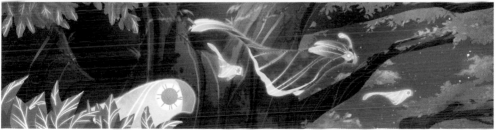

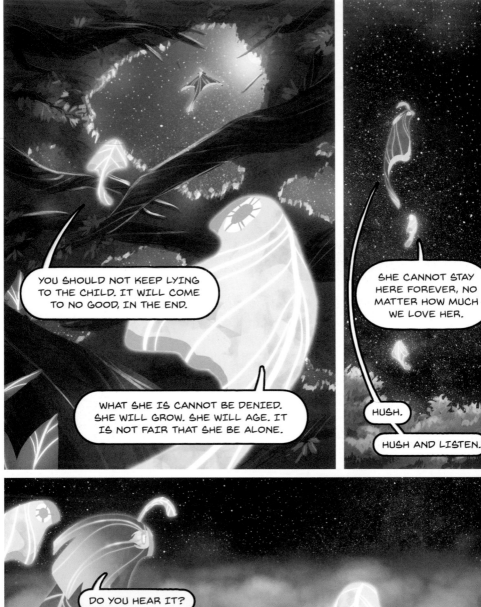

YOU SHOULD NOT KEEP LYING TO THE CHILD. IT WILL COME TO NO GOOD, IN THE END.

WHAT SHE IS CANNOT BE DENIED. SHE WILL GROW. SHE WILL AGE. IT IS NOT FAIR THAT SHE BE ALONE.

SHE CANNOT STAY HERE FOREVER, NO MATTER HOW MUCH WE LOVE HER.

HUSH.

HUSH AND LISTEN.

DO YOU HEAR IT?

THE SILENCE.

THERE ARE NO SOULS IN THE WIND.

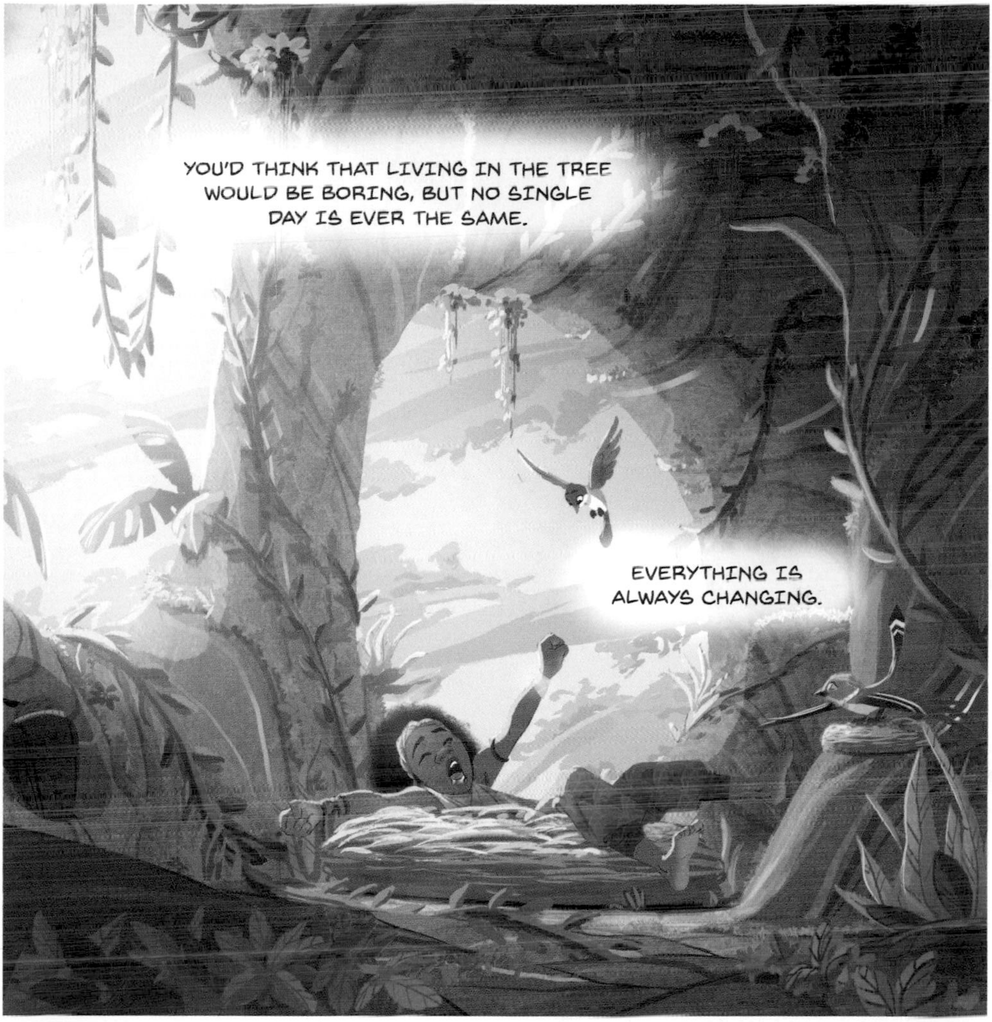
YOU'D THINK THAT LIVING IN THE TREE WOULD BE BORING, BUT NO SINGLE DAY IS EVER THE SAME.
EVERYTHING IS ALWAYS CHANGING.

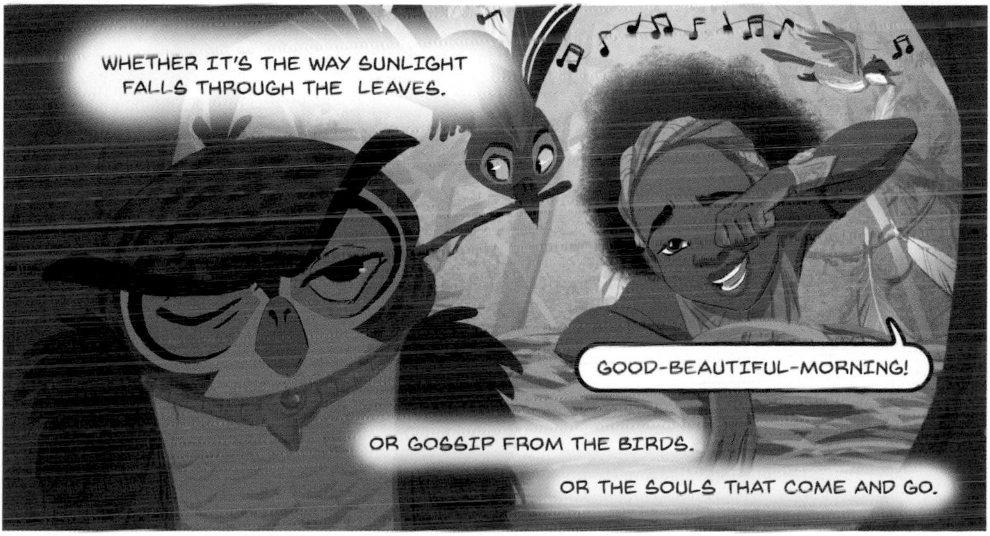
WHETHER IT'S THE WAY SUNLIGHT FALLS THROUGH THE LEAVES.
GOOD-BEAUTIFUL-MORNING!
OR GOSSIP FROM THE BIRDS.
OR THE SOULS THAT COME AND GO.

12

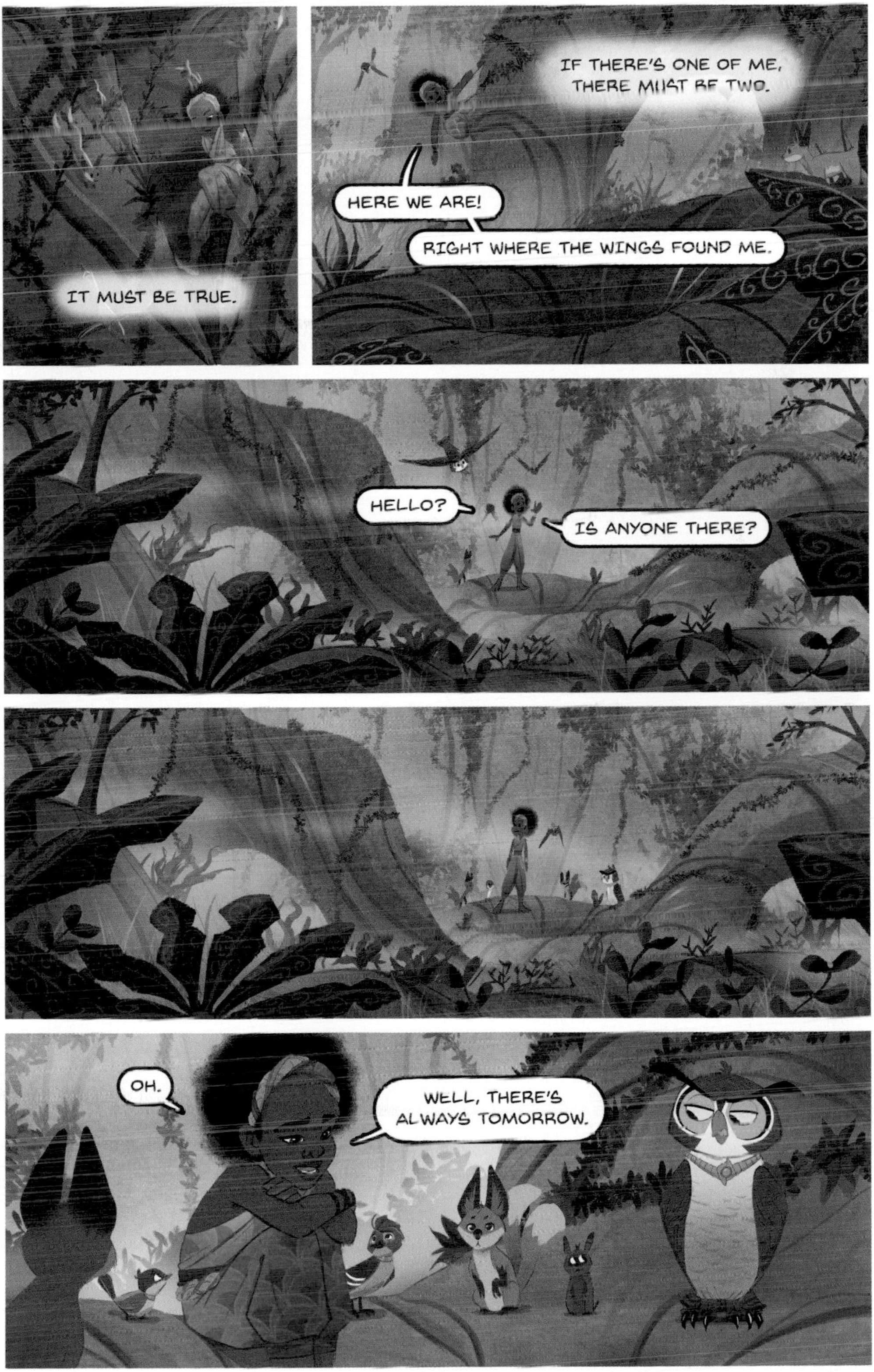
IT MUST BE TRUE.
IF THERE'S ONE OF ME, THERE MUST BE TWO.
HERE WE ARE!
RIGHT WHERE THE WINGS FOUND ME.
HELLO?
IS ANYONE THERE?
OH.
WELL, THERE'S ALWAYS TOMORROW.

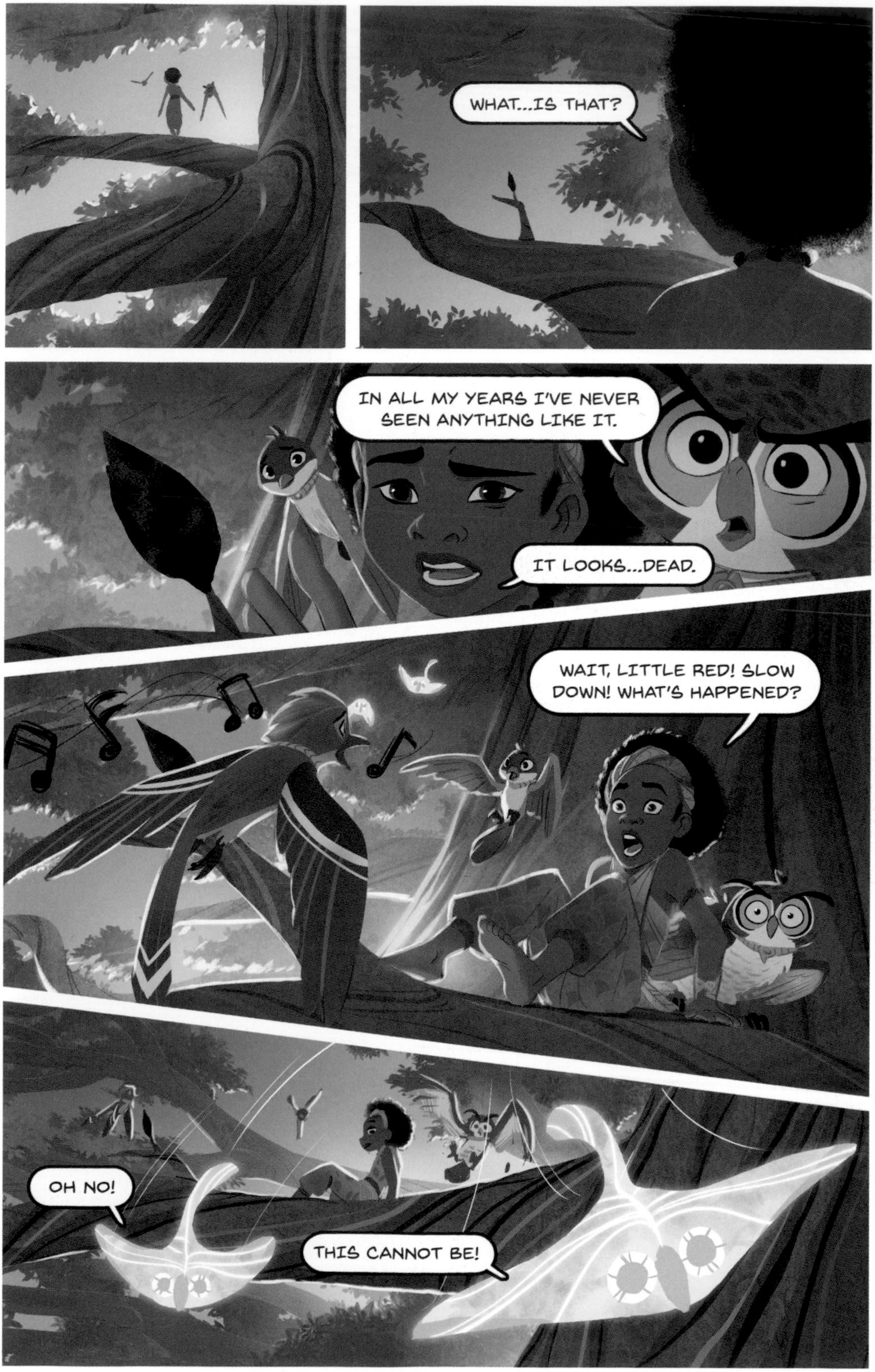
WHAT...IS THAT?
IN ALL MY YEARS I'VE NEVER SEEN ANYTHING LIKE IT.
IT LOOKS...DEAD.
WAIT, LITTLE RED! SLOW DOWN! WHAT'S HAPPENED?
OH NO!
THIS CANNOT BE!

16

NO, LITTLE ONE. FROM WHAT THE TREE TELLS US, THE WORLD OUTSIDE IS UNCHANGED.

BIRDS STILL LIVE AND DIE.

MAYBE...MAYBE BIRDS AREN'T DYING? JUST FOR A NIGHT...?

T'AIA, I'M GETTING REALLY SCARED.

I SUPPOSE YOU ARE RIGHT TO BE.

IF DEATH HAS NOT BEEN STOPPED...

...THEN SOMETHING IS HAPPENING TO THE SOULS OF THE BIRDS.

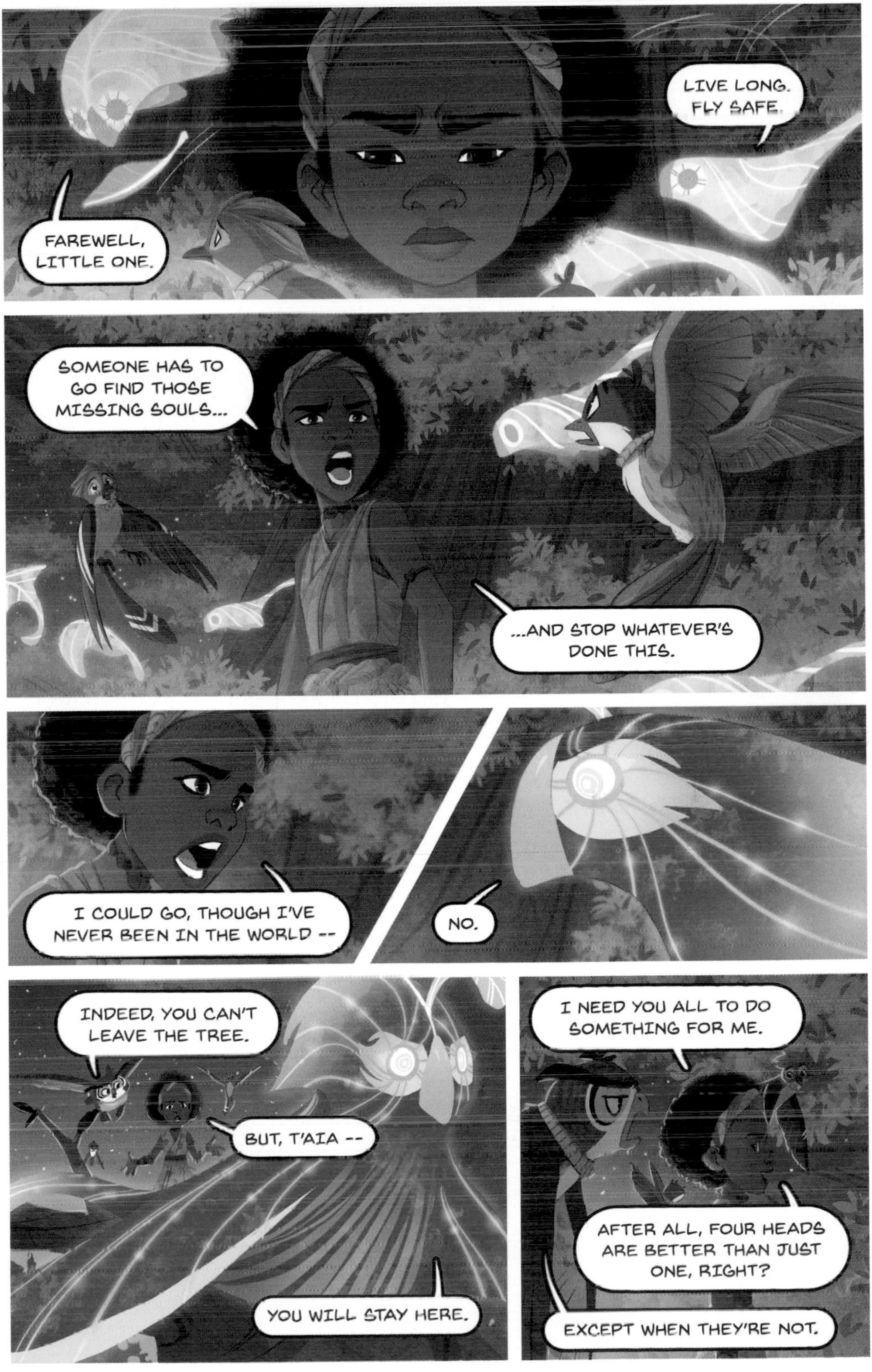
LIVE LONG. FLY SAFE.
FAREWELL, LITTLE ONE.
SOMEONE HAS TO GO FIND THOSE MISSING SOULS...
...AND STOP WHATEVER'S DONE THIS.
I COULD GO, THOUGH I'VE NEVER BEEN IN THE WORLD --
NO.
INDEED, YOU CAN'T LEAVE THE TREE.
BUT, T'AIA --
YOU WILL STAY HERE.
I NEED YOU ALL TO DO SOMETHING FOR ME.
AFTER ALL, FOUR HEADS ARE BETTER THAN JUST ONE, RIGHT?
EXCEPT WHEN THEY'RE NOT.

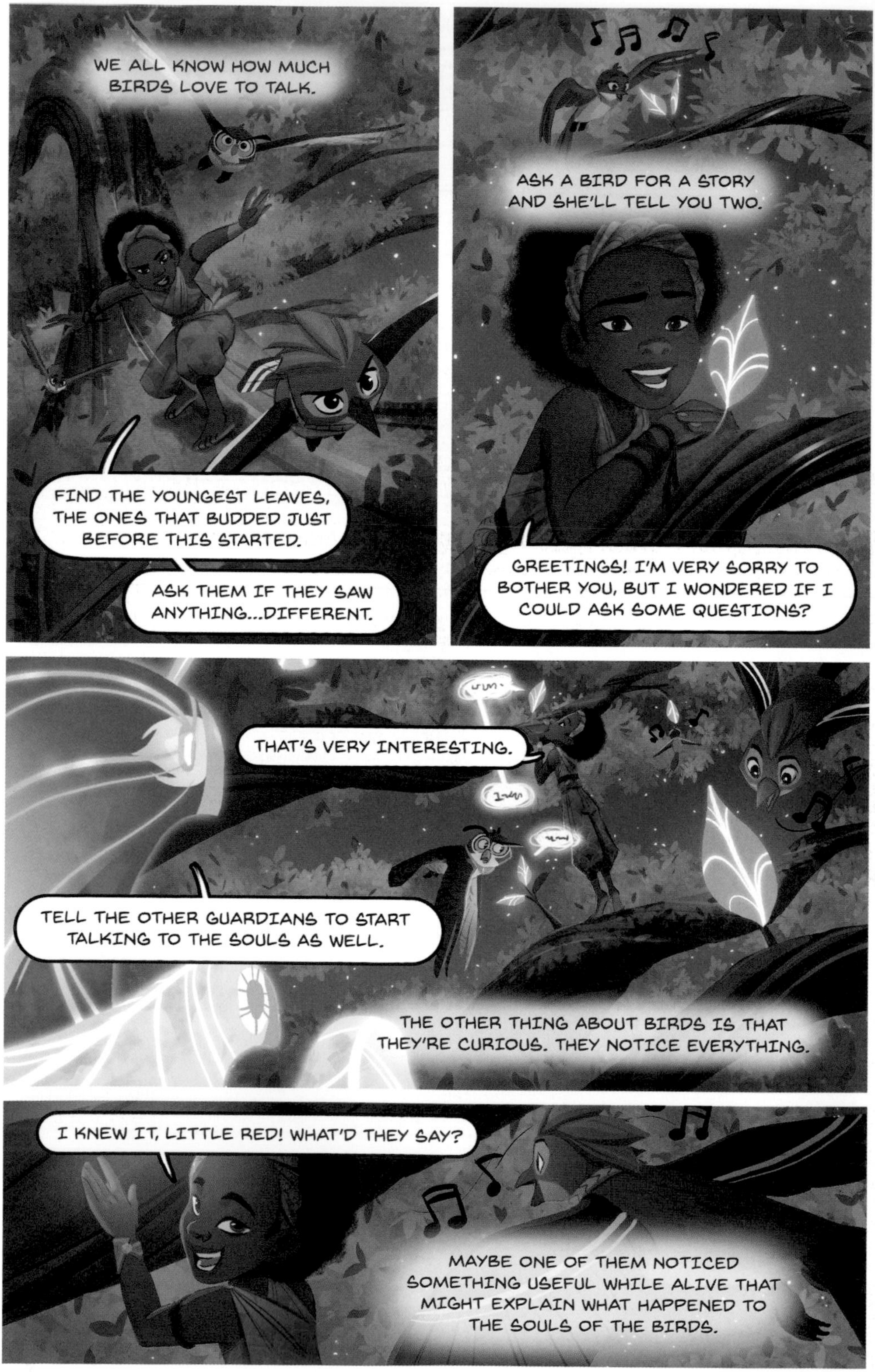
WE ALL KNOW HOW MUCH BIRDS LOVE TO TALK.
FIND THE YOUNGEST LEAVES, THE ONES THAT BUDDED JUST BEFORE THIS STARTED.
ASK THEM IF THEY SAW ANYTHING...DIFFERENT.
ASK A BIRD FOR A STORY AND SHE'LL TELL YOU TWO.
GREETINGS! I'M VERY SORRY TO BOTHER YOU, BUT I WONDERED IF I COULD ASK SOME QUESTIONS?
THAT'S VERY INTERESTING.
TELL THE OTHER GUARDIANS TO START TALKING TO THE SOULS AS WELL.
THE OTHER THING ABOUT BIRDS IS THAT THEY'RE CURIOUS. THEY NOTICE EVERYTHING.
I KNEW IT, LITTLE RED! WHAT'D THEY SAY?
MAYBE ONE OF THEM NOTICED SOMETHING USEFUL WHILE ALIVE THAT MIGHT EXPLAIN WHAT HAPPENED TO THE SOULS OF THE BIRDS.

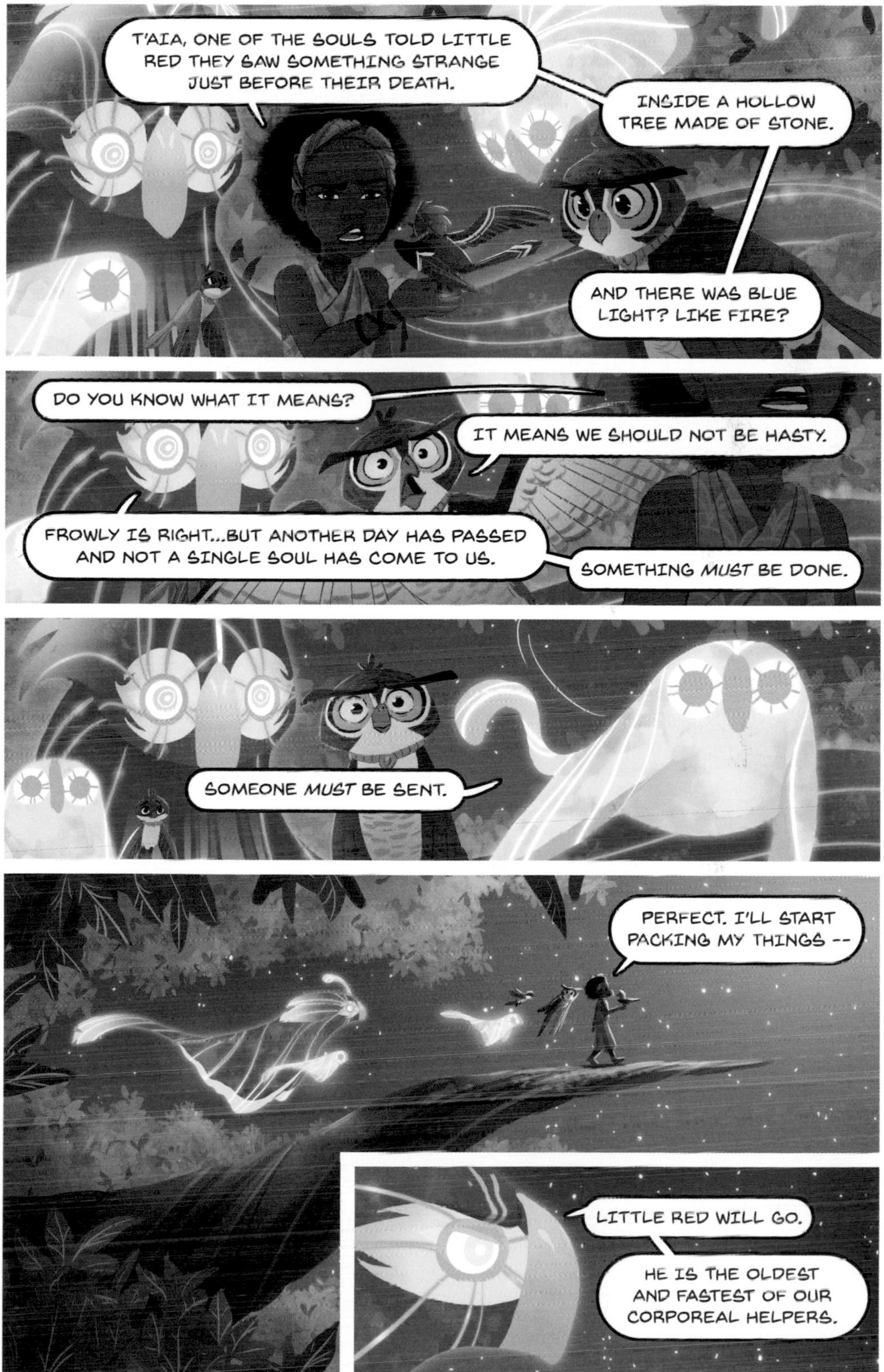
T'AIA, ONE OF THE SOULS TOLD LITTLE RED THEY SAW SOMETHING STRANGE JUST BEFORE THEIR DEATH.
INSIDE A HOLLOW TREE MADE OF STONE.
AND THERE WAS BLUE LIGHT? LIKE FIRE?
DO YOU KNOW WHAT IT MEANS?
IT MEANS WE SHOULD NOT BE HASTY.
FROWLY IS RIGHT...BUT ANOTHER DAY HAS PASSED AND NOT A SINGLE SOUL HAS COME TO US.
SOMETHING *MUST* BE DONE.
SOMEONE *MUST* BE SENT.
PERFECT. I'LL START PACKING MY THINGS --
LITTLE RED WILL GO.
HE IS THE OLDEST AND FASTEST OF OUR CORPOREAL HELPERS.

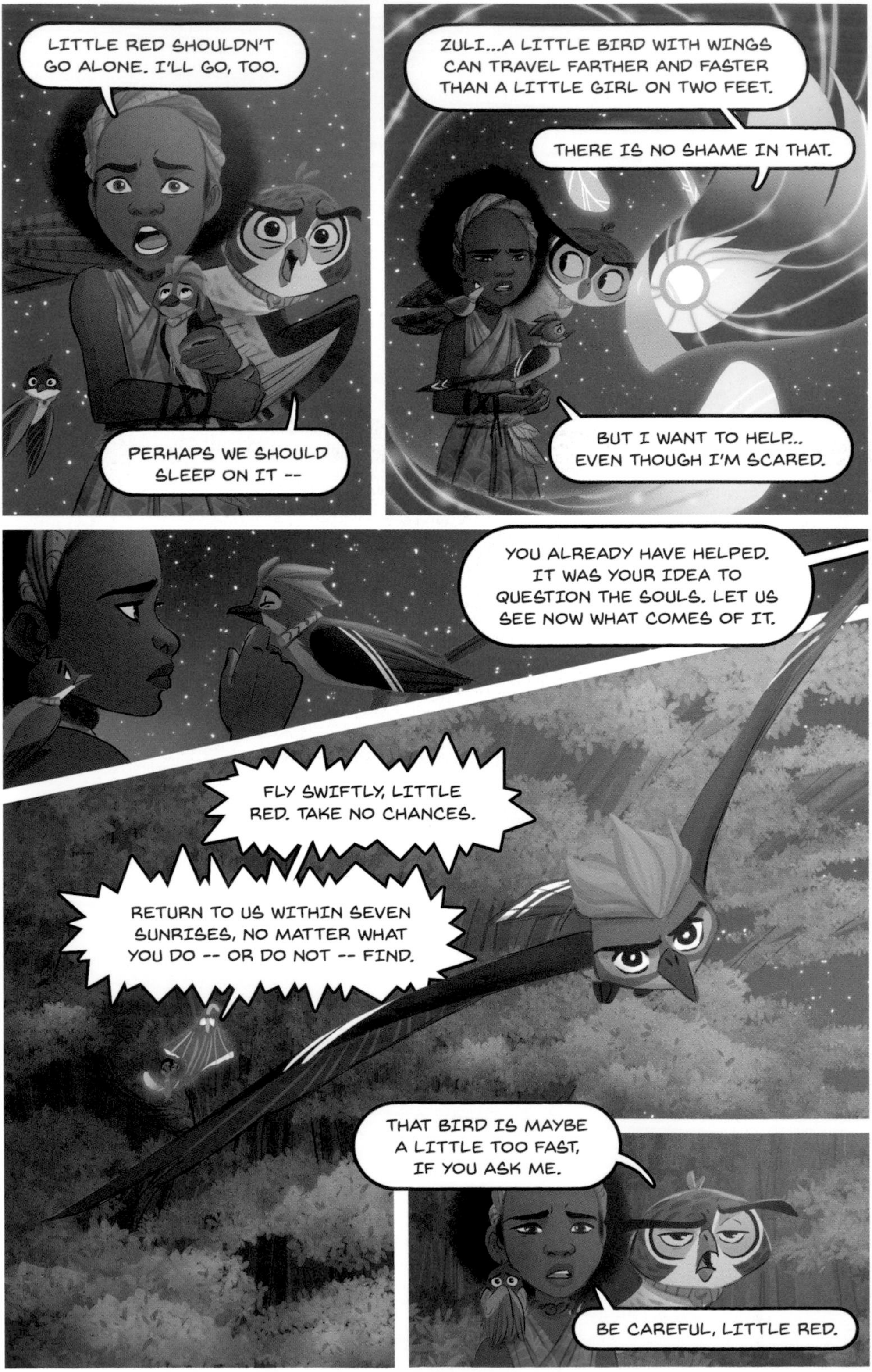
LITTLE RED SHOULDN'T GO ALONE. I'LL GO, TOO.
PERHAPS WE SHOULD SLEEP ON IT --
ZULI...A LITTLE BIRD WITH WINGS CAN TRAVEL FARTHER AND FASTER THAN A LITTLE GIRL ON TWO FEET.
THERE IS NO SHAME IN THAT.
BUT I WANT TO HELP... EVEN THOUGH I'M SCARED.
YOU ALREADY HAVE HELPED. IT WAS YOUR IDEA TO QUESTION THE SOULS. LET US SEE NOW WHAT COMES OF IT.
FLY SWIFTLY, LITTLE RED. TAKE NO CHANCES.
RETURN TO US WITHIN SEVEN SUNRISES, NO MATTER WHAT YOU DO -- OR DO NOT -- FIND.
THAT BIRD IS MAYBE A LITTLE TOO FAST, IF YOU ASK ME.
BE CAREFUL, LITTLE RED.

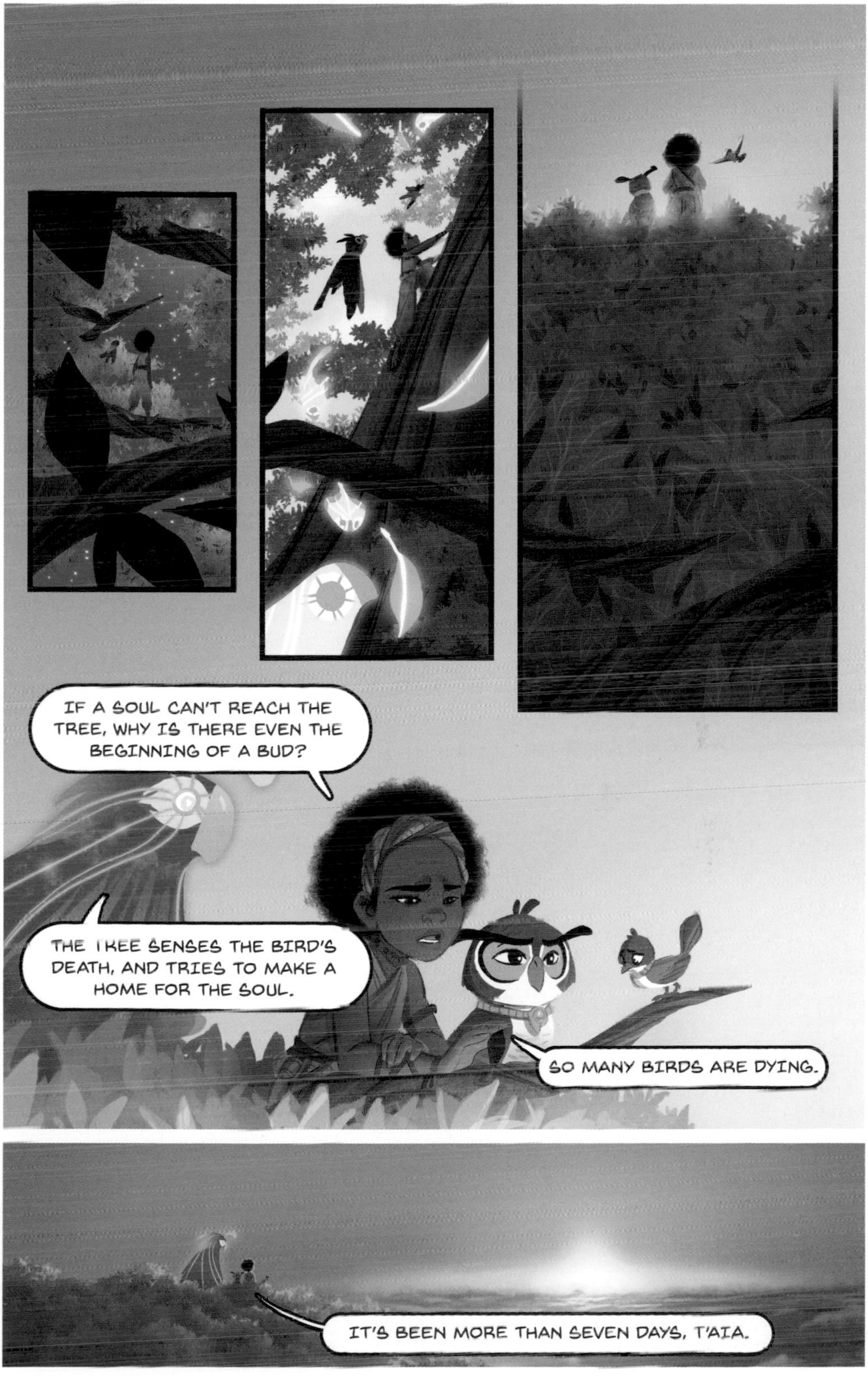
IF A SOUL CAN'T REACH THE TREE, WHY IS THERE EVEN THE BEGINNING OF A BUD?
THE TREE SENSES THE BIRD'S DEATH, AND TRIES TO MAKE A HOME FOR THE SOUL.
SO MANY BIRDS ARE DYING.
IT'S BEEN MORE THAN SEVEN DAYS, T'AIA.

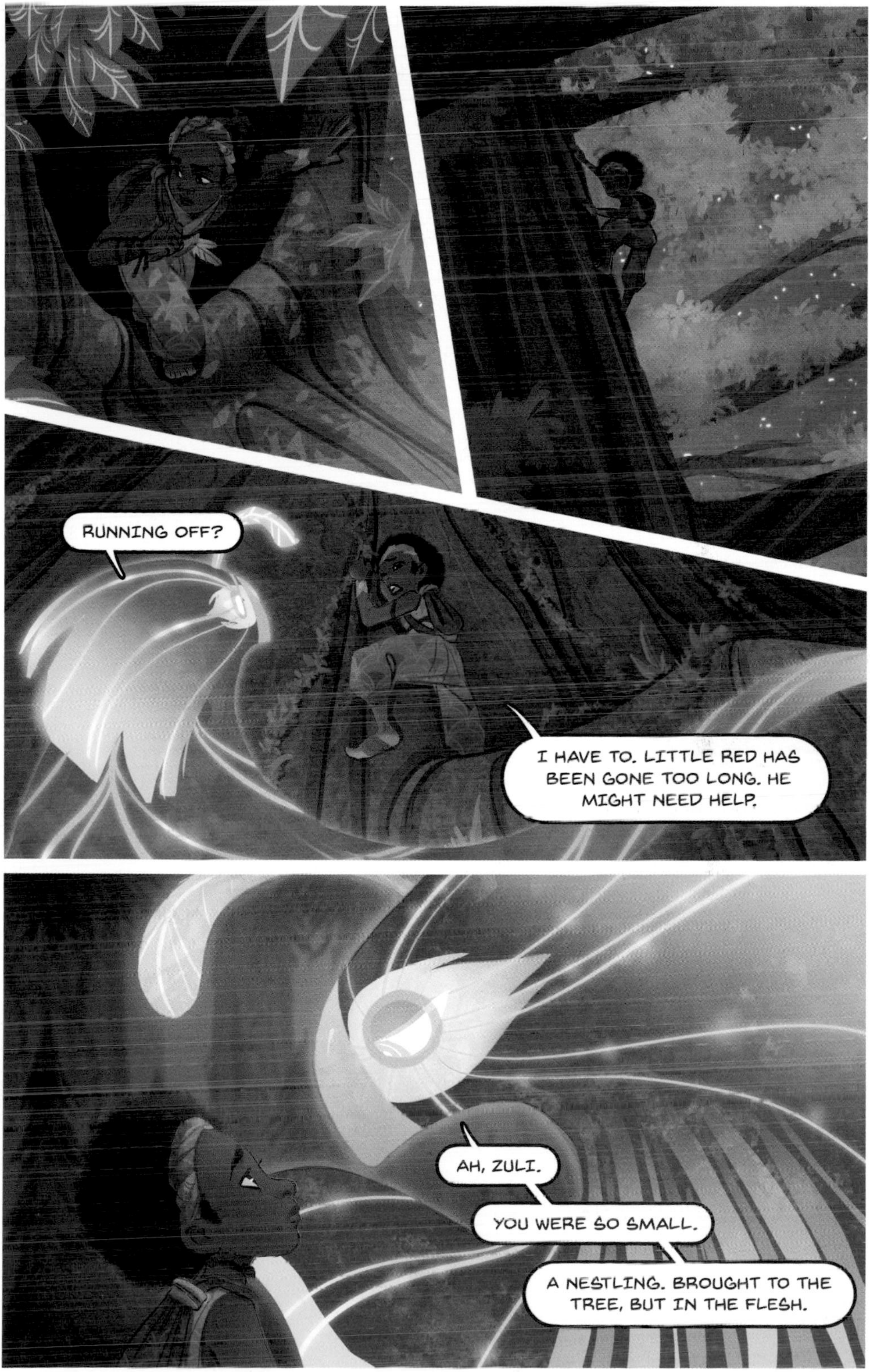
RUNNING OFF?
I HAVE TO. LITTLE RED HAS BEEN GONE TOO LONG. HE MIGHT NEED HELP.
AH, ZULI.
YOU WERE SO SMALL.
A NESTLING. BROUGHT TO THE TREE, BUT IN THE FLESH.

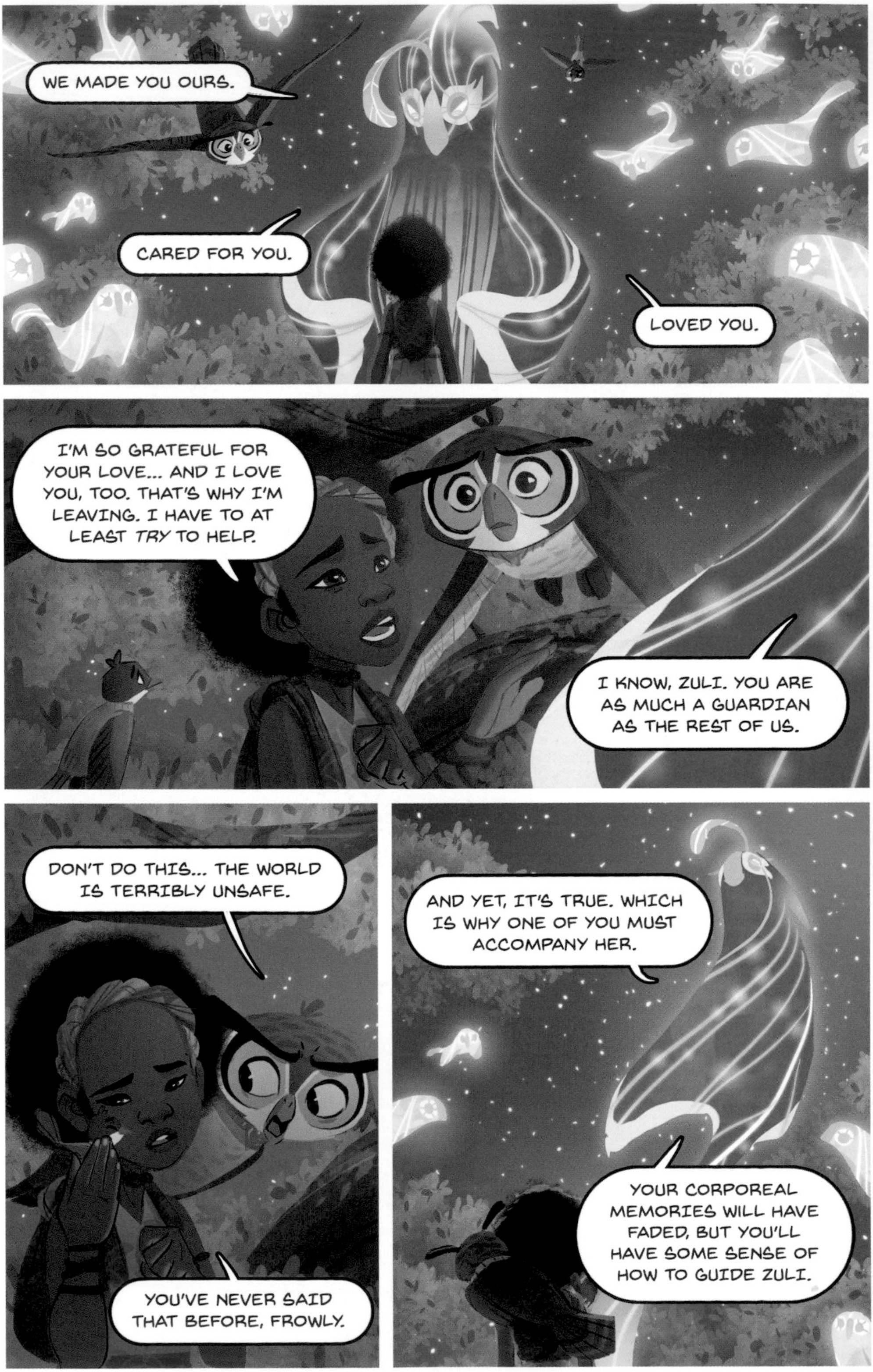
WE MADE YOU OURS.
CARED FOR YOU.
LOVED YOU.
I'M SO GRATEFUL FOR YOUR LOVE... AND I LOVE YOU, TOO. THAT'S WHY I'M LEAVING. I HAVE TO AT LEAST *TRY* TO HELP.
I KNOW, ZULI. YOU ARE AS MUCH A GUARDIAN AS THE REST OF US.
DON'T DO THIS... THE WORLD IS TERRIBLY UNSAFE.
YOU'VE NEVER SAID THAT BEFORE, FROWLY.
AND YET, IT'S TRUE. WHICH IS WHY ONE OF YOU MUST ACCOMPANY HER.
YOUR CORPOREAL MEMORIES WILL HAVE FADED, BUT YOU'LL HAVE SOME SENSE OF HOW TO GUIDE ZULI.

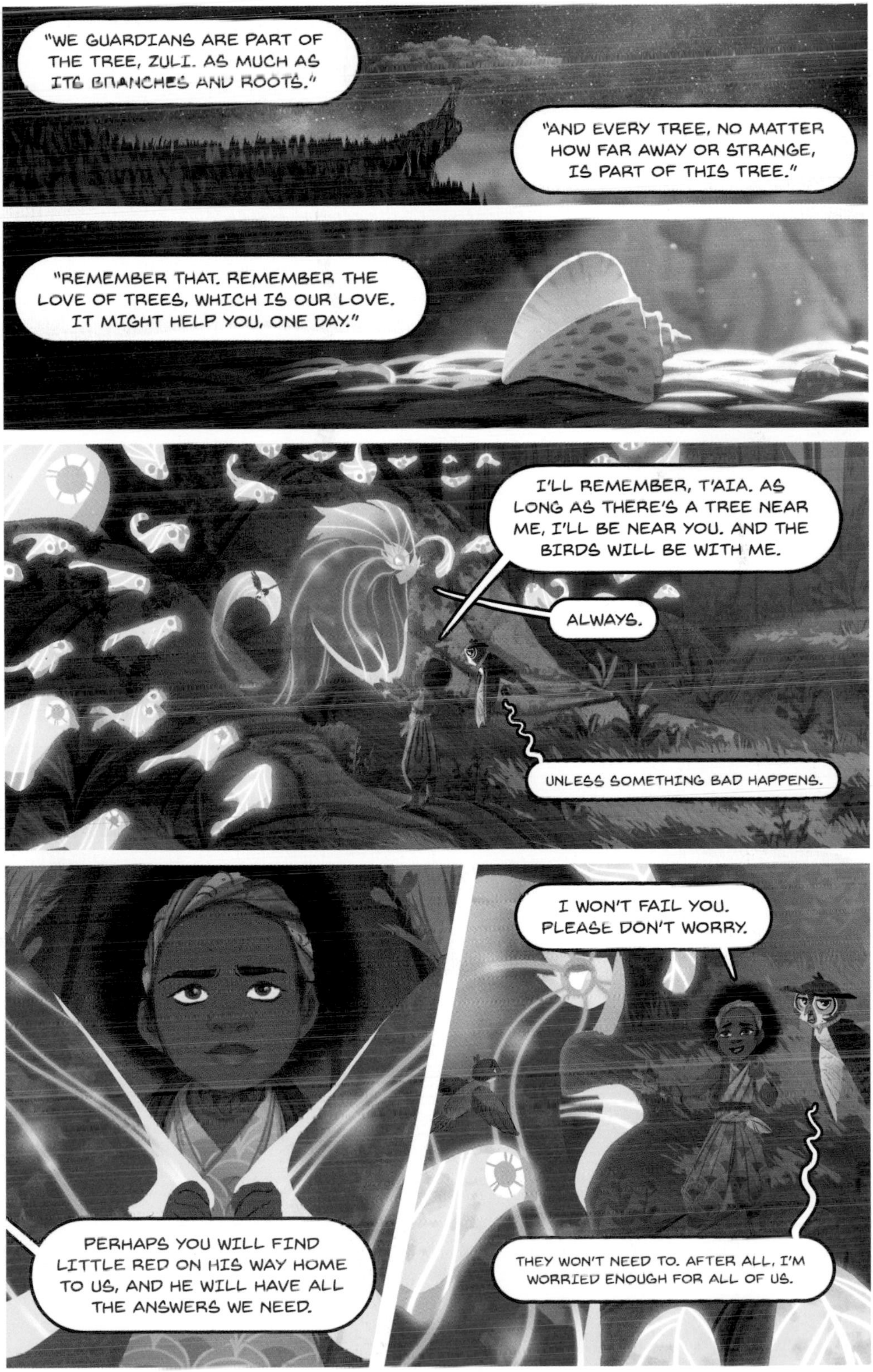
"WE GUARDIANS ARE PART OF THE TREE, ZULI. AS MUCH AS ITS BRANCHES AND ROOTS."
"AND EVERY TREE, NO MATTER HOW FAR AWAY OR STRANGE, IS PART OF THIS TREE."
"REMEMBER THAT. REMEMBER THE LOVE OF TREES, WHICH IS OUR LOVE. IT MIGHT HELP YOU, ONE DAY."
I'LL REMEMBER, T'AIA. AS LONG AS THERE'S A TREE NEAR ME, I'LL BE NEAR YOU. AND THE BIRDS WILL BE WITH ME.
ALWAYS.
UNLESS SOMETHING BAD HAPPENS.
I WON'T FAIL YOU. PLEASE DON'T WORRY.
PERHAPS YOU WILL FIND LITTLE RED ON HIS WAY HOME TO US, AND HE WILL HAVE ALL THE ANSWERS WE NEED.
THEY WON'T NEED TO. AFTER ALL, I'M WORRIED ENOUGH FOR ALL OF US.

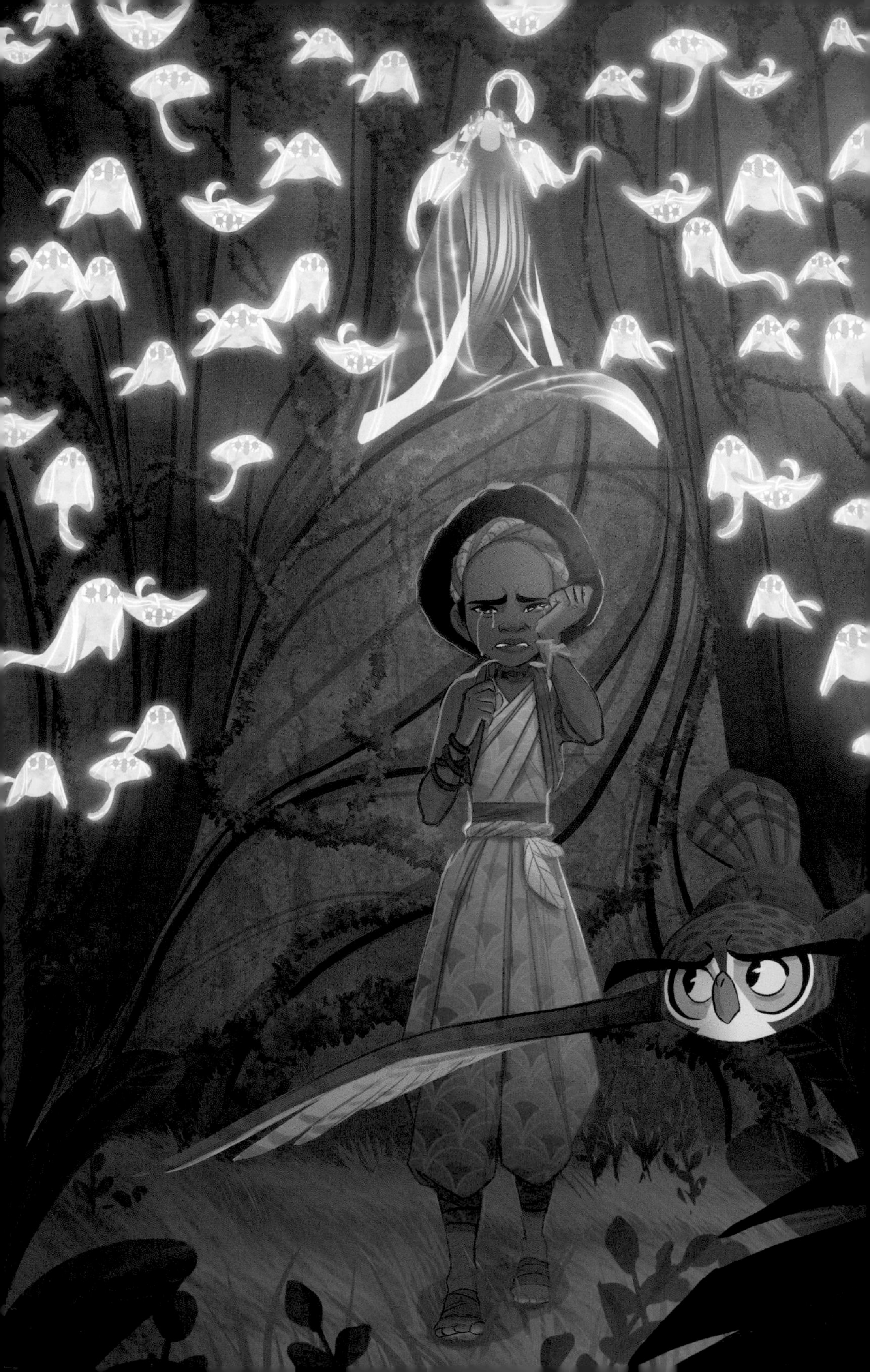

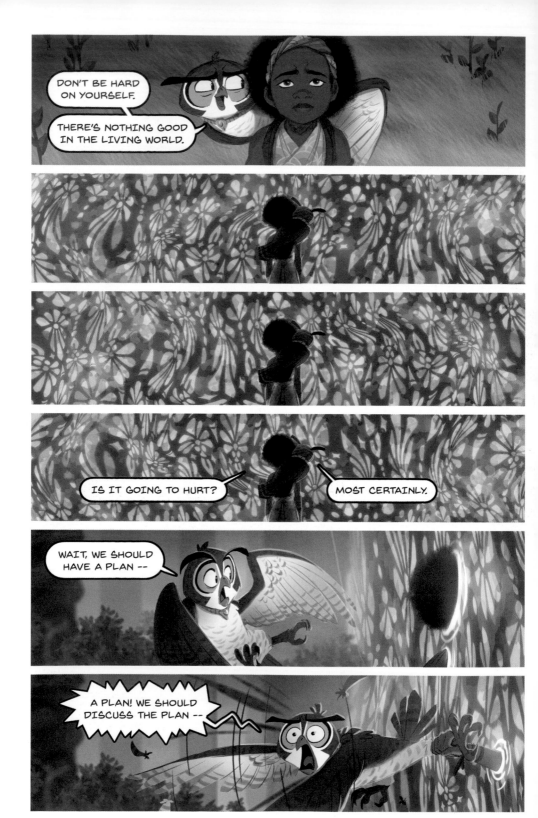

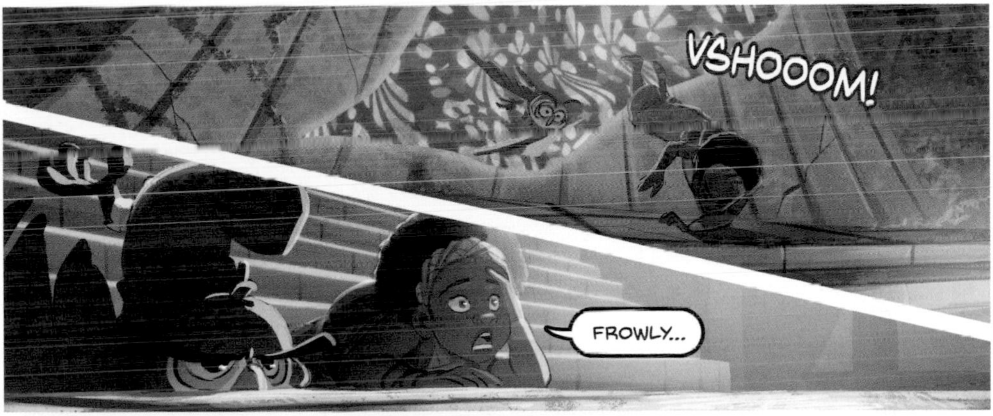
VSHOOOM!
FROWLY...

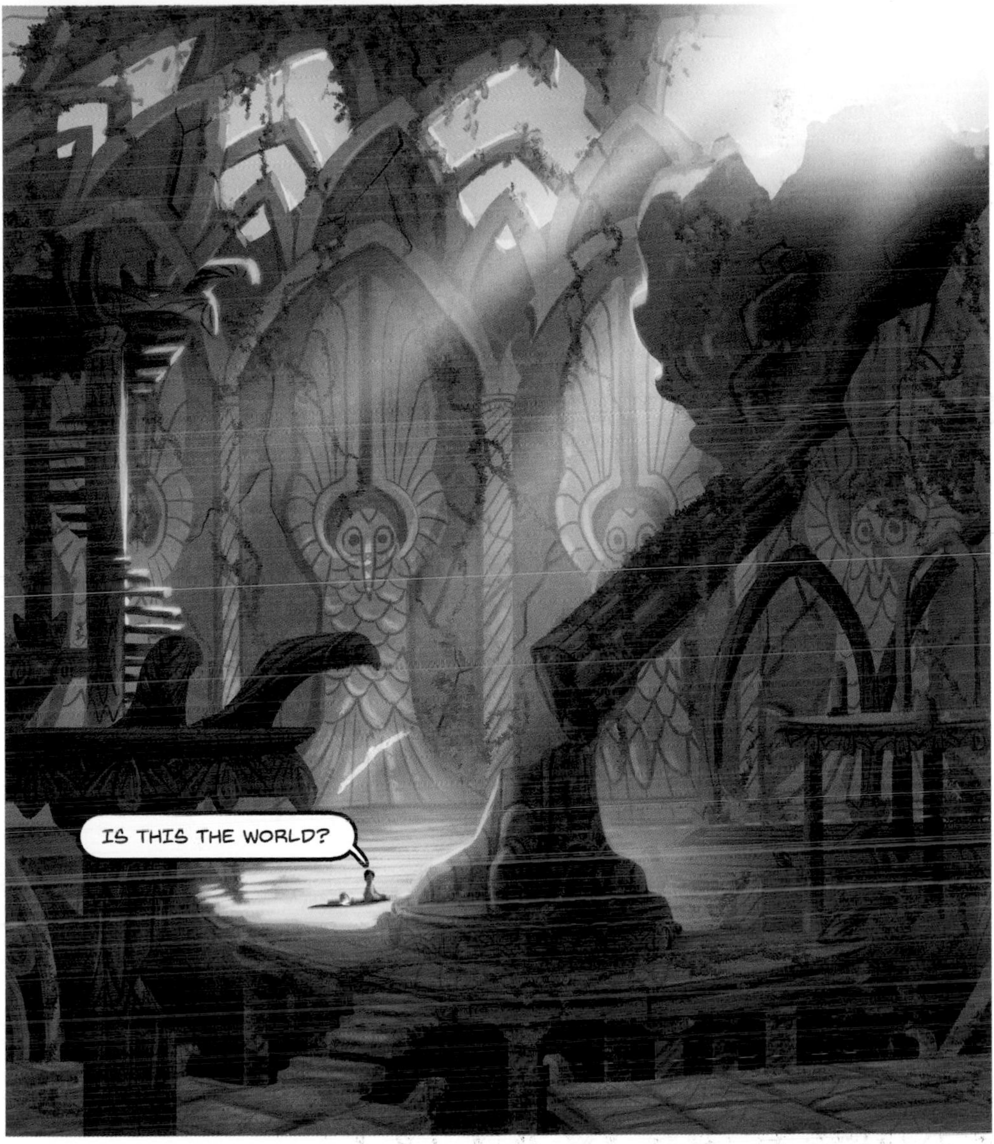
IS THIS THE WORLD?

36

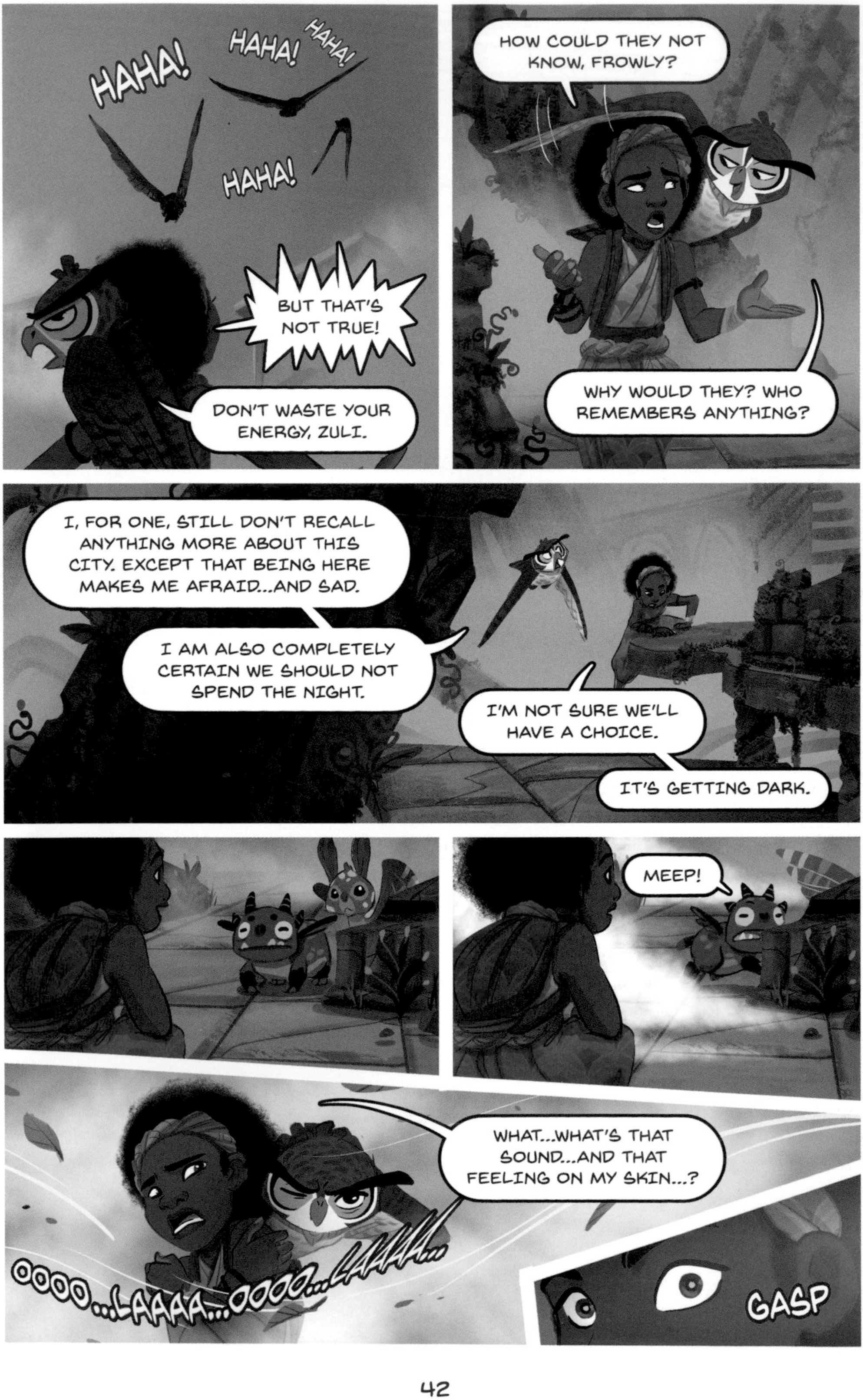
HAHA!
HAHA!
HAHA!
HAHA!
BUT THAT'S NOT TRUE!
DON'T WASTE YOUR ENERGY, ZULI.
HOW COULD THEY NOT KNOW, FROWLY?
WHY WOULD THEY? WHO REMEMBERS ANYTHING?
I, FOR ONE, STILL DON'T RECALL ANYTHING MORE ABOUT THIS CITY. EXCEPT THAT BEING HERE MAKES ME AFRAID...AND SAD.
I AM ALSO COMPLETELY CERTAIN WE SHOULD NOT SPEND THE NIGHT.
I'M NOT SURE WE'LL HAVE A CHOICE.
IT'S GETTING DARK.
MEEP!
WHAT...WHAT'S THAT SOUND...AND THAT FEELING ON MY SKIN...?
OOOO...LAAAA...OOOO...LAAAA...
GASP

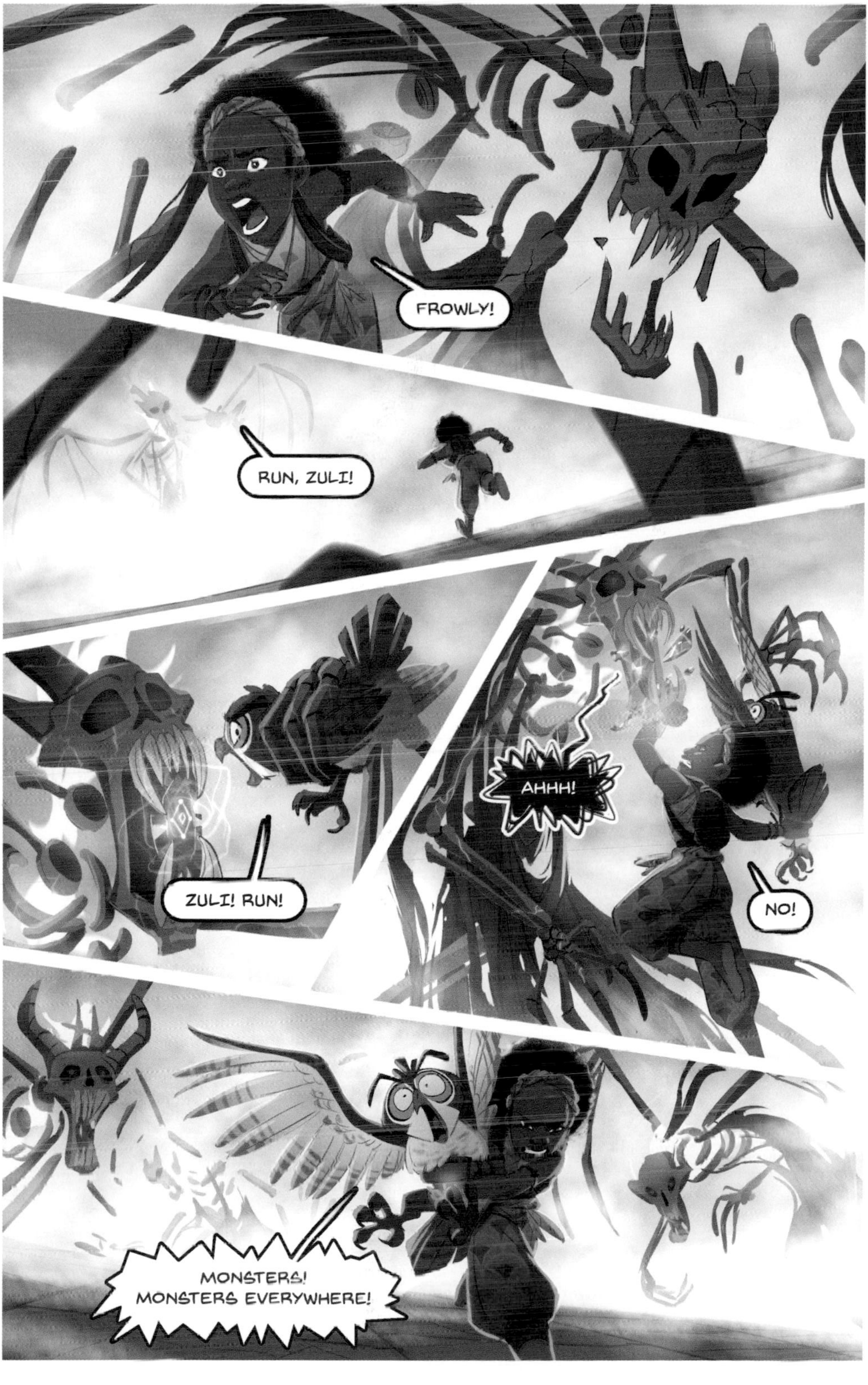
FROWLY!
RUN, ZULI!
ZULI! RUN!
AHHH!
NO!
MONSTERS! MONSTERS EVERYWHERE!

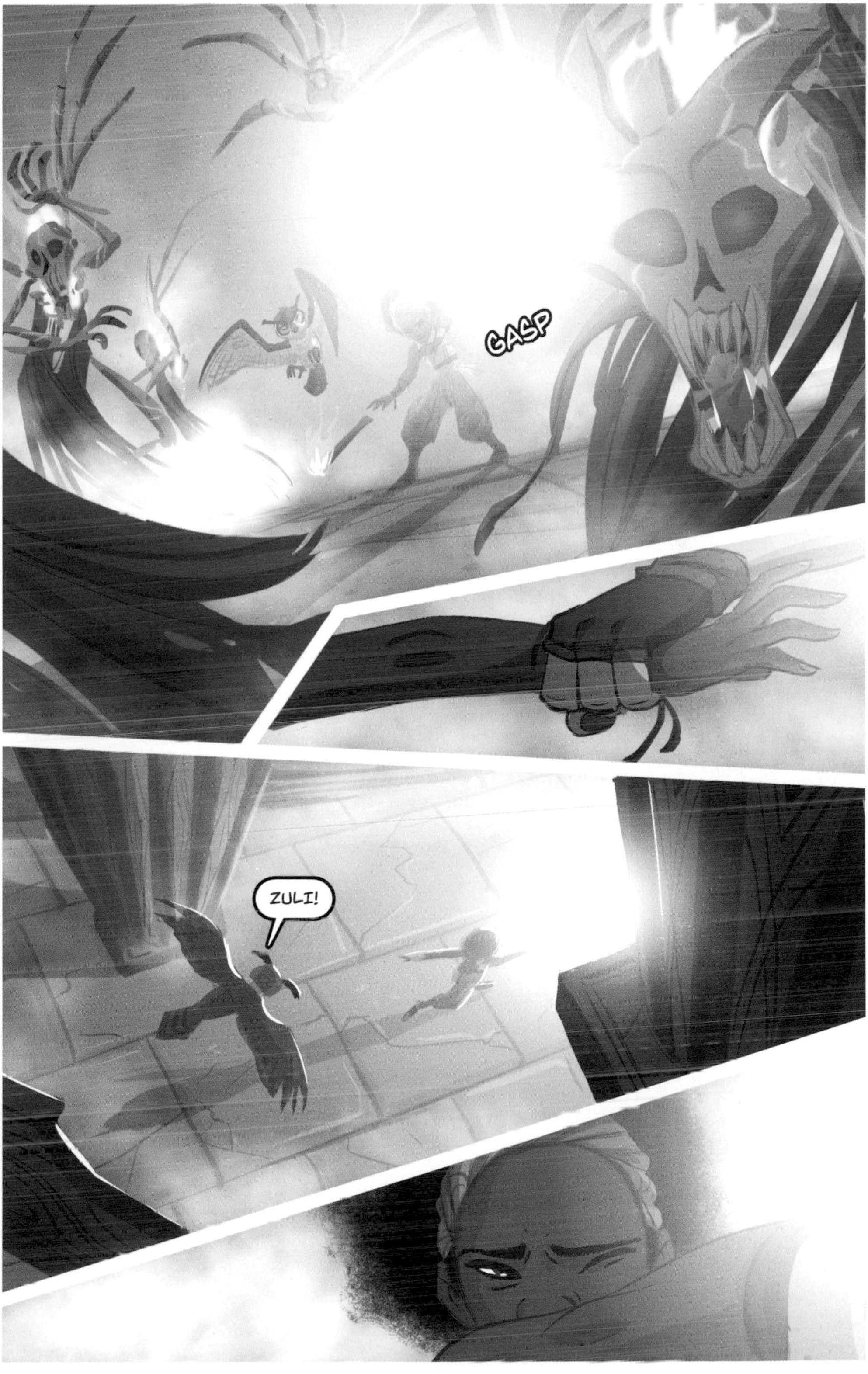
GASP
ZULI!

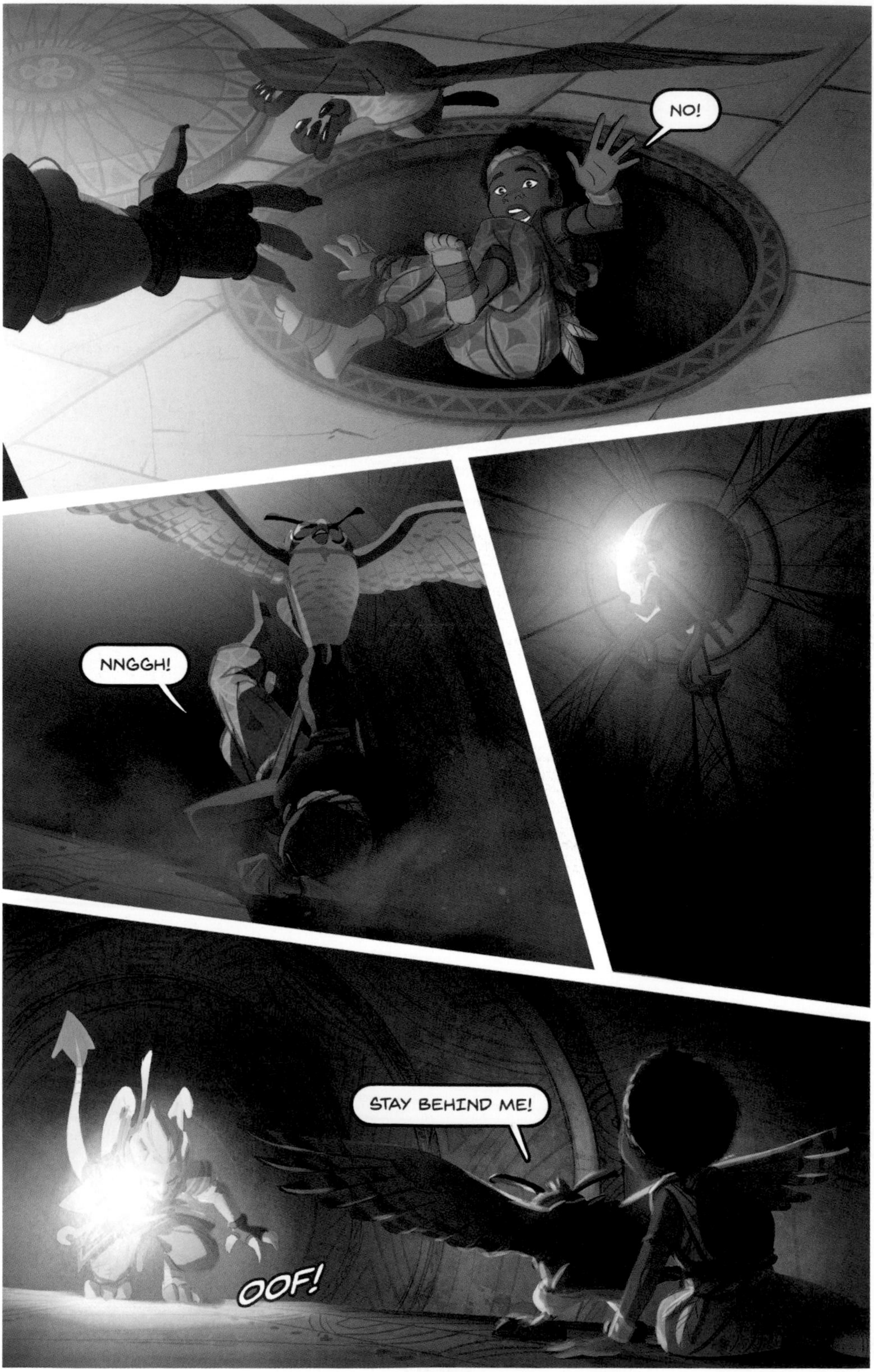
NO!
NNGGH!
STAY BEHIND ME!
OOF!

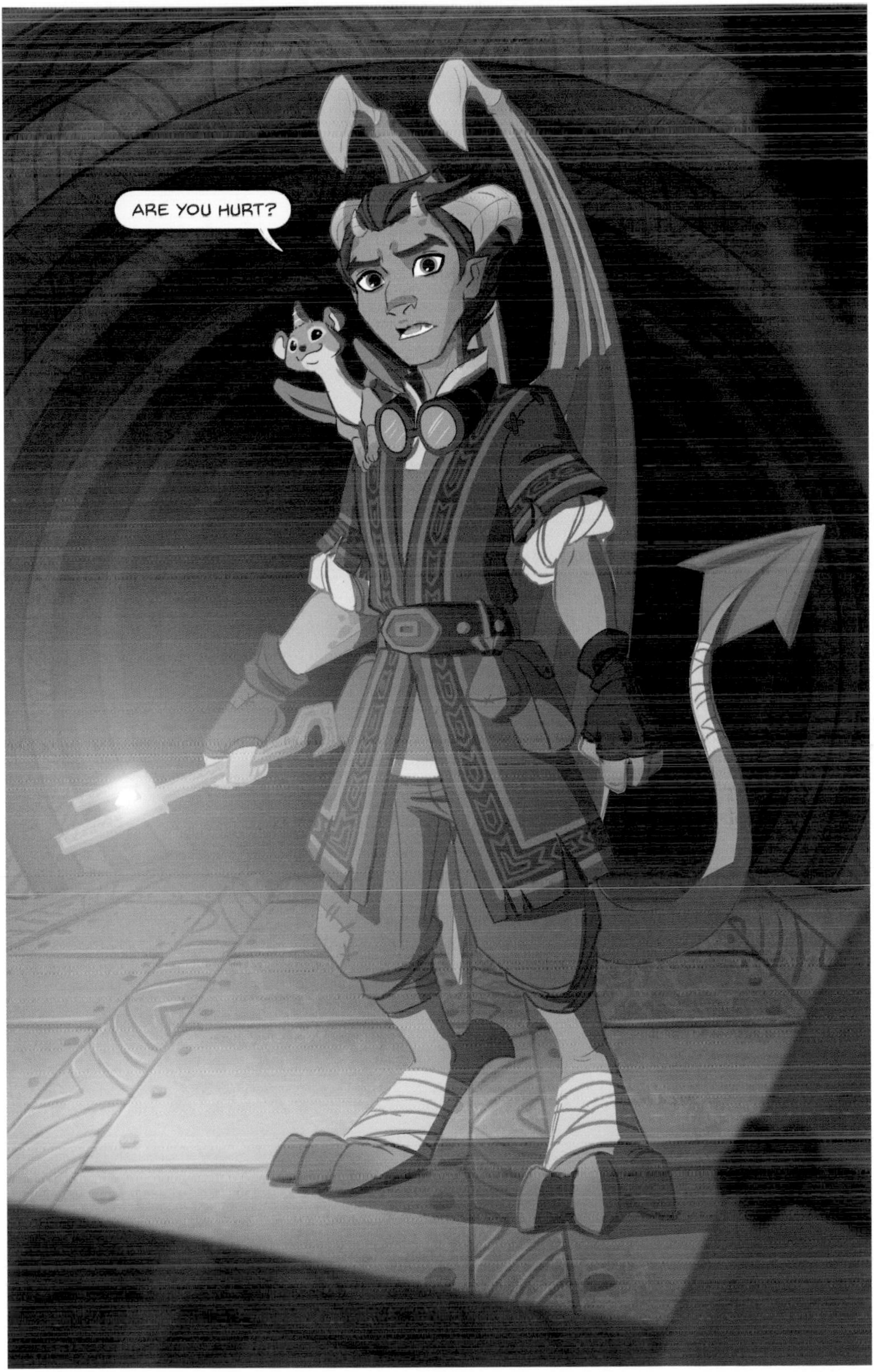
ARE YOU HURT?

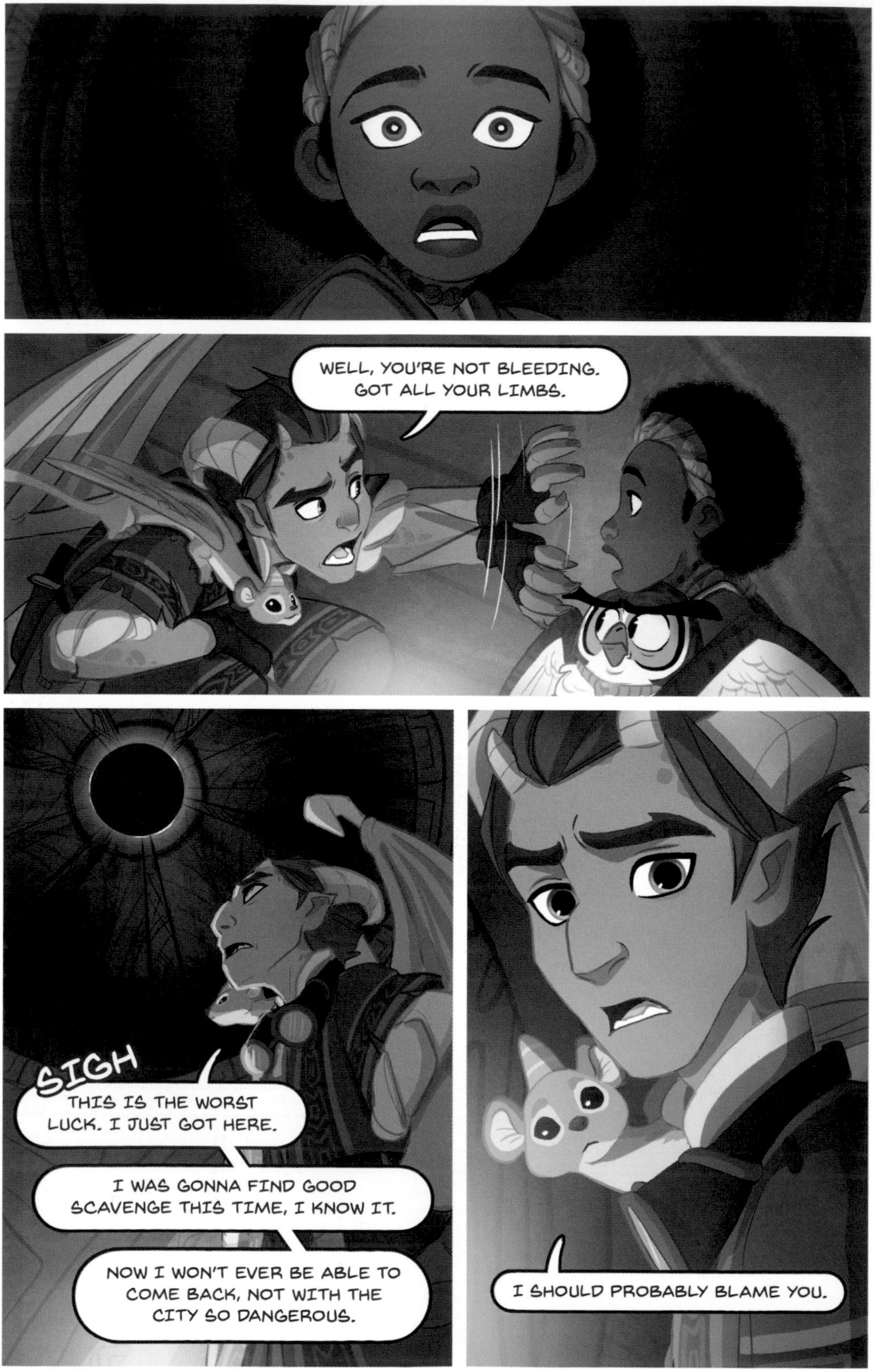
WELL, YOU'RE NOT BLEEDING. GOT ALL YOUR LIMBS.
SIGH
THIS IS THE WORST LUCK. I JUST GOT HERE.
I WAS GONNA FIND GOOD SCAVENGE THIS TIME, I KNOW IT.
NOW I WON'T EVER BE ABLE TO COME BACK, NOT WITH THE CITY SO DANGEROUS.
I SHOULD PROBABLY BLAME YOU.

COME ON. I KNOW YOUR LEGS STILL WORK. WE HAVE TO GET OUT OF THE CITY.

WHAT ARE YOU DOING?

WE CAN'T STAY HERE, FROWLY.

BUT HE'S A STRANGER! JUST BECAUSE HE HELPED US DOES NOT MAKE HIM SAFE.

MAYBE NOT.

BUT HE CAN'T BE MORE DANGEROUS THAN THOSE THINGS UP THERE.

I'M NOT SURE ABOUT THAT. THERE'S SOMETHING FAMILIAR ABOUT HIM... I WISH I COULD REMEMBER WHAT IT IS...

I DO KNOW I DON'T LIKE IT.

51

IS THAT OWL...*TALKING*?

OF COURSE I AM TALKING. HOW ELSE AM I TO COMMUNICATE?

ALL BIRDS TALK.

BIRDS *SING*. THEY DON'T USE --

BANG! BANG! BANG! BAN

I THOUGHT WE'D HAVE MORE TIME.

WHAT ARE THEY?

DEAD THINGS KEPT ALIVE WITH MAGIC. WE CALL 'EM WRAITHS.

AND WHO ARE YOU?

MY NAME IS ORIEN.

YOU?

I'M...ZULI.

54

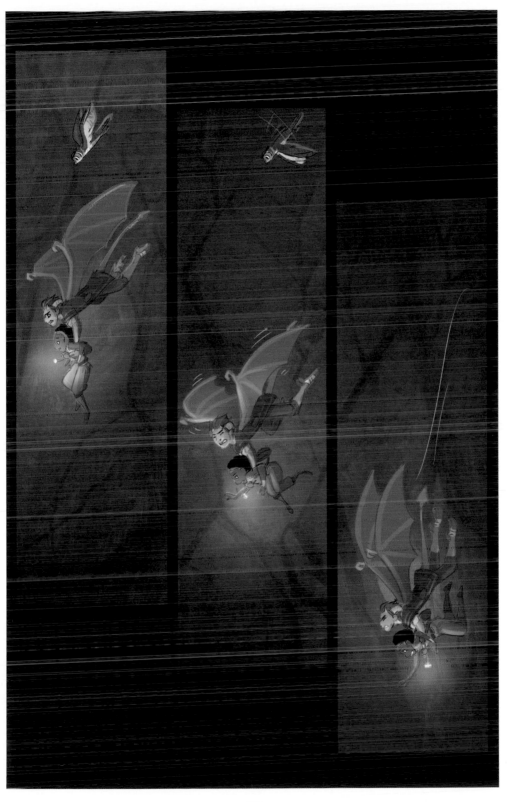

58

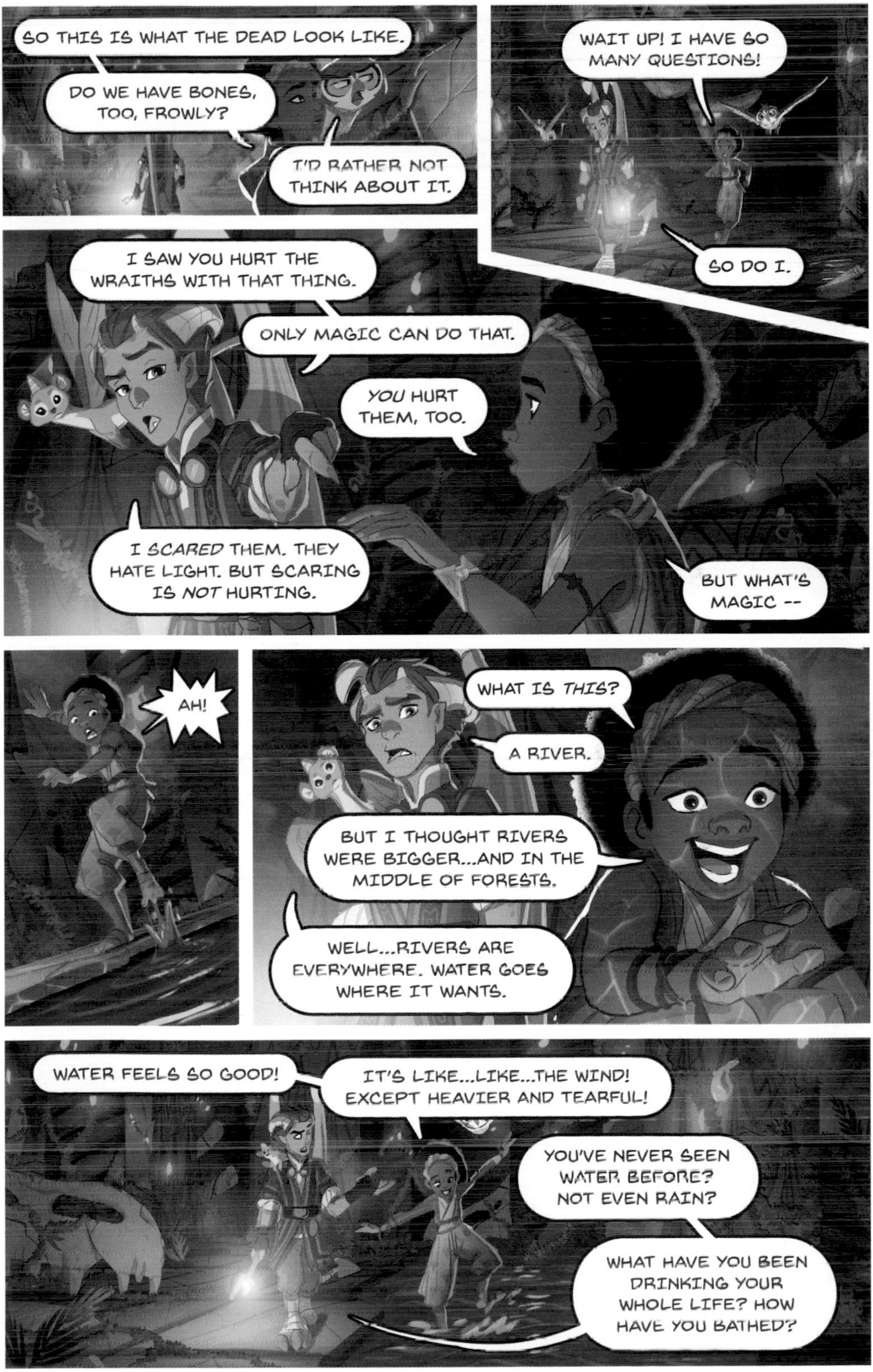
SO THIS IS WHAT THE DEAD LOOK LIKE.
DO WE HAVE BONES, TOO, FROWLY?
I'D RATHER NOT THINK ABOUT IT.
WAIT UP! I HAVE SO MANY QUESTIONS!
SO DO I.
I SAW YOU HURT THE WRAITHS WITH THAT THING.
ONLY MAGIC CAN DO THAT.
YOU HURT THEM, TOO.
I *SCARED* THEM. THEY HATE LIGHT. BUT SCARING IS *NOT* HURTING.
BUT WHAT'S MAGIC --
AH!
WHAT IS *THIS*?
A RIVER.
BUT I THOUGHT RIVERS WERE BIGGER...AND IN THE MIDDLE OF FORESTS.
WELL...RIVERS ARE EVERYWHERE. WATER GOES WHERE IT WANTS.
WATER FEELS SO GOOD!
IT'S LIKE...LIKE...THE WIND! EXCEPT HEAVIER AND TEARFUL!
YOU'VE NEVER SEEN WATER BEFORE? NOT EVEN RAIN?
WHAT HAVE YOU BEEN DRINKING YOUR WHOLE LIFE? HOW HAVE YOU BATHED?

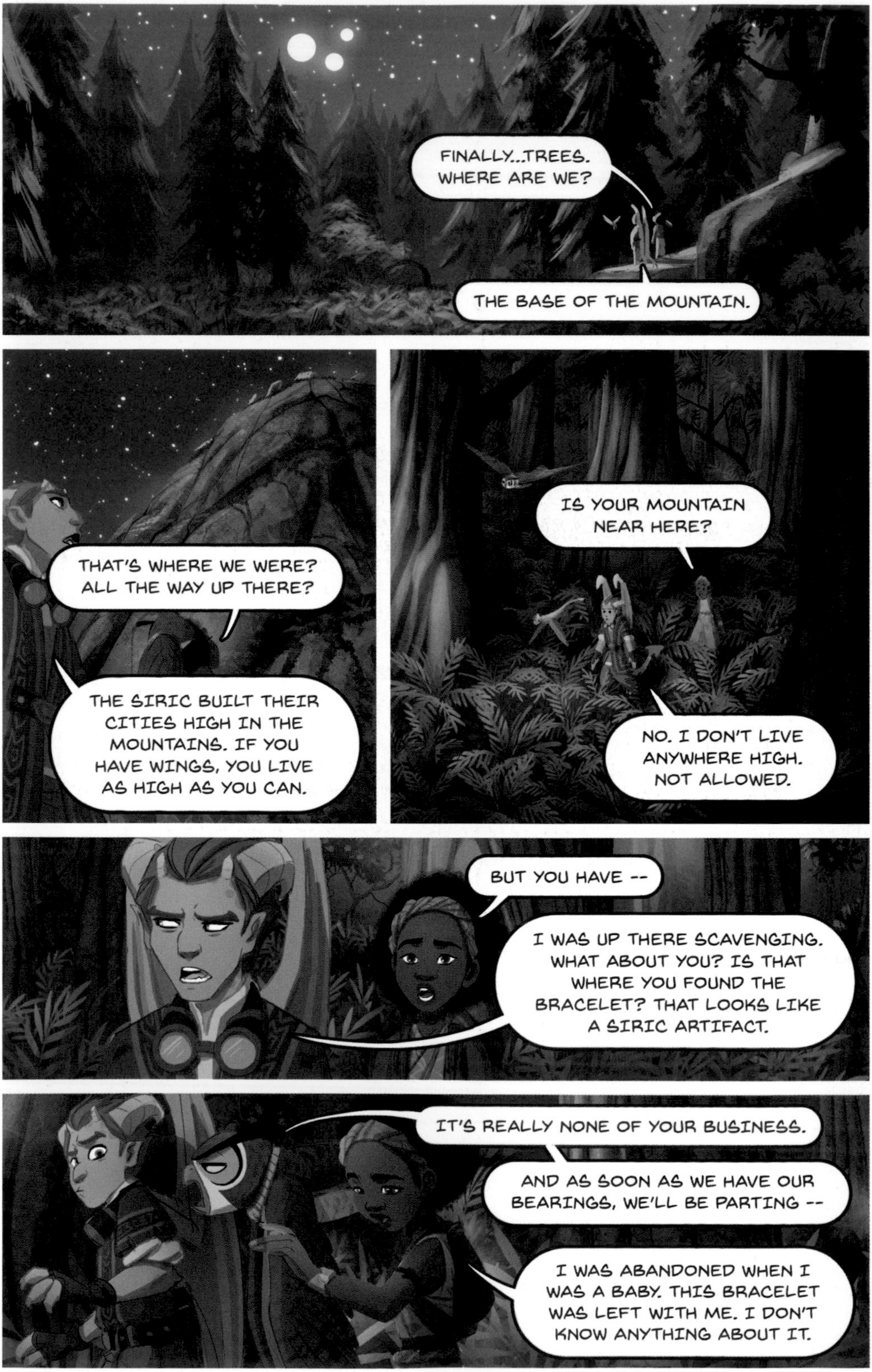
FINALLY...TREES. WHERE ARE WE?
THE BASE OF THE MOUNTAIN.
THAT'S WHERE WE WERE? ALL THE WAY UP THERE?
THE SIRIC BUILT THEIR CITIES HIGH IN THE MOUNTAINS. IF YOU HAVE WINGS, YOU LIVE AS HIGH AS YOU CAN.
IS YOUR MOUNTAIN NEAR HERE?
NO. I DON'T LIVE ANYWHERE HIGH. NOT ALLOWED.
BUT YOU HAVE --
I WAS UP THERE SCAVENGING. WHAT ABOUT YOU? IS THAT WHERE YOU FOUND THE BRACELET? THAT LOOKS LIKE A SIRIC ARTIFACT.
IT'S REALLY NONE OF YOUR BUSINESS.
AND AS SOON AS WE HAVE OUR BEARINGS, WE'LL BE PARTING --
I WAS ABANDONED WHEN I WAS A BABY. THIS BRACELET WAS LEFT WITH ME. I DON'T KNOW ANYTHING ABOUT IT.

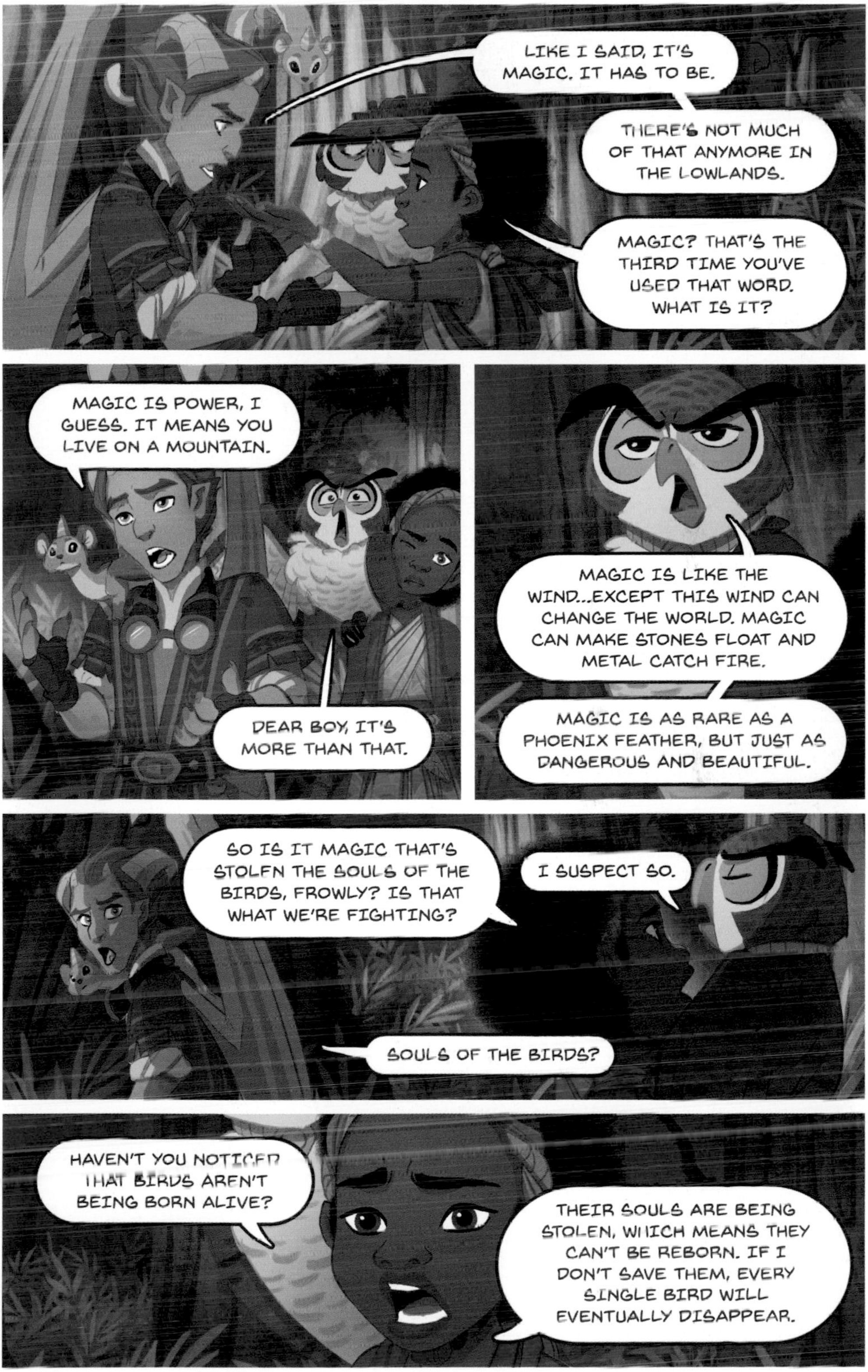
LIKE I SAID, IT'S MAGIC. IT HAS TO BE.
THERE'S NOT MUCH OF THAT ANYMORE IN THE LOWLANDS.
MAGIC? THAT'S THE THIRD TIME YOU'VE USED THAT WORD. WHAT IS IT?
MAGIC IS POWER, I GUESS. IT MEANS YOU LIVE ON A MOUNTAIN.
DEAR BOY, IT'S MORE THAN THAT.
MAGIC IS LIKE THE WIND...EXCEPT THIS WIND CAN CHANGE THE WORLD. MAGIC CAN MAKE STONES FLOAT AND METAL CATCH FIRE.
MAGIC IS AS RARE AS A PHOENIX FEATHER, BUT JUST AS DANGEROUS AND BEAUTIFUL.
SO IS IT MAGIC THAT'S STOLEN THE SOULS OF THE BIRDS, FROWLY? IS THAT WHAT WE'RE FIGHTING?
I SUSPECT SO.
SOULS OF THE BIRDS?
HAVEN'T YOU NOTICED THAT BIRDS AREN'T BEING BORN ALIVE?
THEIR SOULS ARE BEING STOLEN, WHICH MEANS THEY CAN'T BE REBORN. IF I DON'T SAVE THEM, EVERY SINGLE BIRD WILL EVENTUALLY DISAPPEAR.

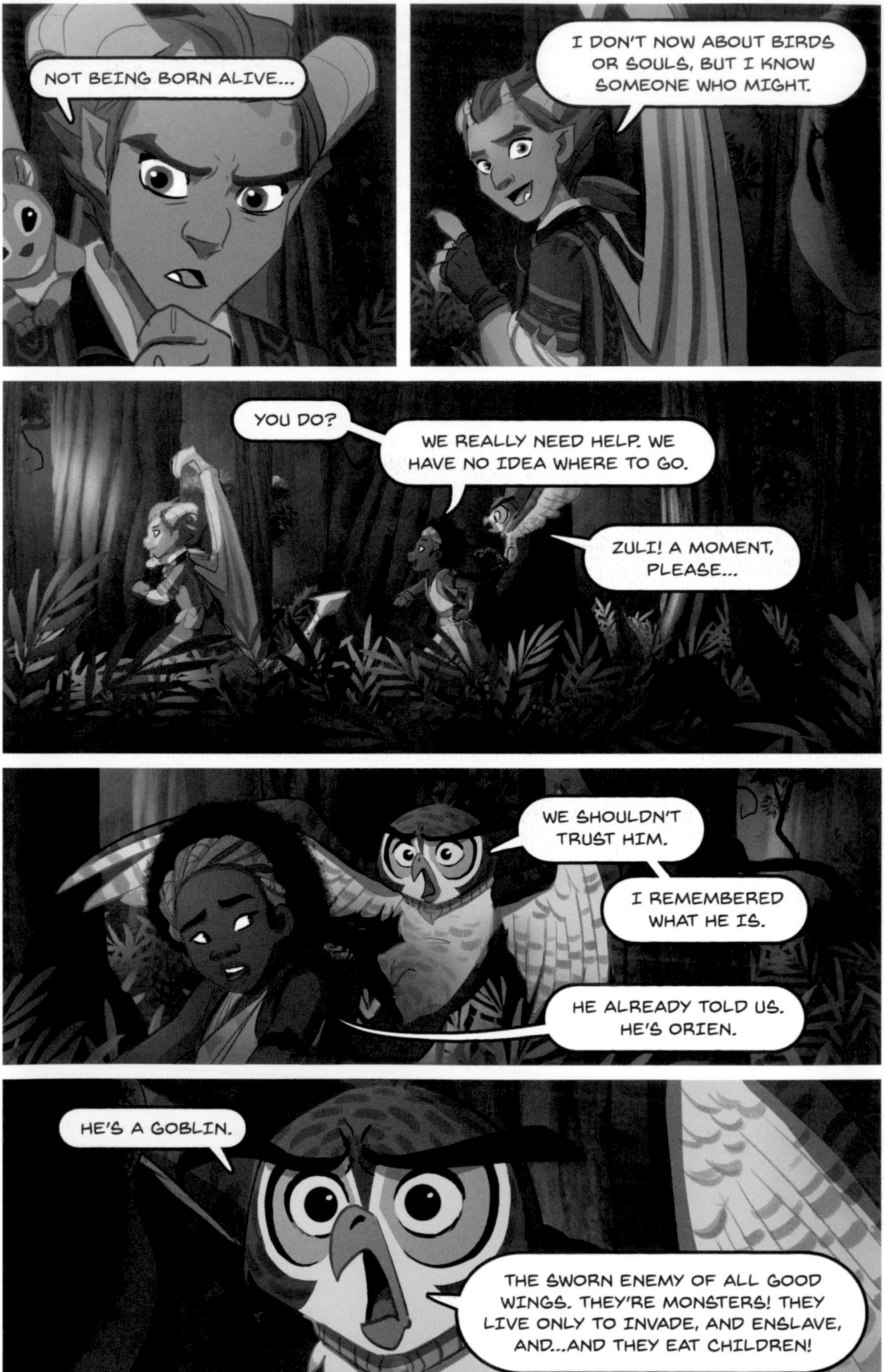
NOT BEING BORN ALIVE...
I DON'T NOW ABOUT BIRDS OR SOULS, BUT I KNOW SOMEONE WHO MIGHT.
YOU DO?
WE REALLY NEED HELP. WE HAVE NO IDEA WHERE TO GO.
ZULI! A MOMENT, PLEASE...
WE SHOULDN'T TRUST HIM.
I REMEMBERED WHAT HE IS.
HE ALREADY TOLD US. HE'S ORIEN.
HE'S A GOBLIN.
THE SWORN ENEMY OF ALL GOOD WINGS. THEY'RE MONSTERS! THEY LIVE ONLY TO INVADE, AND ENSLAVE, AND...AND THEY EAT CHILDREN!

65

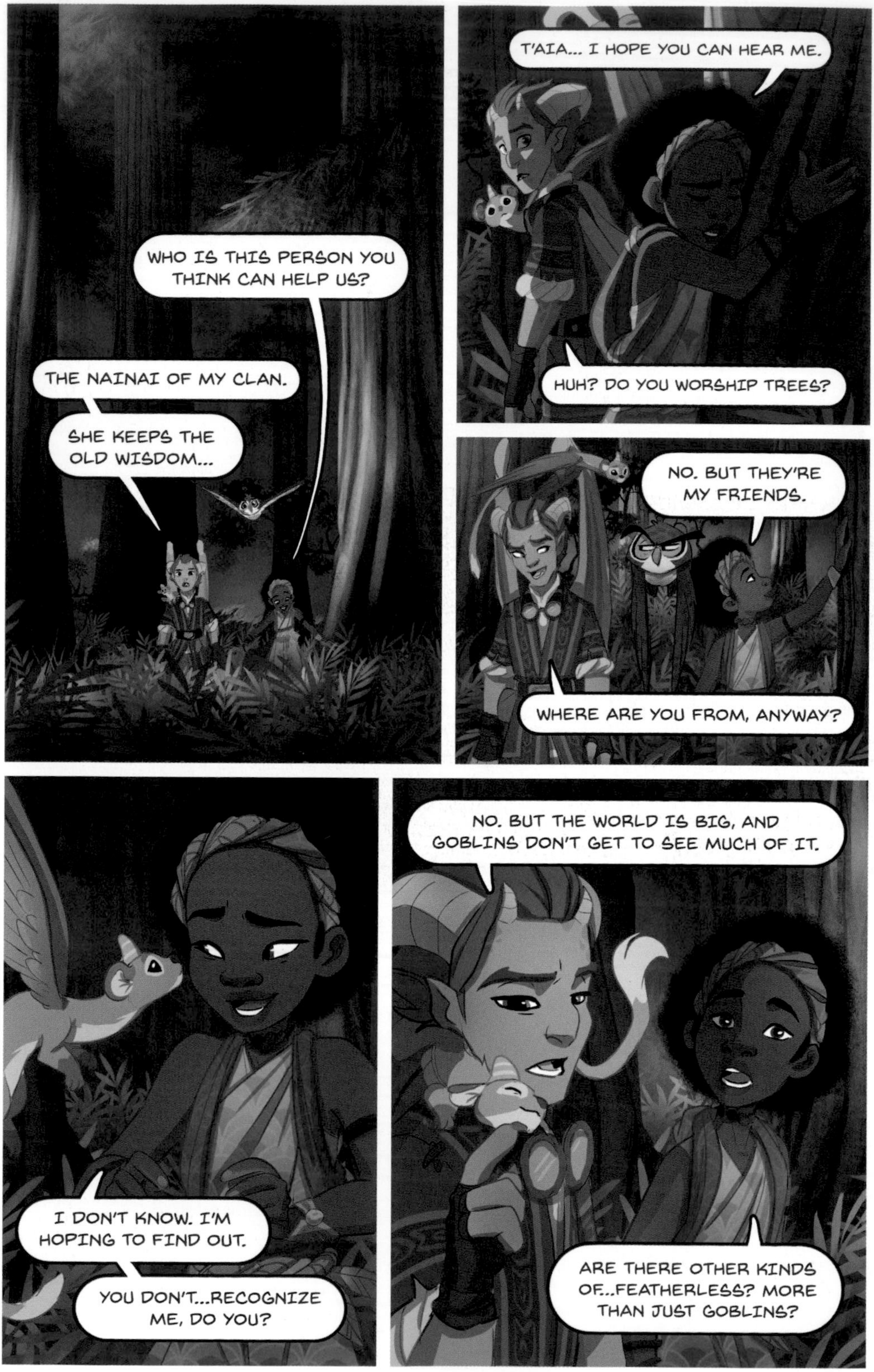
WHO IS THIS PERSON YOU THINK CAN HELP US?
THE NAINAI OF MY CLAN.
SHE KEEPS THE OLD WISDOM...
T'AIA... I HOPE YOU CAN HEAR ME.
HUH? DO YOU WORSHIP TREES?
NO. BUT THEY'RE MY FRIENDS.
WHERE ARE YOU FROM, ANYWAY?
I DON'T KNOW. I'M HOPING TO FIND OUT.
YOU DON'T...RECOGNIZE ME, DO YOU?
NO. BUT THE WORLD IS BIG, AND GOBLINS DON'T GET TO SEE MUCH OF IT.
ARE THERE OTHER KINDS OF...FEATHERLESS? MORE THAN JUST GOBLINS?

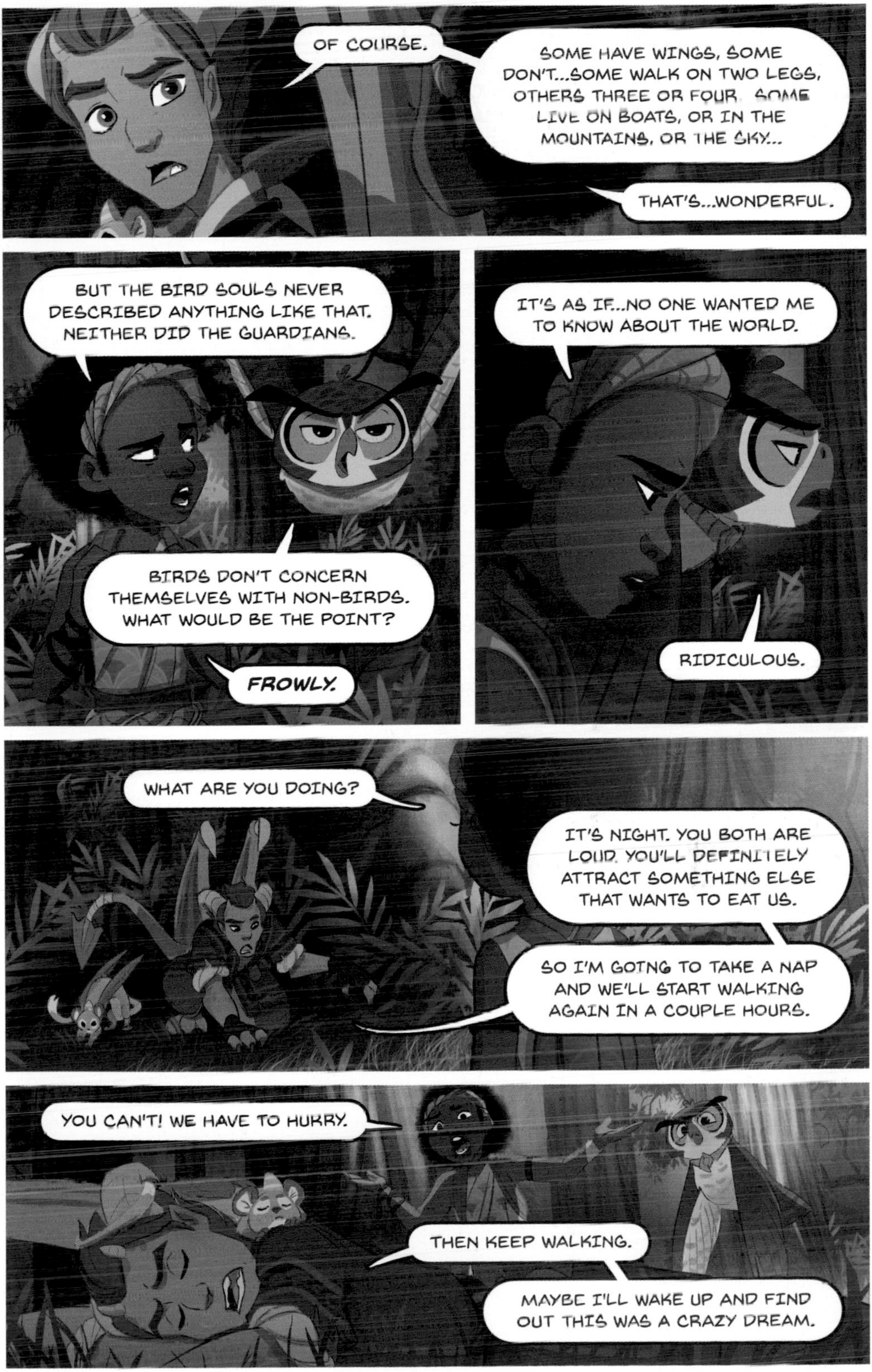
OF COURSE.
SOME HAVE WINGS, SOME DON'T...SOME WALK ON TWO LEGS, OTHERS THREE OR FOUR. SOME LIVE ON BOATS, OR IN THE MOUNTAINS, OR THE SKY...
THAT'S...WONDERFUL.
BUT THE BIRD SOULS NEVER DESCRIBED ANYTHING LIKE THAT. NEITHER DID THE GUARDIANS.
BIRDS DON'T CONCERN THEMSELVES WITH NON-BIRDS. WHAT WOULD BE THE POINT?
FROWLY.
IT'S AS IF...NO ONE WANTED ME TO KNOW ABOUT THE WORLD.
RIDICULOUS.
WHAT ARE YOU DOING?
IT'S NIGHT. YOU BOTH ARE LOUD. YOU'LL DEFINITELY ATTRACT SOMETHING ELSE THAT WANTS TO EAT US.
SO I'M GOING TO TAKE A NAP AND WE'LL START WALKING AGAIN IN A COUPLE HOURS.
YOU CAN'T! WE HAVE TO HURRY.
THEN KEEP WALKING.
MAYBE I'LL WAKE UP AND FIND OUT THIS WAS A CRAZY DREAM.

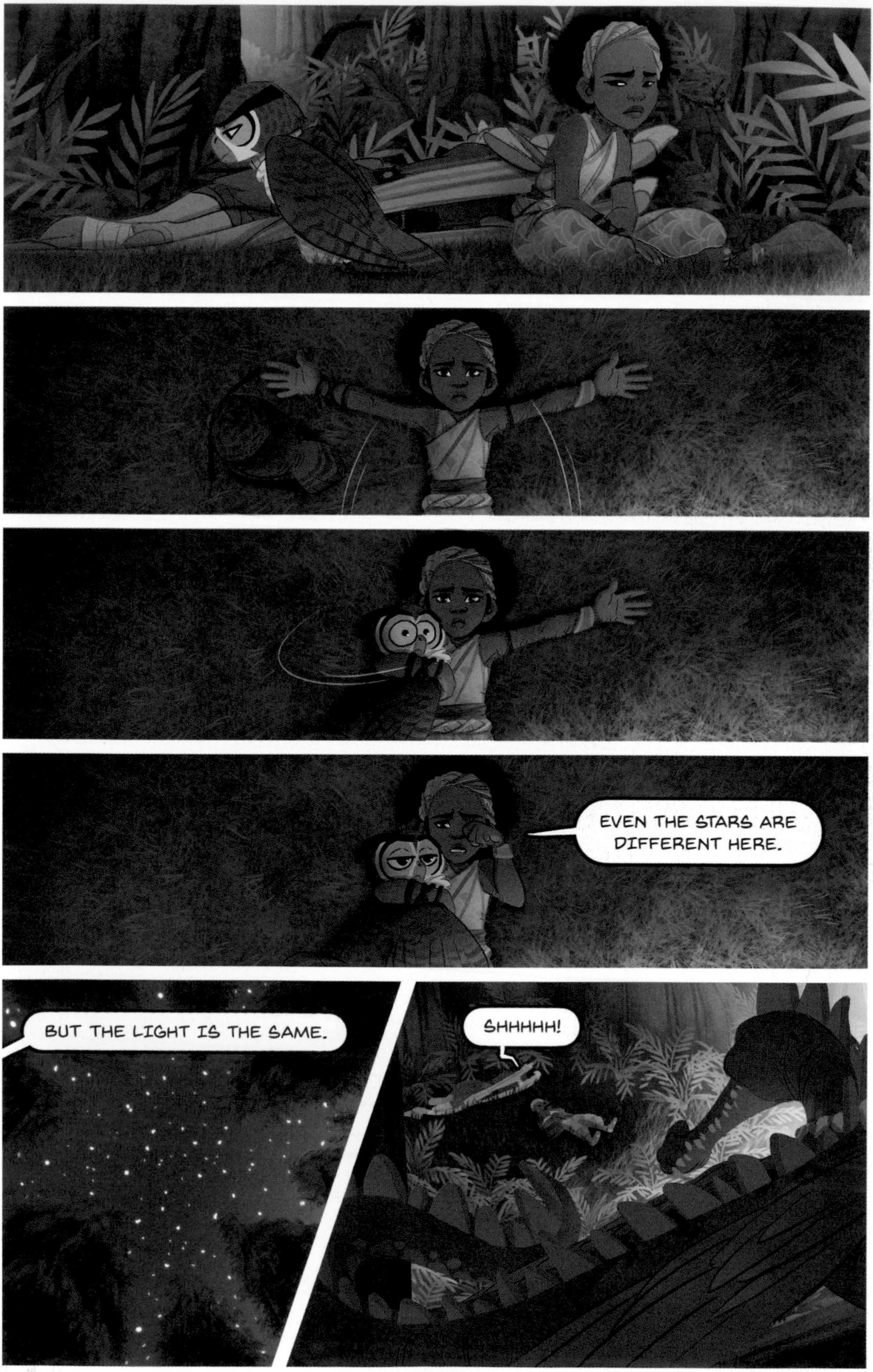
EVEN THE STARS ARE DIFFERENT HERE.
BUT THE LIGHT IS THE SAME.
SHHHHH!

I DON'T SUPPOSE THAT MAGIC BRACELET OF YOURS IS GOOD AT FINDING SCAVENGE?

ACTUALLY, NEVER MIND.

THIS PLACE HAS BEEN PICKED OVER FOR A THOUSAND YEARS. NOTHING LEFT BUT ROCK.

WAS IT A CITY LIKE THE ONE WE WERE IN?

NAH. DRAGON OUTPOST. A FEW OF THEM ALWAYS LIVED NEAR THE SIRIC.

SIGH.

I'M GONNA GET MY WINGS CLIPPED.

WHAT'S WRONG?

I WASN'T BORN INSIDE MY CLAN. THEY ADOPTED ME. BUT THERE WERE CONDITIONS.

I JUST NEED A COUPLE GOOD SCORES, AND I'LL BE SAFE.

OH.

THOSE WRAITHS, MEETING ME...

...MADE THINGS HARDER FOR YOU.

CHOP!

CHOP!. CREEEAK!

WELL, HERE WE ARE.

EH...IT'S OKAY. IF IT HADN'T BEEN YOU, IT WOULD HAVE BEEN SOMETHING ELSE. LIFE ISN'T EVER EASY.

OUTSKIRTS OF CAMP.

YES, THEY ARE! TREES ARE ALIVE! THEY THINK, THEY TALK!

CUTTING THEM DOWN IS MURDER!

WOW. YOU ARE TOO MUCH.

WITHOUT WOOD, WE WOULD DIE. WE USE IT TO BUILD SHELTERS, KEEP WARM, COOK MEALS.

WE BARTER THE LOGS FOR THINGS WE NEED.

THERE'S PLENTY OF TREES. WE DON'T TAKE MORE THAN WE NEED.

IT DOESN'T MATTER. EACH ONE IS SPECIAL. AND IT'S WHERE BIRDS MAKE THEIR HOMES.

CUTTING THEM IS WRONG AND...AND DISGUSTING.

DO YOU STILL WANT TO SEE THE NAINAI?

I DON'T KNOW. IS SHE A TREE-KILLER?

YUP, DEFINITELY.

NUMBER ONE TREE-KILLER, THAT'S HER. SAME AS ME.

JUST ANOTHER EXCUSE NOT TO LIKE A GOBLIN.

FINE. I SHOULDN'T HAVE BROUGHT YOU HERE ANYWAY.

NOTHING IN IT FOR ME.

BUT YOU WON'T LIKE ANYONE IN THIS WORLD IF YOU CAN'T STAND SEEING A TREE CUT DOWN.

IGNORE HIM. GOOD RIDDANCE!

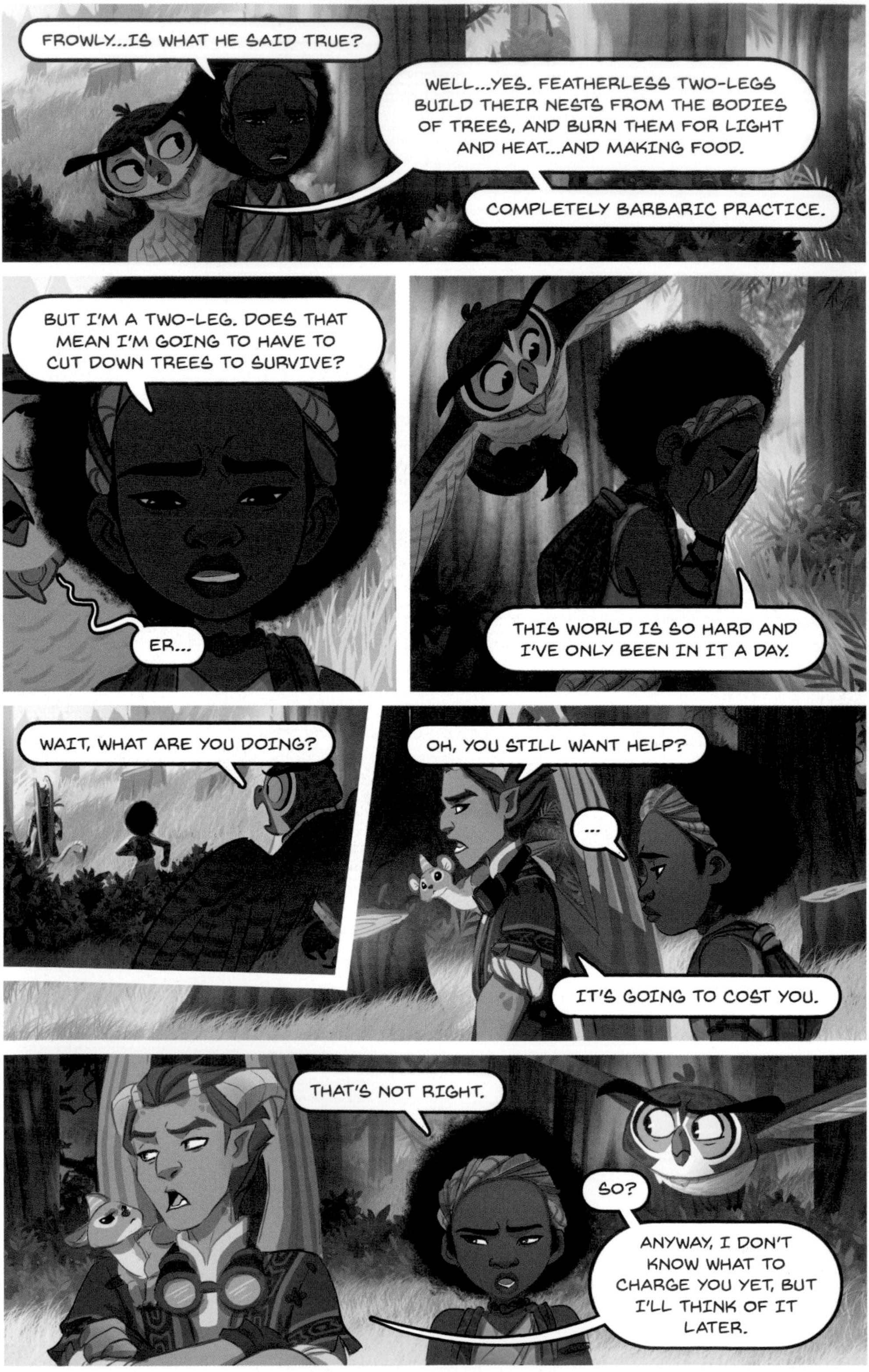
FROWLY...IS WHAT HE SAID TRUE?
WELL...YES. FEATHERLESS TWO-LEGS BUILD THEIR NESTS FROM THE BODIES OF TREES, AND BURN THEM FOR LIGHT AND HEAT...AND MAKING FOOD.
COMPLETELY BARBARIC PRACTICE.
BUT I'M A TWO-LEG. DOES THAT MEAN I'M GOING TO HAVE TO CUT DOWN TREES TO SURVIVE?
ER...
THIS WORLD IS SO HARD AND I'VE ONLY BEEN IN IT A DAY.
WAIT, WHAT ARE YOU DOING?
OH, YOU STILL WANT HELP?
...
IT'S GOING TO COST YOU.
THAT'S NOT RIGHT.
SO?
ANYWAY, I DON'T KNOW WHAT TO CHARGE YOU YET, BUT I'LL THINK OF IT LATER.

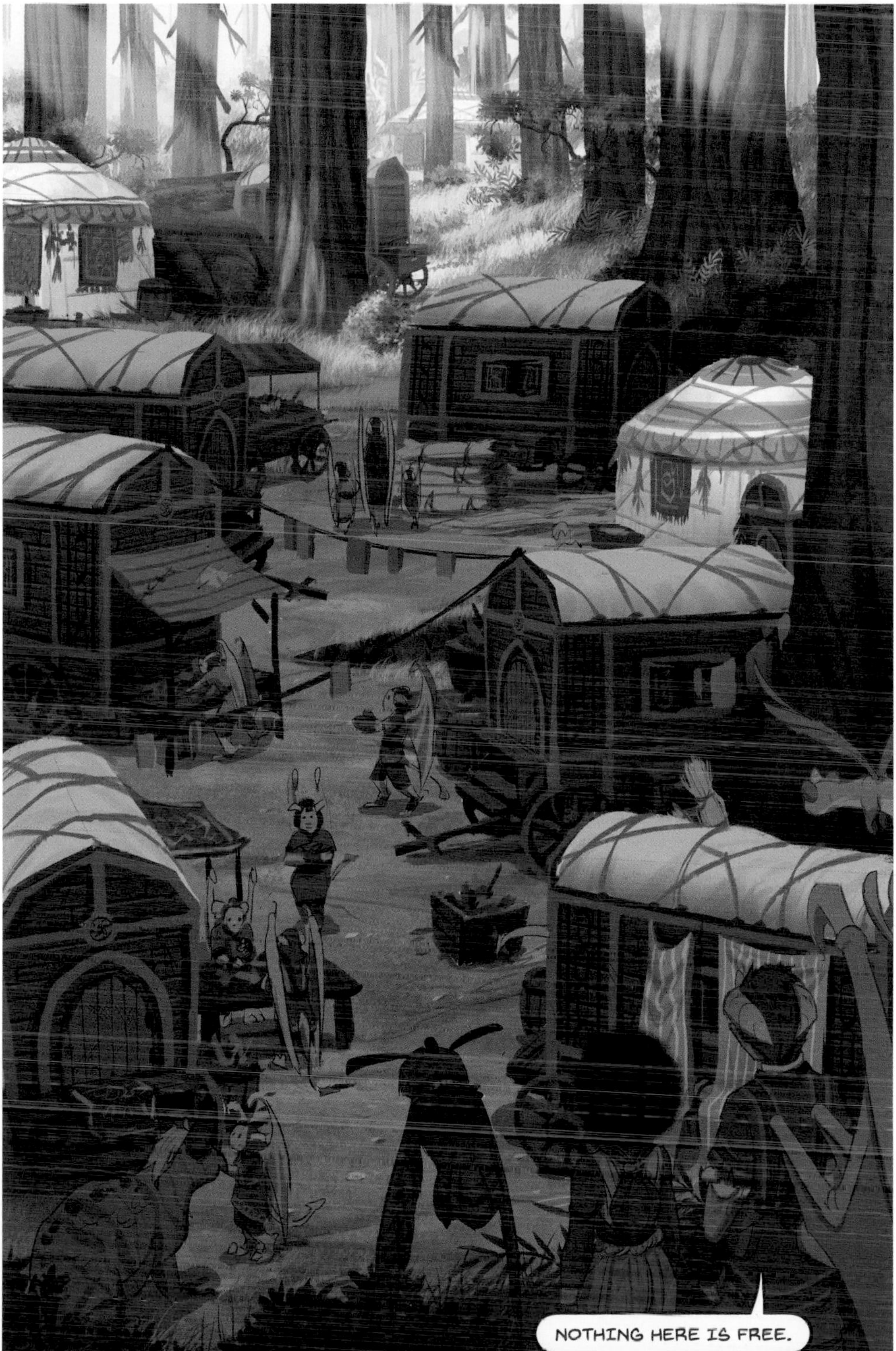
NOTHING HERE IS FREE.

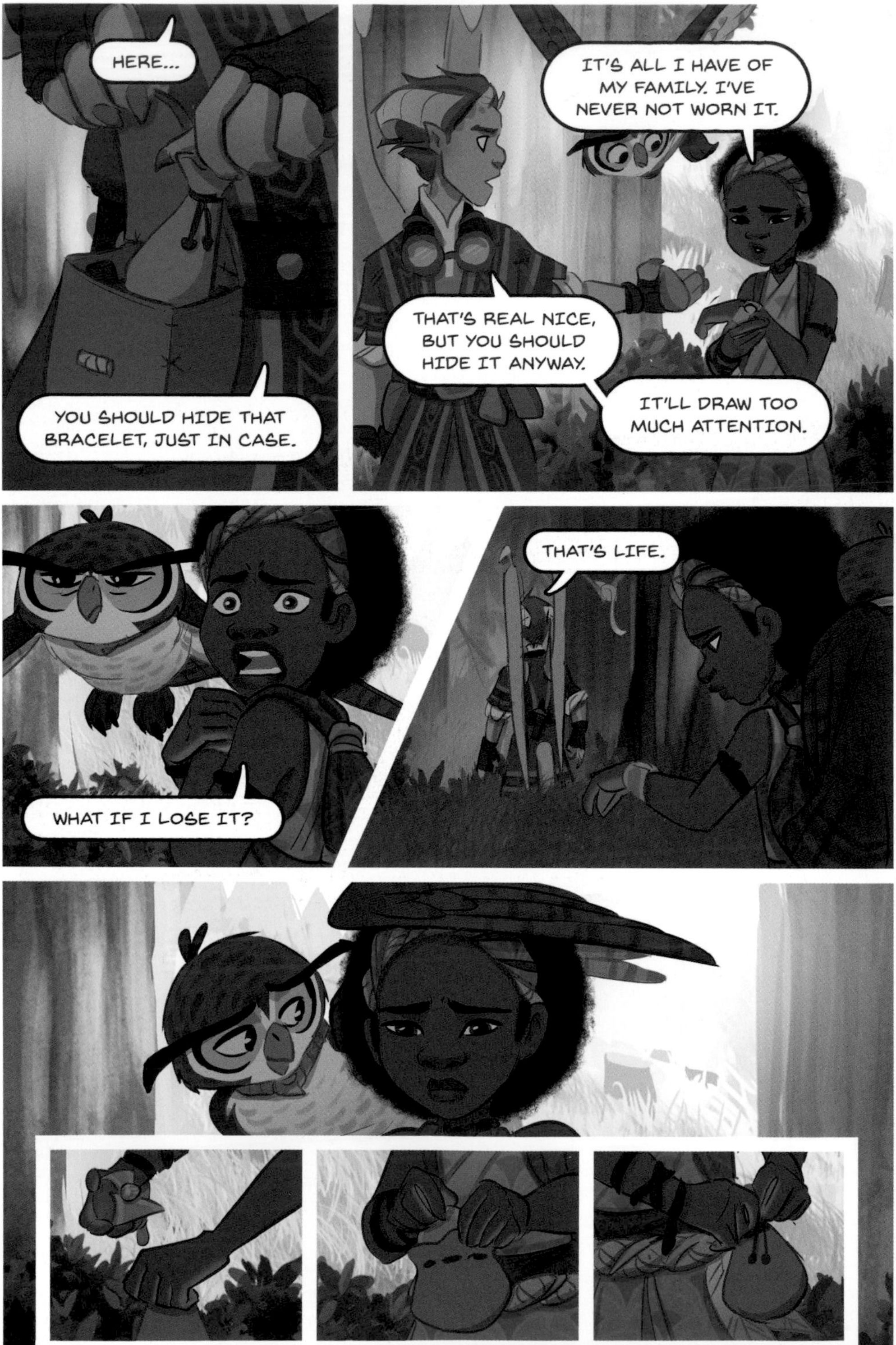
HERE...
YOU SHOULD HIDE THAT BRACELET, JUST IN CASE.
IT'S ALL I HAVE OF MY FAMILY. I'VE NEVER NOT WORN IT.
THAT'S REAL NICE, BUT YOU SHOULD HIDE IT ANYWAY.
IT'LL DRAW TOO MUCH ATTENTION.
WHAT IF I LOSE IT?
THAT'S LIFE.

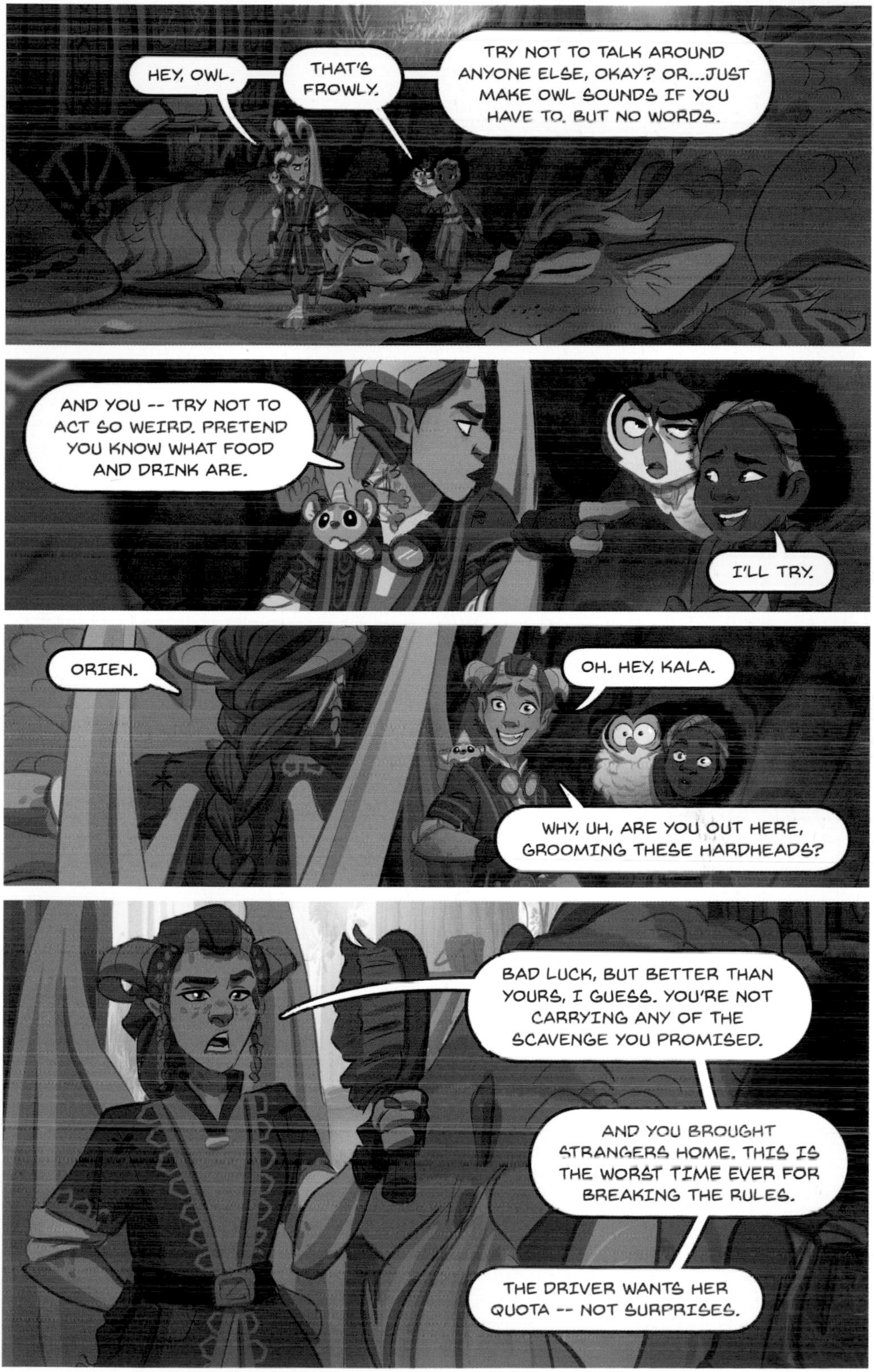
HEY, OWL.
THAT'S FROWLY.
TRY NOT TO TALK AROUND ANYONE ELSE, OKAY? OR...JUST MAKE OWL SOUNDS IF YOU HAVE TO. BUT NO WORDS.
AND YOU -- TRY NOT TO ACT SO WEIRD. PRETEND YOU KNOW WHAT FOOD AND DRINK ARE.
I'LL TRY.
ORIEN.
OH. HEY, KALA.
WHY, UH, ARE YOU OUT HERE, GROOMING THESE HARDHEADS?
BAD LUCK, BUT BETTER THAN YOURS, I GUESS. YOU'RE NOT CARRYING ANY OF THE SCAVENGE YOU PROMISED.
AND YOU BROUGHT STRANGERS HOME. THIS IS THE WORST TIME EVER FOR BREAKING THE RULES.
THE DRIVER WANTS HER QUOTA -- NOT SURPRISES.

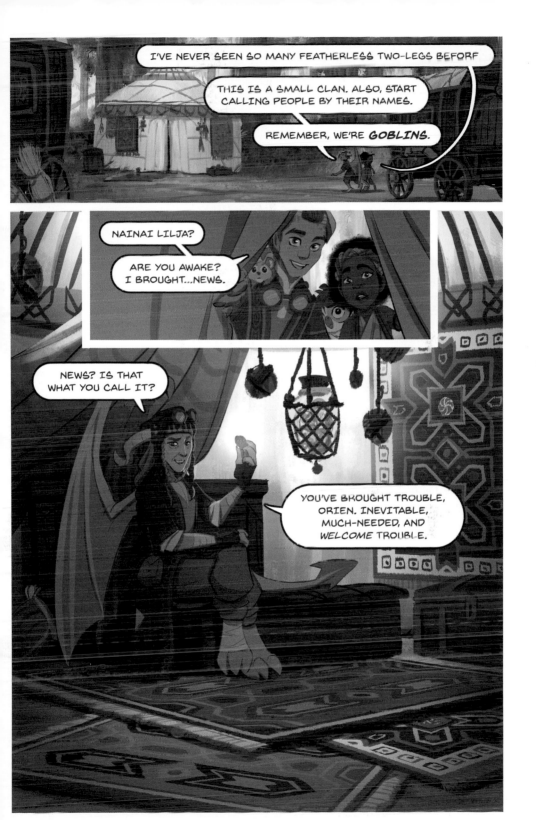

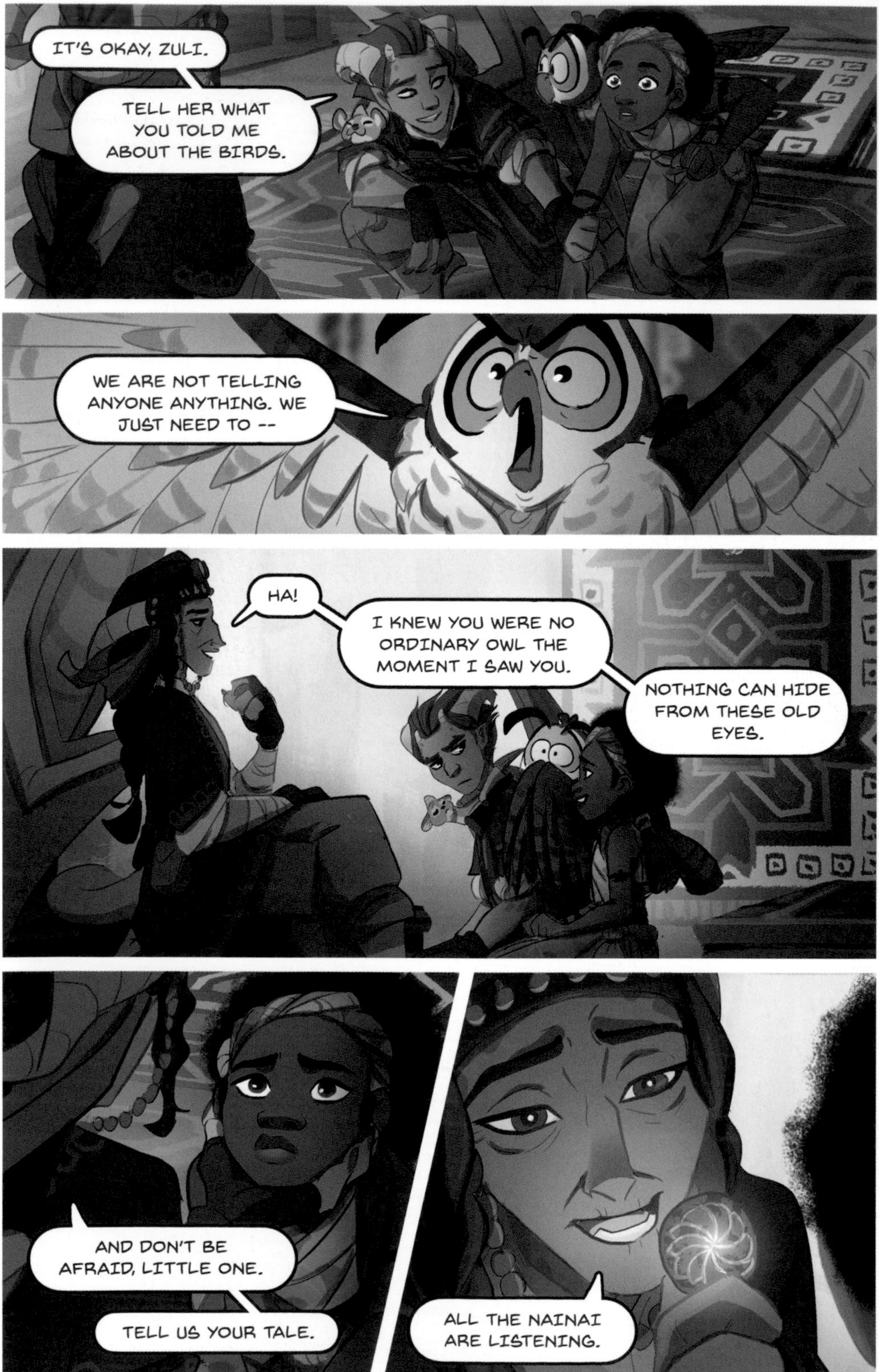
IT'S OKAY, ZULI.
TELL HER WHAT YOU TOLD ME ABOUT THE BIRDS.
WE ARE NOT TELLING ANYONE ANYTHING. WE JUST NEED TO --
HA!
I KNEW YOU WERE NO ORDINARY OWL THE MOMENT I SAW YOU.
NOTHING CAN HIDE FROM THESE OLD EYES.
AND DON'T BE AFRAID, LITTLE ONE.
TELL US YOUR TALE.
ALL THE NAINAI ARE LISTENING.

THE SOULS OF DEAD BIRDS HAVE BEEN STOLEN. I LEFT THE GREAT TREE TO FIND OUT WHY, BUT I DON'T KNOW WHERE THEY ARE, OR WHO'S RESPONSIBLE.

NO BIRDS WILL EVER BE BORN AGAIN UNLESS ME AND FROWL' SAVE THEM.

IT'S NOT JUST THE BIRDS, LITTLE ONE.

A BAD YEAR, SOME SAY. GOBLINS ARE SICK, THEY SAY. OTHERS BLAME THE WINGS WHO LIVE IN THE HIGH PLACES, AND THINK OF HOW TO GET REVENGE.

BUT THE NAINAIS KNOW DIFFERENT.

NO GOBLINS WERE BORN LAST SEASON.

WE CAN TASTE THE WIND COMING FROM THE NORTH, AND IT IS PART OF A SPREADING SICKNESS.

AN OLD AND GREEDY HUNGER.

THIS IS WHAT WE KNOW: MAGIC BEGAN THIS. MAGIC WILL END IT.

YOU HAVE TO GO NORTH. THAT'S WHAT I'M CERTAIN OF.

BUT THE NORTH IS A PRETTY BIG PLACE, AND IT'S NOT VERY FRIENDLY.

HOW WILL SHE FIND ANYTHING UP THERE?

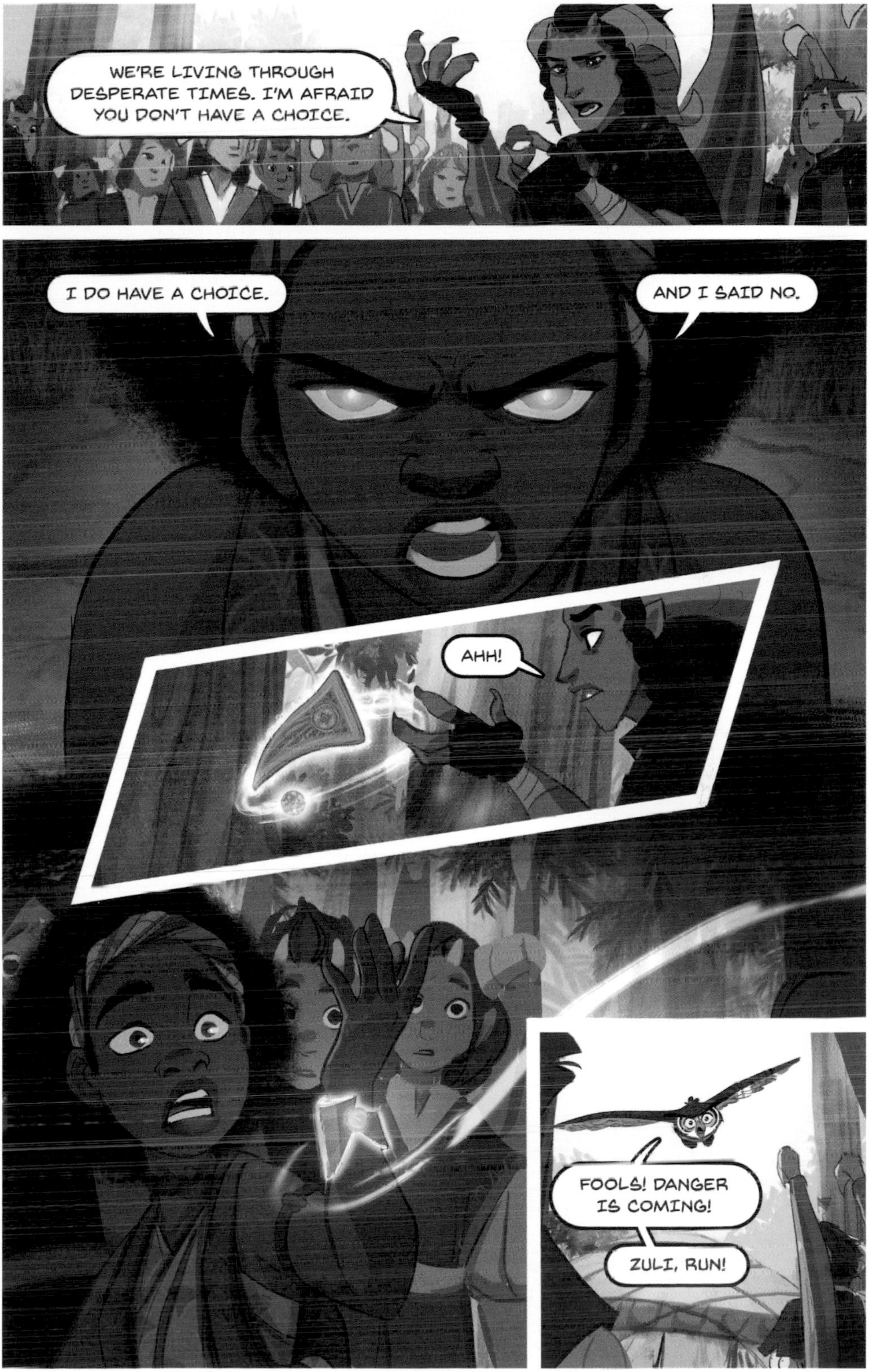
WE'RE LIVING THROUGH DESPERATE TIMES. I'M AFRAID YOU DON'T HAVE A CHOICE.
I DO HAVE A CHOICE.
AND I SAID NO.
AHH!
FOOLS! DANGER IS COMING!
ZULI, RUN!

86

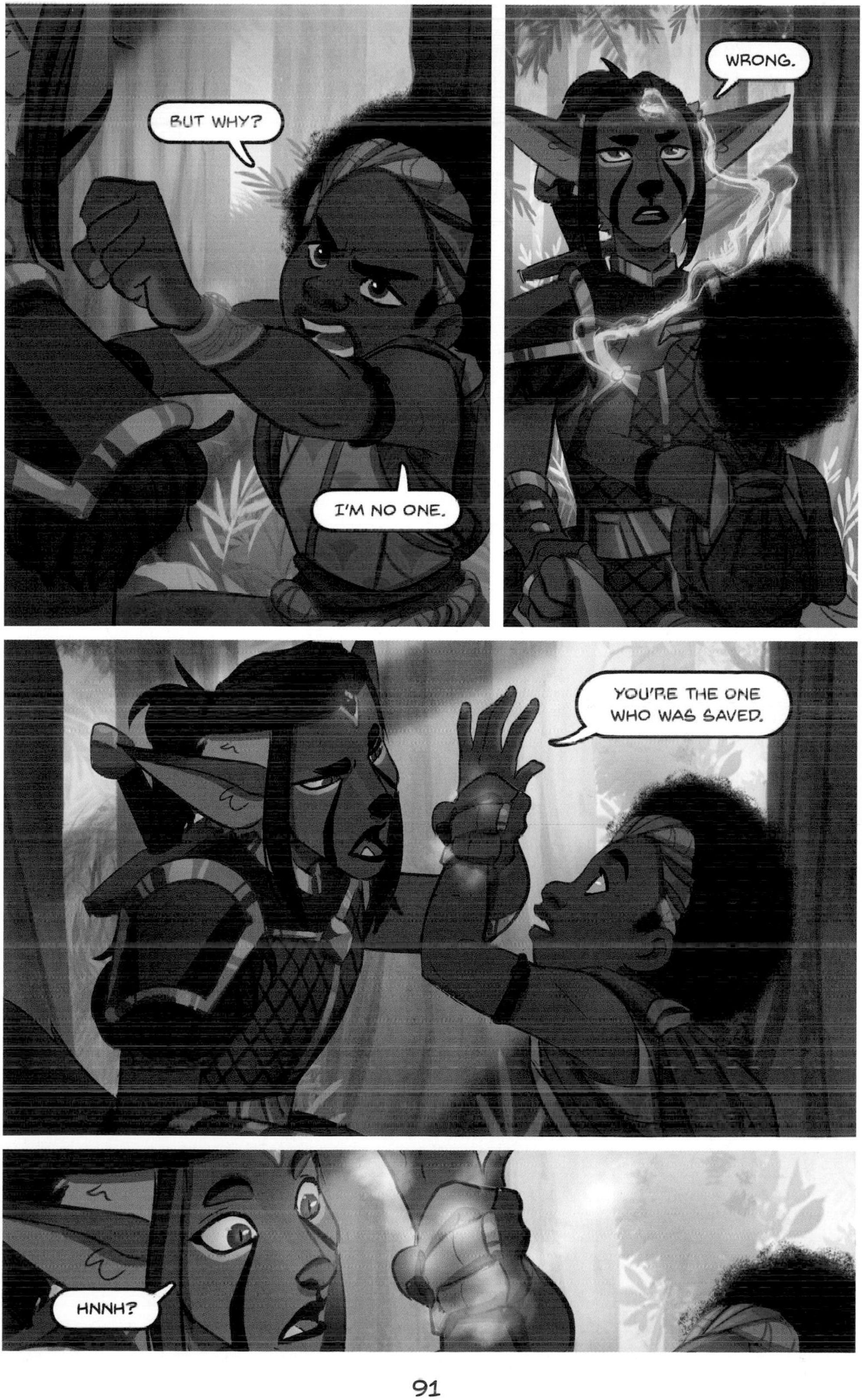
BUT WHY?
I'M NO ONE.
WRONG.
YOU'RE THE ONE WHO WAS SAVED.
HNNH?

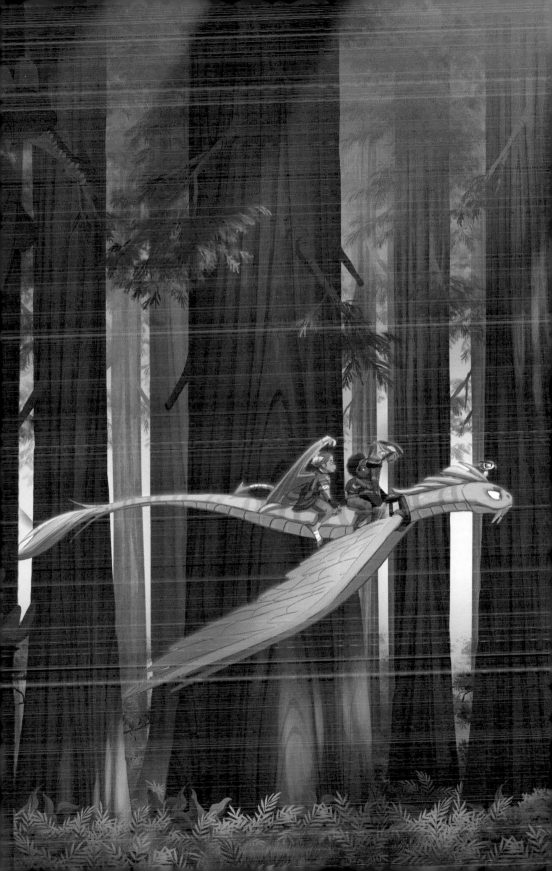

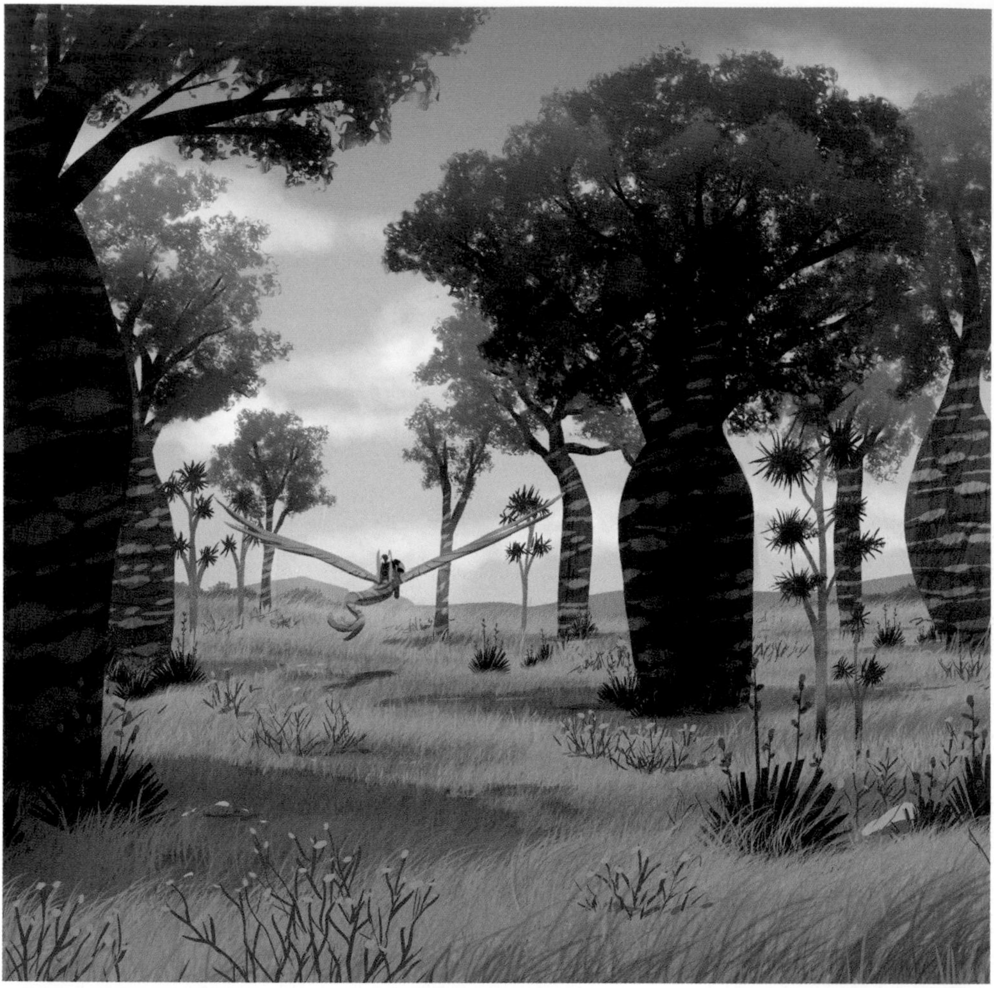

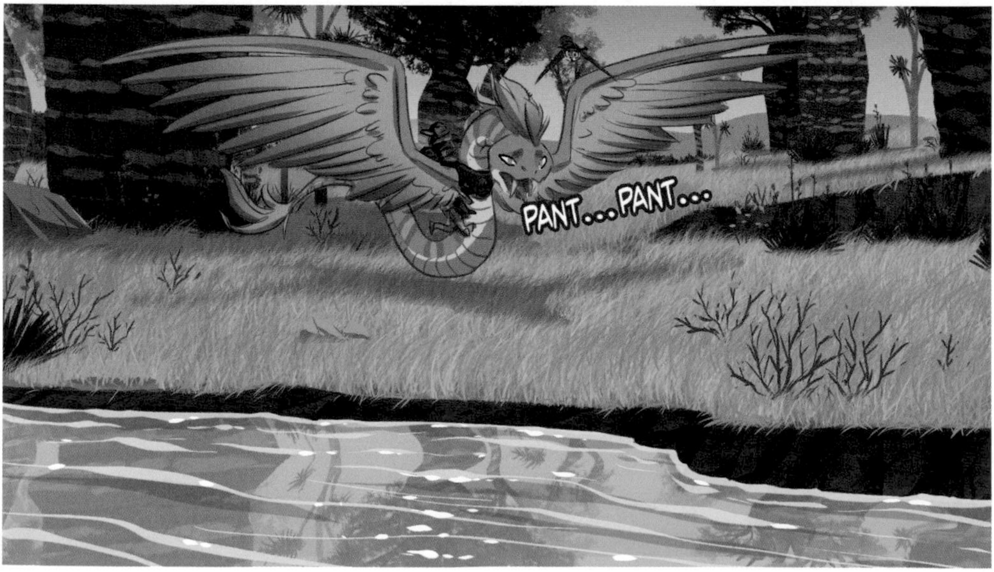
PANT... PANT...

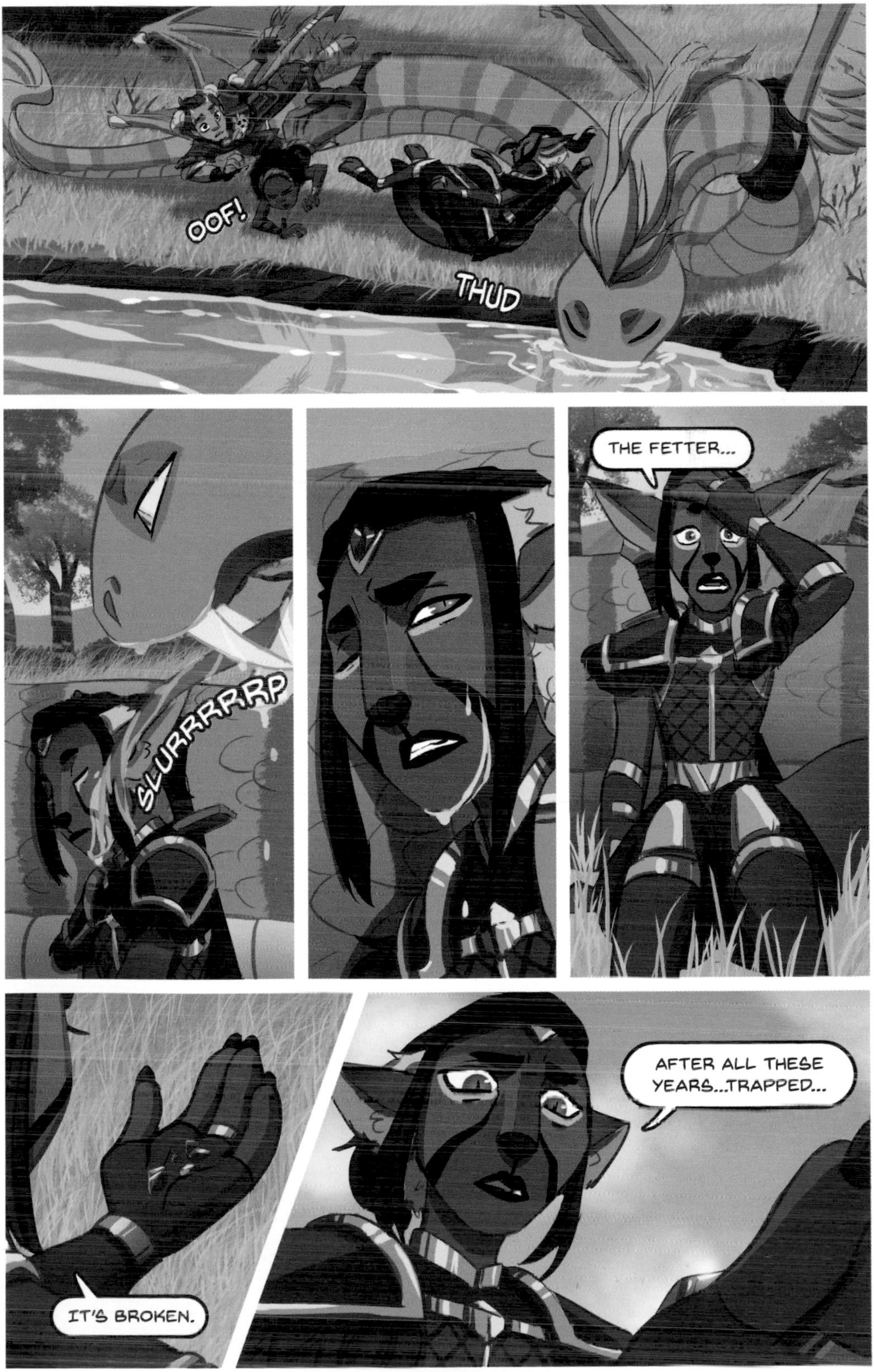
OOF!
THUD
SLURRRRRP
THE FETTER...
IT'S BROKEN.
AFTER ALL THESE YEARS...TRAPPED...

NEVER AGAIN!

THE OTHERS SHOULD BE ON OUR HEELS. THEY SHOULD NEVER HAVE ALLOWED US TO ESCAPE.

WHO ARE YOU...AND WHO IS THIS WITCH-QUEEN?

WERE THOSE RED STONES CONTROLLING YOU?

BUT PERHAPS LOSING ME AND JAX HAS MADE THE WITCH-QUEEN CAUTIOUS.

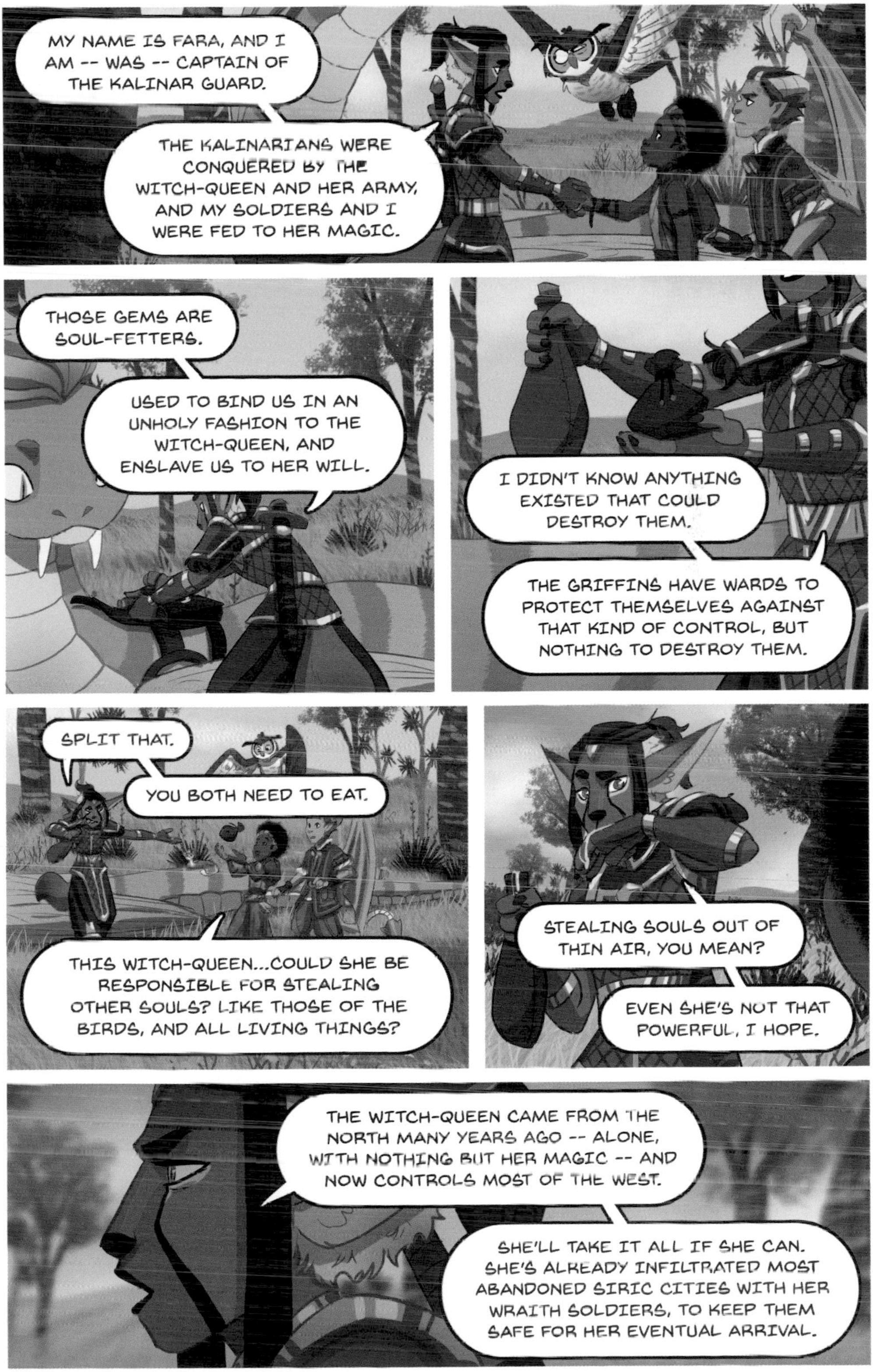
MY NAME IS FARA, AND I AM -- WAS -- CAPTAIN OF THE KALINAR GUARD.
THE KALINARIANS WERE CONQUERED BY THE WITCH-QUEEN AND HER ARMY, AND MY SOLDIERS AND I WERE FED TO HER MAGIC.
THOSE GEMS ARE SOUL-FETTERS.
USED TO BIND US IN AN UNHOLY FASHION TO THE WITCH-QUEEN, AND ENSLAVE US TO HER WILL.
I DIDN'T KNOW ANYTHING EXISTED THAT COULD DESTROY THEM.
THE GRIFFINS HAVE WARDS TO PROTECT THEMSELVES AGAINST THAT KIND OF CONTROL, BUT NOTHING TO DESTROY THEM.
SPLIT THAT.
YOU BOTH NEED TO EAT.
THIS WITCH-QUEEN...COULD SHE BE RESPONSIBLE FOR STEALING OTHER SOULS? LIKE THOSE OF THE BIRDS, AND ALL LIVING THINGS?
STEALING SOULS OUT OF THIN AIR, YOU MEAN?
EVEN SHE'S NOT THAT POWERFUL, I HOPE.
THE WITCH-QUEEN CAME FROM THE NORTH MANY YEARS AGO -- ALONE, WITH NOTHING BUT HER MAGIC -- AND NOW CONTROLS MOST OF THE WEST.
SHE'LL TAKE IT ALL IF SHE CAN. SHE'S ALREADY INFILTRATED MOST ABANDONED SIRIC CITIES WITH HER WRAITH SOLDIERS, TO KEEP THEM SAFE FOR HER EVENTUAL ARRIVAL.

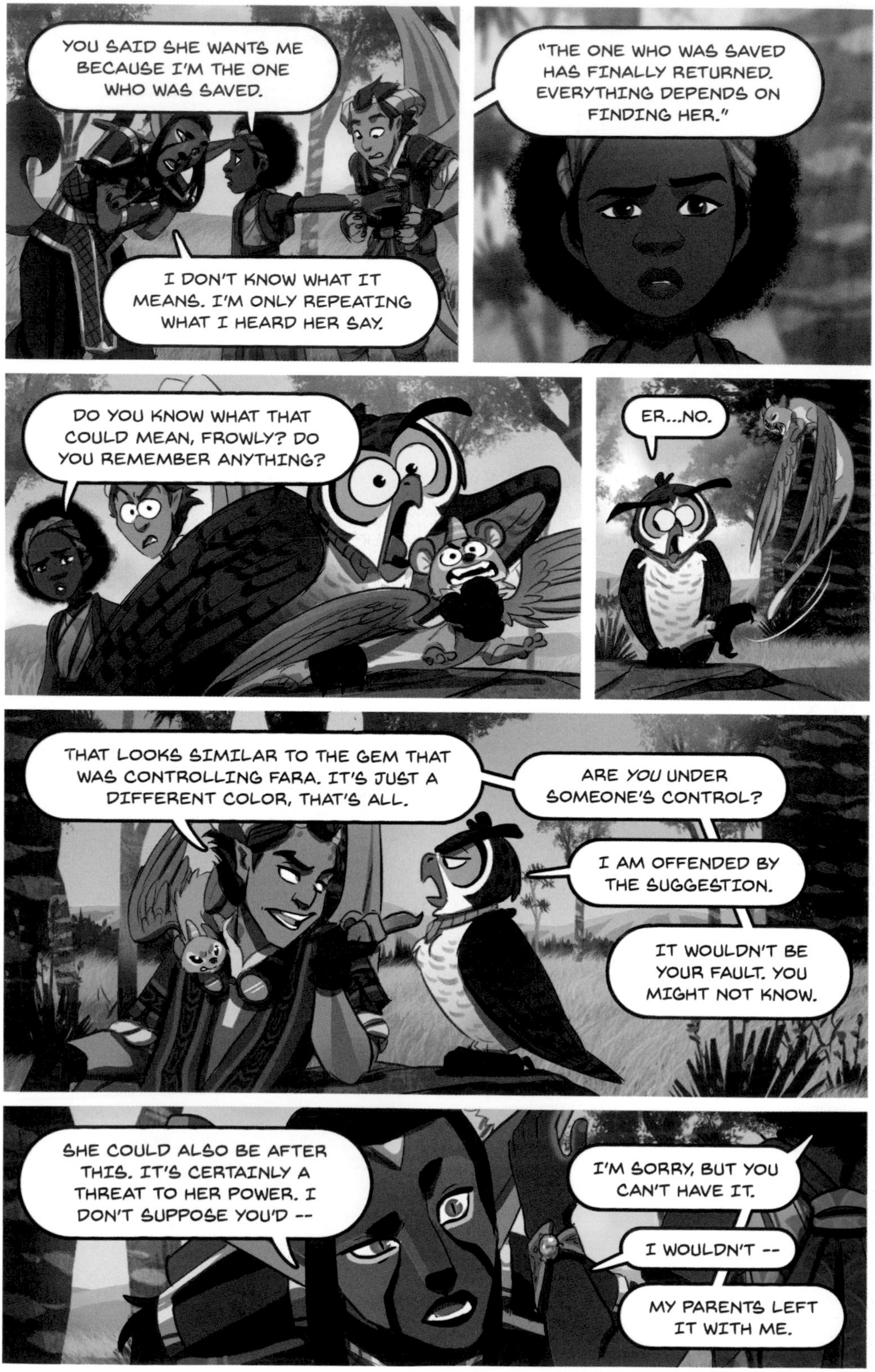
YOU SAID SHE WANTS ME BECAUSE I'M THE ONE WHO WAS SAVED.
I DON'T KNOW WHAT IT MEANS. I'M ONLY REPEATING WHAT I HEARD HER SAY.
"THE ONE WHO WAS SAVED HAS FINALLY RETURNED. EVERYTHING DEPENDS ON FINDING HER."
DO YOU KNOW WHAT THAT COULD MEAN, FROWLY? DO YOU REMEMBER ANYTHING?
ER...NO.
THAT LOOKS SIMILAR TO THE GEM THAT WAS CONTROLLING FARA. IT'S JUST A DIFFERENT COLOR, THAT'S ALL.
ARE *YOU* UNDER SOMEONE'S CONTROL?
I AM OFFENDED BY THE SUGGESTION.
IT WOULDN'T BE YOUR FAULT. YOU MIGHT NOT KNOW.
SHE COULD ALSO BE AFTER THIS. IT'S CERTAINLY A THREAT TO HER POWER. I DON'T SUPPOSE YOU'D --
I'M SORRY, BUT YOU CAN'T HAVE IT.
I WOULDN'T --
MY PARENTS LEFT IT WITH ME.

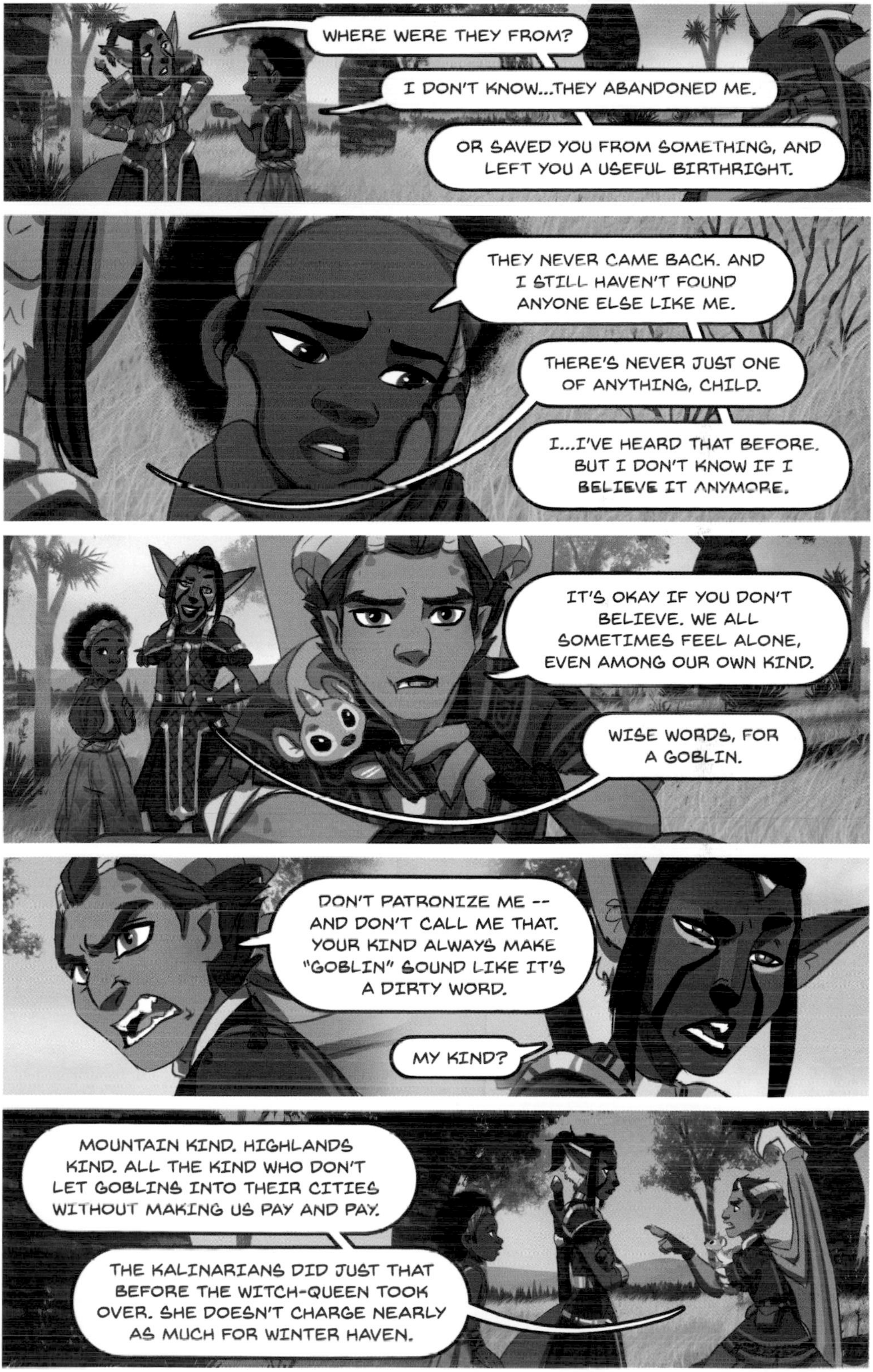
WHERE WERE THEY FROM?
I DON'T KNOW...THEY ABANDONED ME.
OR SAVED YOU FROM SOMETHING, AND LEFT YOU A USEFUL BIRTHRIGHT.
THEY NEVER CAME BACK. AND I STILL HAVEN'T FOUND ANYONE ELSE LIKE ME.
THERE'S NEVER JUST ONE OF ANYTHING, CHILD.
I...I'VE HEARD THAT BEFORE. BUT I DON'T KNOW IF I BELIEVE IT ANYMORE.
IT'S OKAY IF YOU DON'T BELIEVE. WE ALL SOMETIMES FEEL ALONE, EVEN AMONG OUR OWN KIND.
WISE WORDS, FOR A GOBLIN.
DON'T PATRONIZE ME -- AND DON'T CALL ME THAT. YOUR KIND ALWAYS MAKE "GOBLIN" SOUND LIKE IT'S A DIRTY WORD.
MY KIND?
MOUNTAIN KIND. HIGHLANDS KIND. ALL THE KIND WHO DON'T LET GOBLINS INTO THEIR CITIES WITHOUT MAKING US PAY AND PAY.
THE KALINARIANS DID JUST THAT BEFORE THE WITCH-QUEEN TOOK OVER. SHE DOESN'T CHARGE NEARLY AS MUCH FOR WINTER HAVEN.

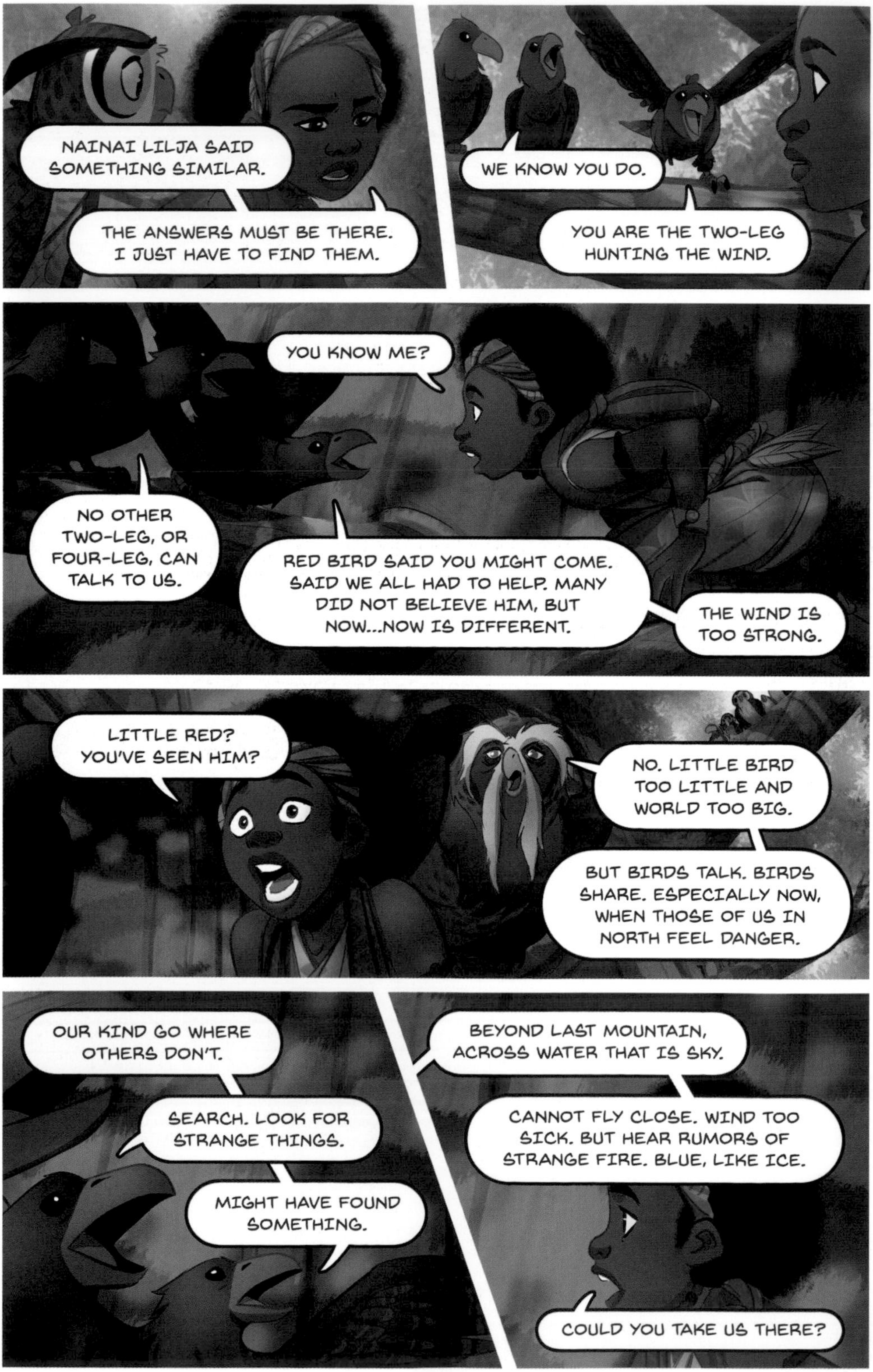
NAINAI LILJA SAID SOMETHING SIMILAR.
THE ANSWERS MUST BE THERE. I JUST HAVE TO FIND THEM.
WE KNOW YOU DO.
YOU ARE THE TWO-LEG HUNTING THE WIND.
YOU KNOW ME?
NO OTHER TWO-LEG, OR FOUR-LEG, CAN TALK TO US.
RED BIRD SAID YOU MIGHT COME. SAID WE ALL HAD TO HELP. MANY DID NOT BELIEVE HIM, BUT NOW...NOW IS DIFFERENT.
THE WIND IS TOO STRONG.
LITTLE RED? YOU'VE SEEN HIM?
NO. LITTLE BIRD TOO LITTLE AND WORLD TOO BIG.
BUT BIRDS TALK. BIRDS SHARE. ESPECIALLY NOW, WHEN THOSE OF US IN NORTH FEEL DANGER.
OUR KIND GO WHERE OTHERS DON'T.
SEARCH. LOOK FOR STRANGE THINGS.
MIGHT HAVE FOUND SOMETHING.
BEYOND LAST MOUNTAIN, ACROSS WATER THAT IS SKY.
CANNOT FLY CLOSE. WIND TOO SICK. BUT HEAR RUMORS OF STRANGE FIRE. BLUE, LIKE ICE.
COULD YOU TAKE US THERE?

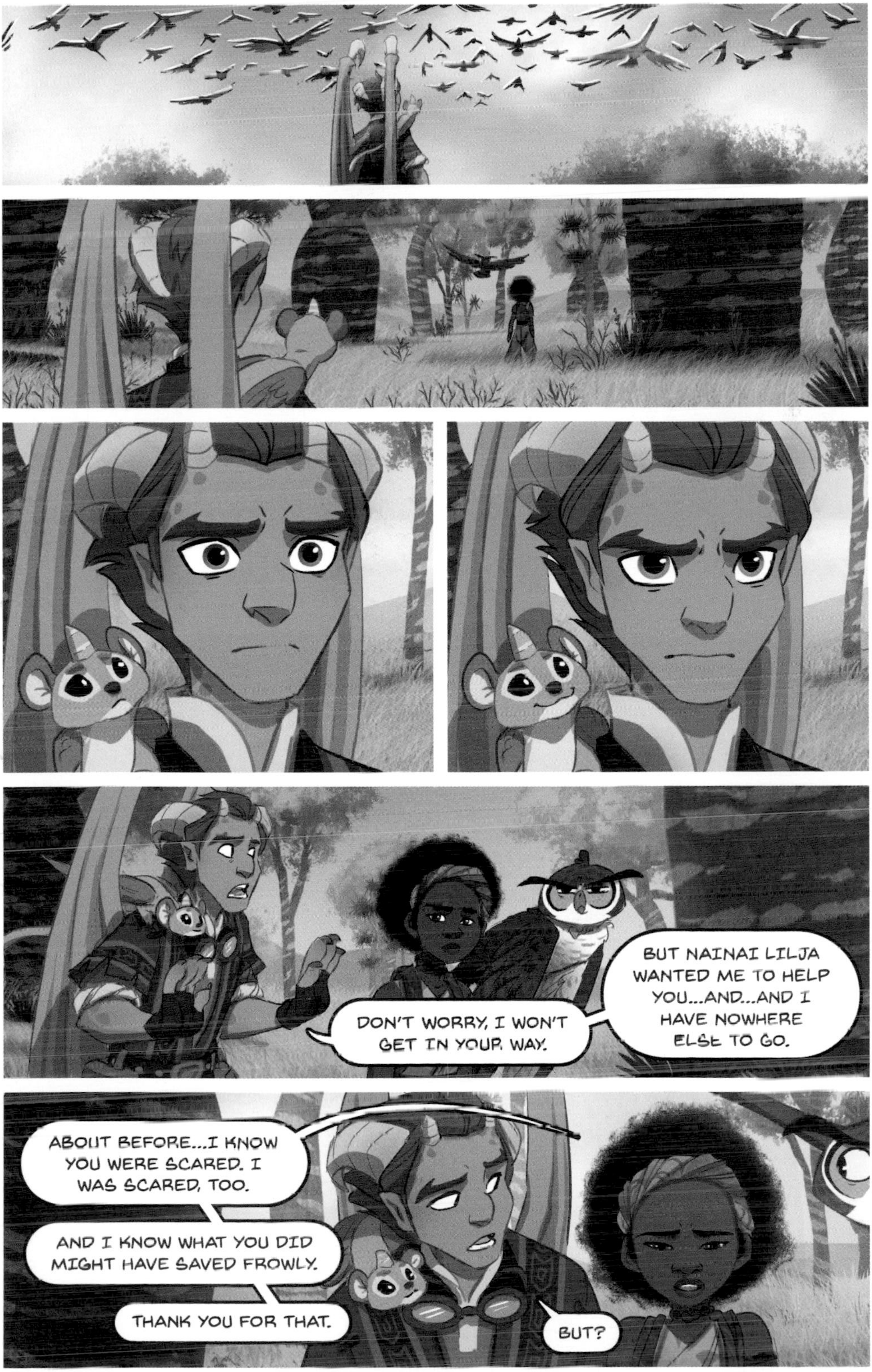
DON'T WORRY, I WON'T GET IN YOUR WAY.
BUT NAINAI LILJA WANTED ME TO HELP YOU...AND...AND I HAVE NOWHERE ELSE TO GO.
ABOUT BEFORE...I KNOW YOU WERE SCARED. I WAS SCARED, TOO.
AND I KNOW WHAT YOU DID MIGHT HAVE SAVED FROWLY.
THANK YOU FOR THAT.
BUT?

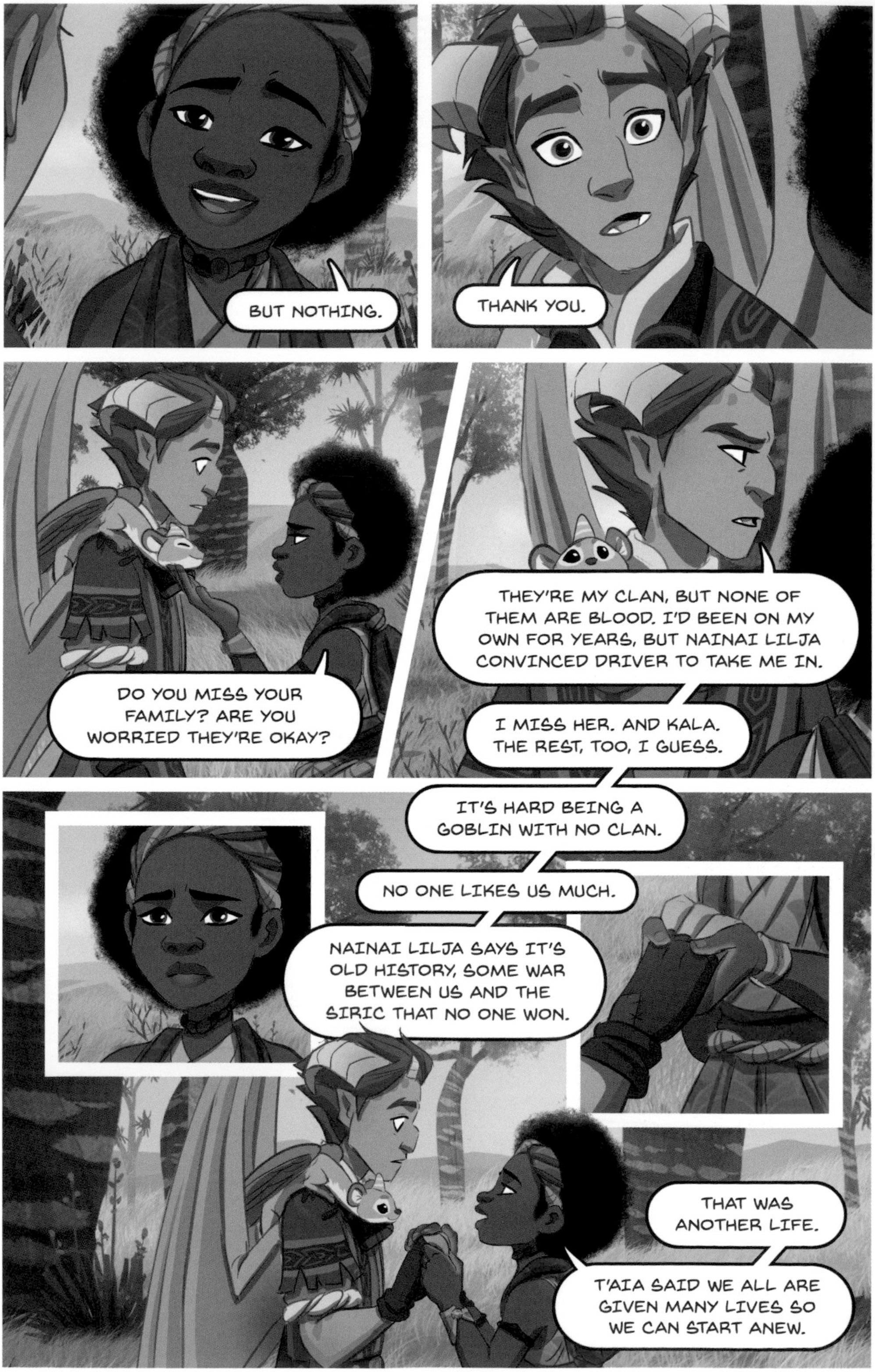
BUT NOTHING.
THANK YOU.
DO YOU MISS YOUR FAMILY? ARE YOU WORRIED THEY'RE OKAY?
THEY'RE MY CLAN, BUT NONE OF THEM ARE BLOOD. I'D BEEN ON MY OWN FOR YEARS, BUT NAINAI LILJA CONVINCED DRIVER TO TAKE ME IN.
I MISS HER. AND KALA. THE REST, TOO, I GUESS.
IT'S HARD BEING A GOBLIN WITH NO CLAN.
NO ONE LIKES US MUCH.
NAINAI LILJA SAYS IT'S OLD HISTORY, SOME WAR BETWEEN US AND THE SIRIC THAT NO ONE WON.
THAT WAS ANOTHER LIFE.
T'AIA SAID WE ALL ARE GIVEN MANY LIVES SO WE CAN START ANEW.

111

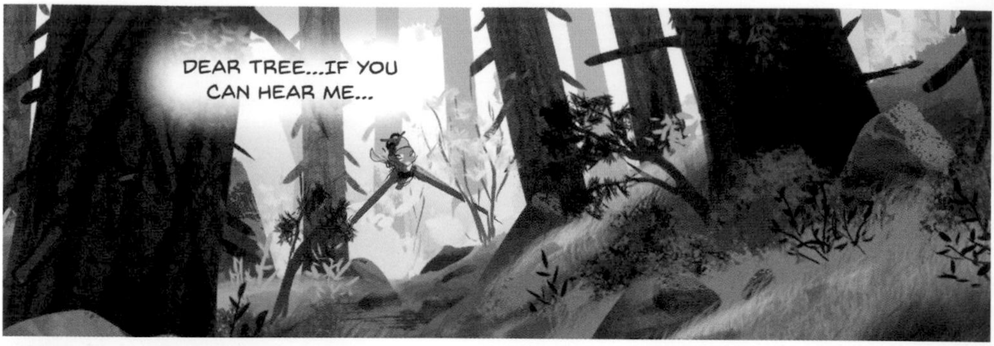
DEAR TREE...IF YOU CAN HEAR ME...

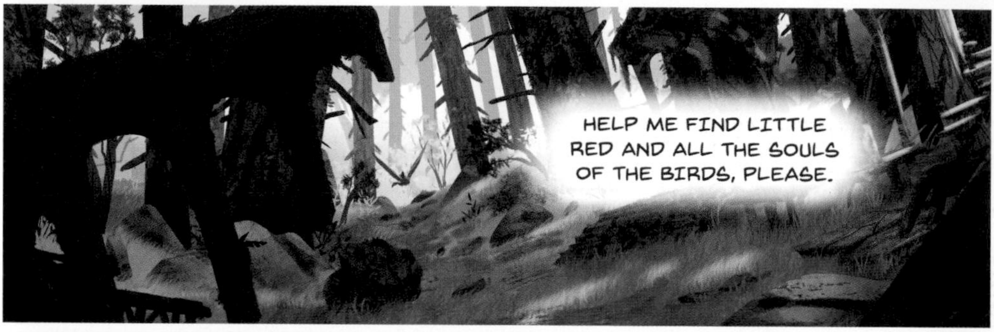
HELP ME FIND LITTLE RED AND ALL THE SOULS OF THE BIRDS, PLEASE.

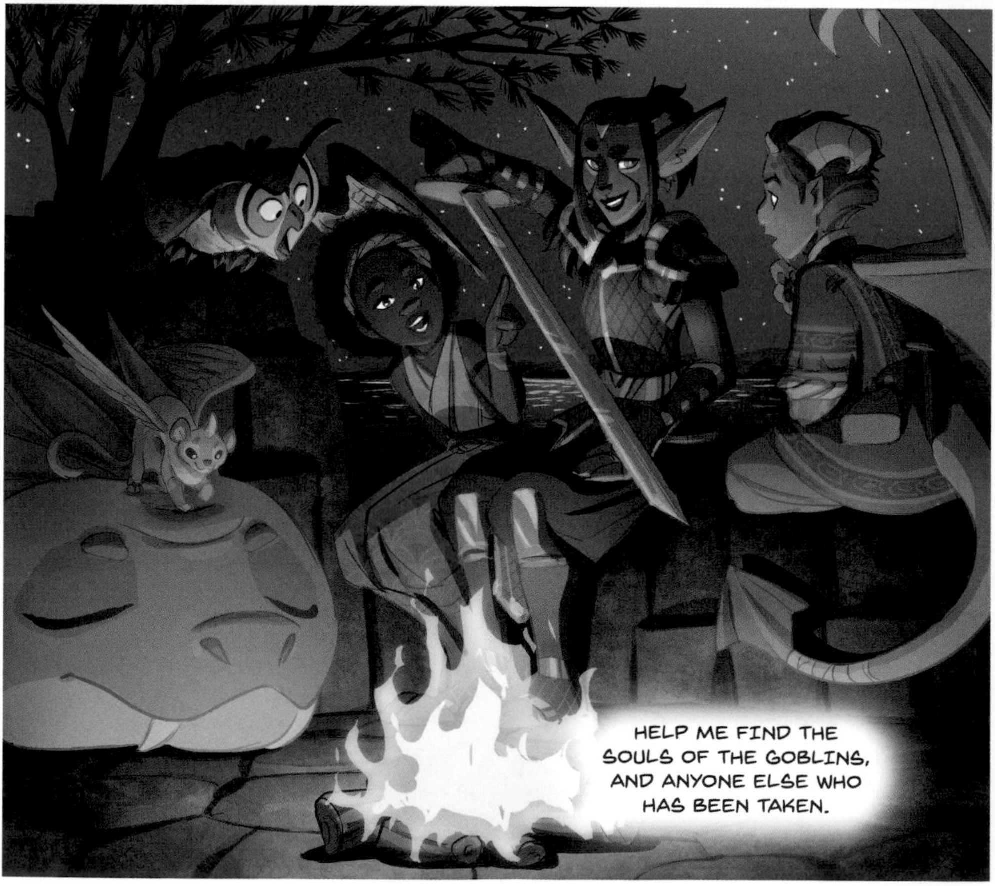
HELP ME FIND THE SOULS OF THE GOBLINS, AND ANYONE ELSE WHO HAS BEEN TAKEN.

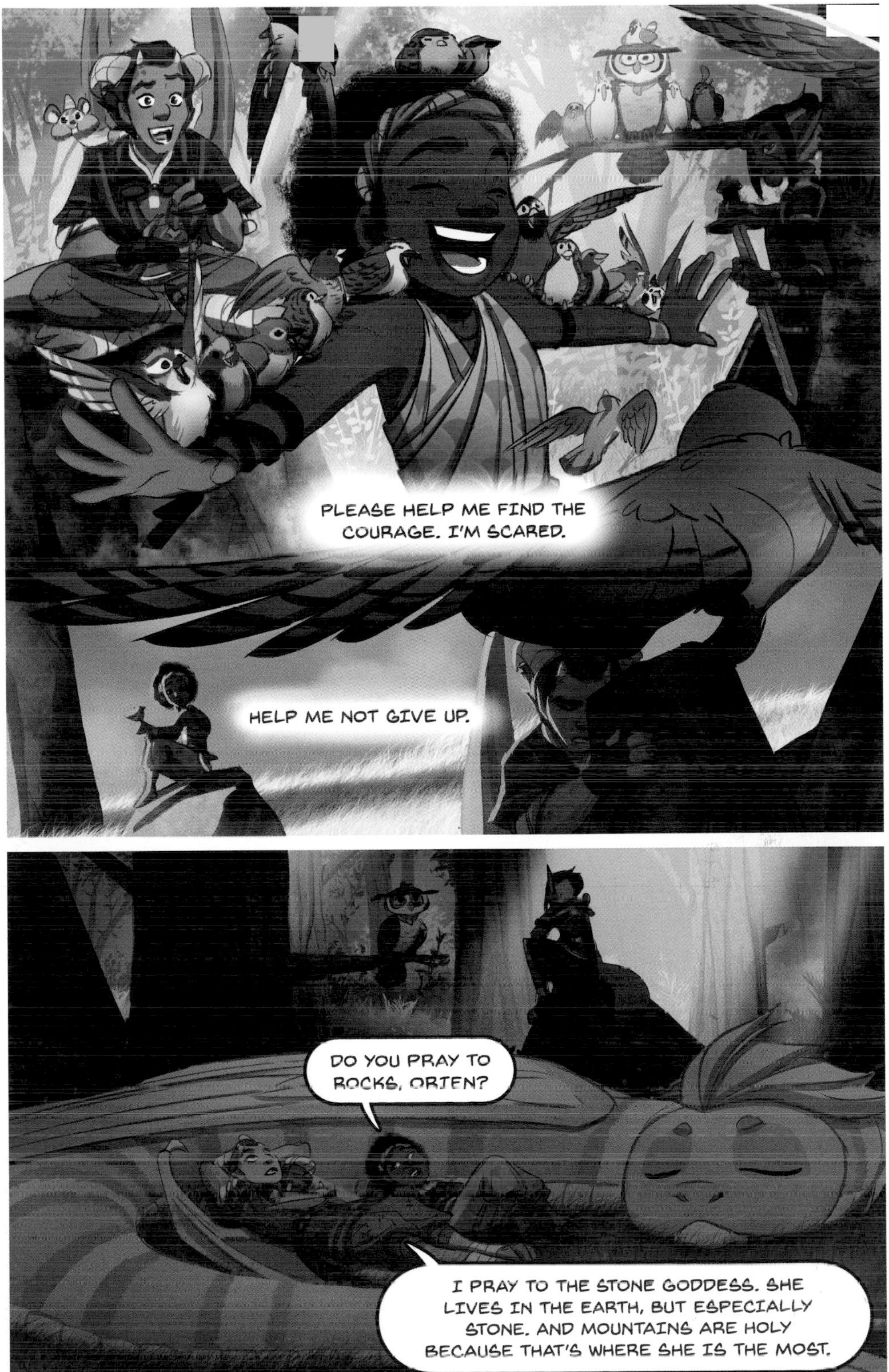
PLEASE HELP ME FIND THE COURAGE. I'M SCARED.
HELP ME NOT GIVE UP.
DO YOU PRAY TO ROCKS, ORIEN?
I PRAY TO THE STONE GODDESS. SHE LIVES IN THE EARTH, BUT ESPECIALLY STONE. AND MOUNTAINS ARE HOLY BECAUSE THAT'S WHERE SHE IS THE MOST.

WHAT DO YOU KNOW ABOUT THE SIRIC?

NOT MUCH. THEY MADE ART, MAGIC, MUSIC. THAT KIND OF STUFF DOESN'T SURVIVE WELL, ESPECIALLY WHEN EVERYONE WHO MADE IT DISAPPEARS ALL AT ONCE.

WHAT DO YOU MEAN... ALL AT ONCE?

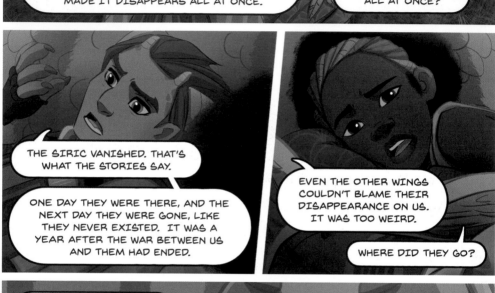

THE SIRIC VANISHED. THAT'S WHAT THE STORIES SAY.

ONE DAY THEY WERE THERE, AND THE NEXT DAY THEY WERE GONE, LIKE THEY NEVER EXISTED. IT WAS A YEAR AFTER THE WAR BETWEEN US AND THEM HAD ENDED.

EVEN THE OTHER WINGS COULDN'T BLAME THEIR DISAPPEARANCE ON US. IT WAS TOO WEIRD.

WHERE DID THEY GO?

DUNNO. BUT THEY LEFT EVERYTHING BEHIND.

A LOT HAS BEEN PICKED OVER BY NOW, BUT I SCAVENGE FOR ANYTHING THAT COULD STILL BE INTERESTING.

ONE TIME I FOUND PARTS OF A NECKLACE. I DON'T KNOW IF IT WAS MAGIC, BUT THAT GOT ME ON DRIVER'S GOOD SIDE FOR A WHILE.

GOBLINS ARE THE ONLY ONES WHO STILL GO INTO SIRIC CITIES. IT'S FORBIDDEN, BUT EVERYONE PRETENDS NOT TO NOTICE BECAUSE THEY LOVE OLD SIRIC STUFF.

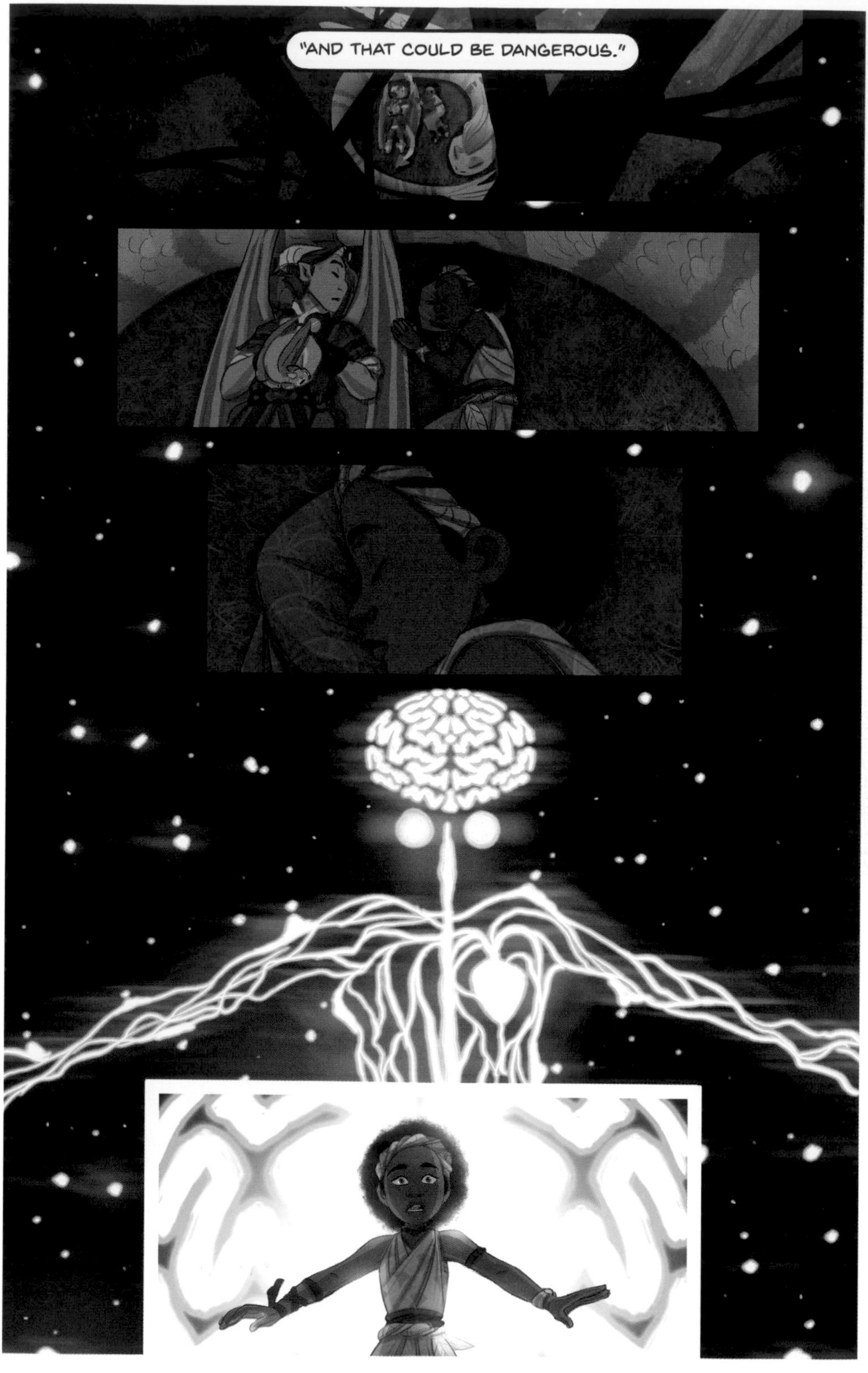
"AND THAT COULD BE DANGEROUS."

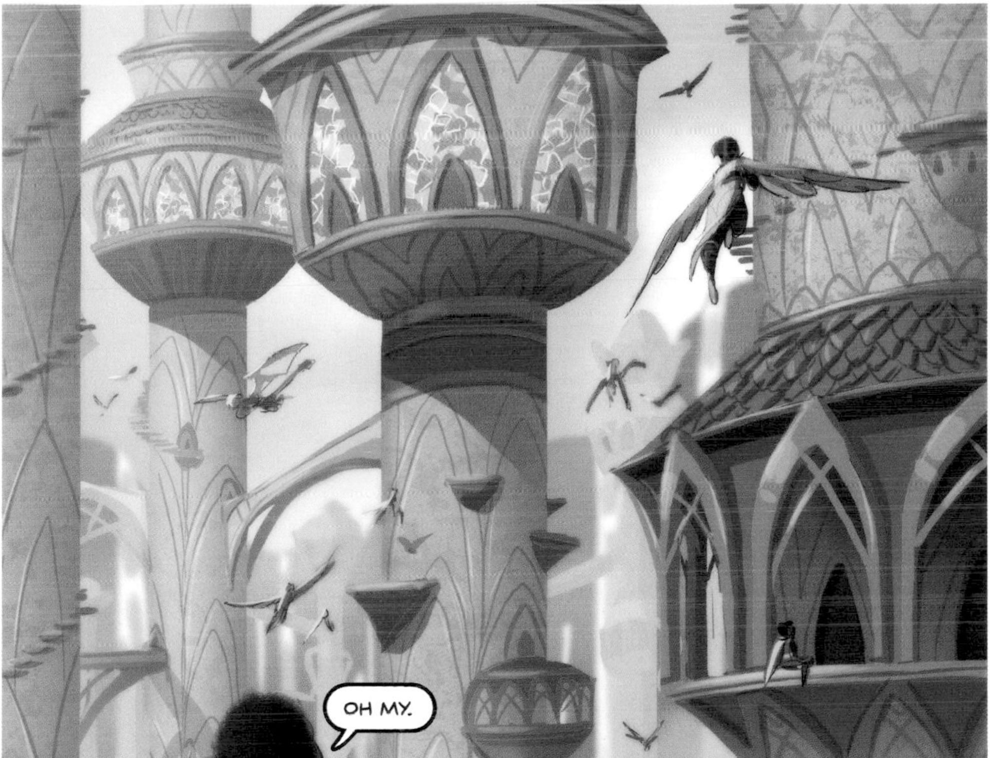
OH MY.
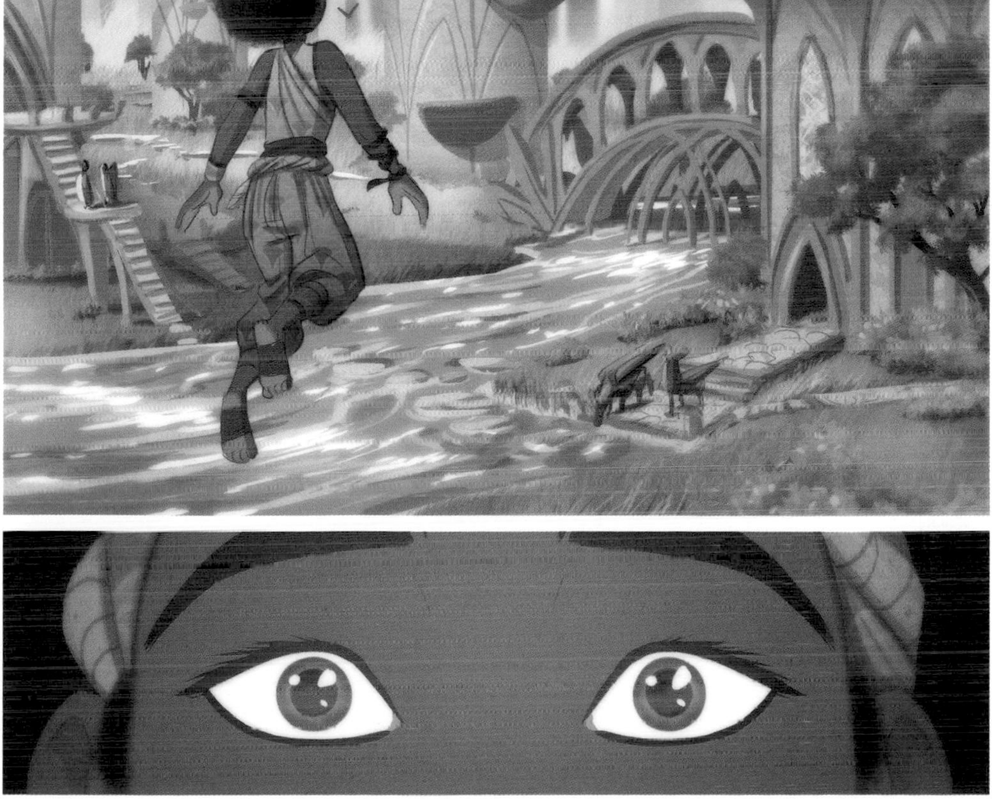

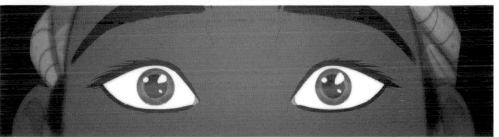

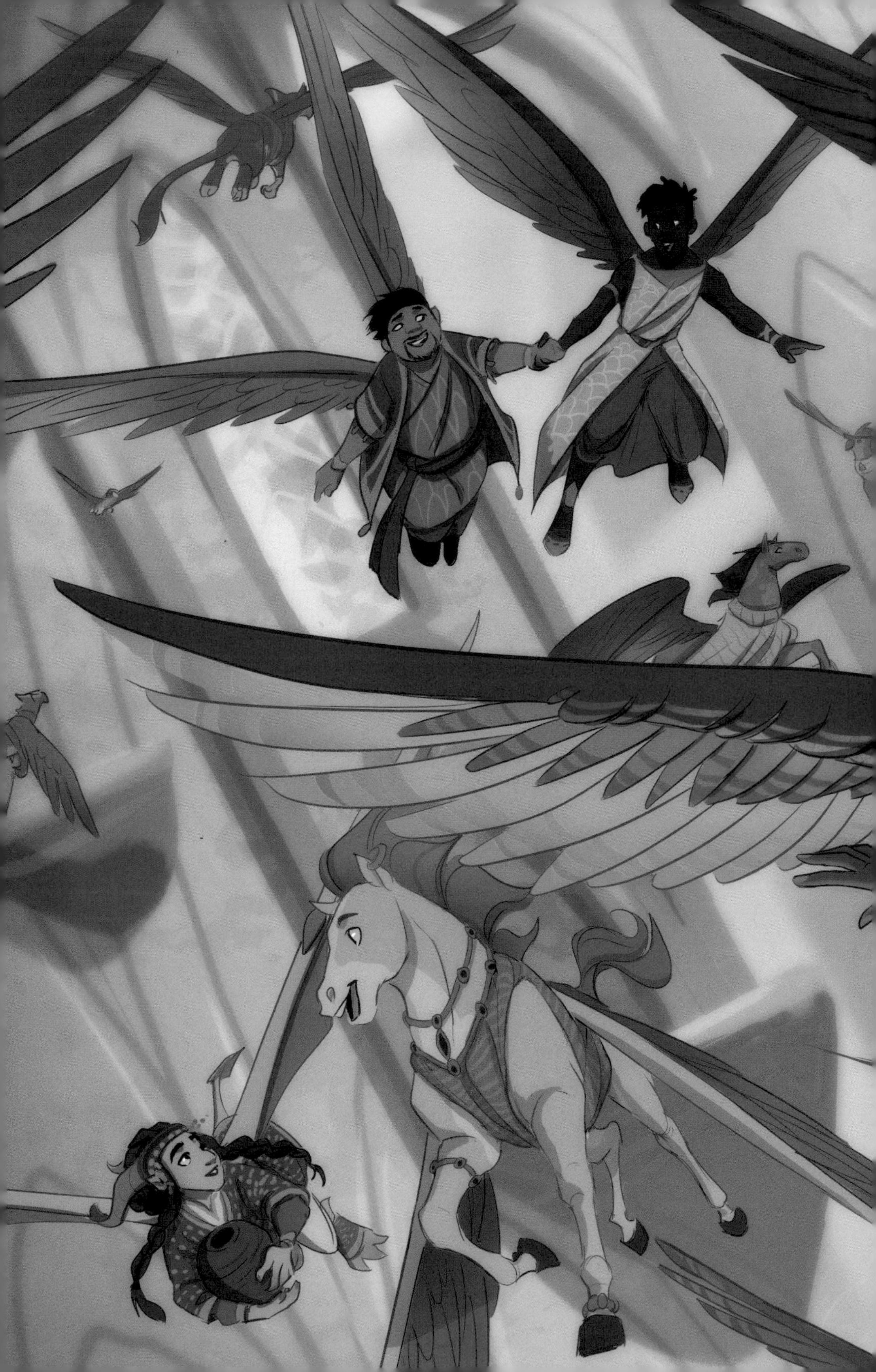

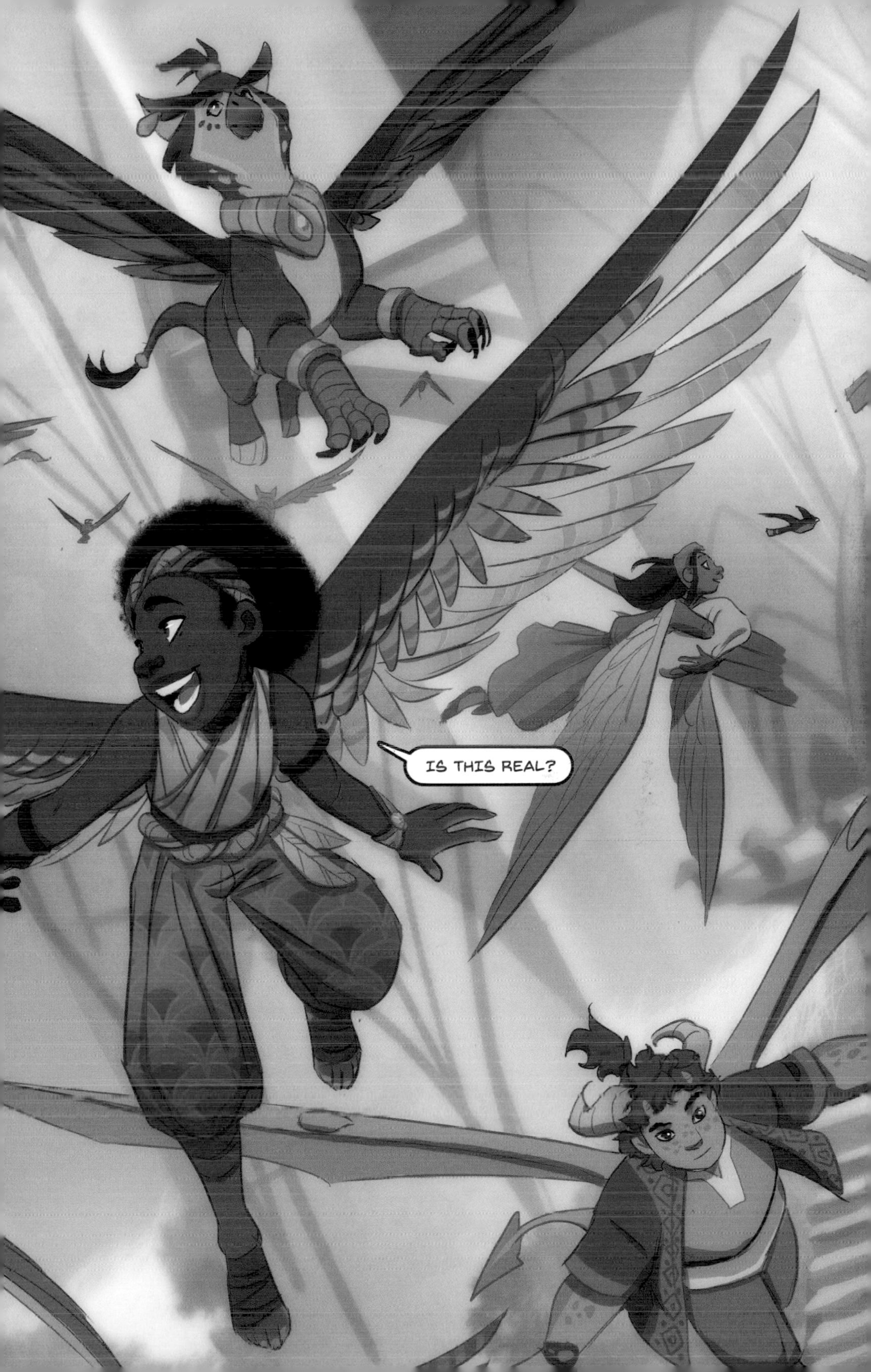
IS THIS REAL?

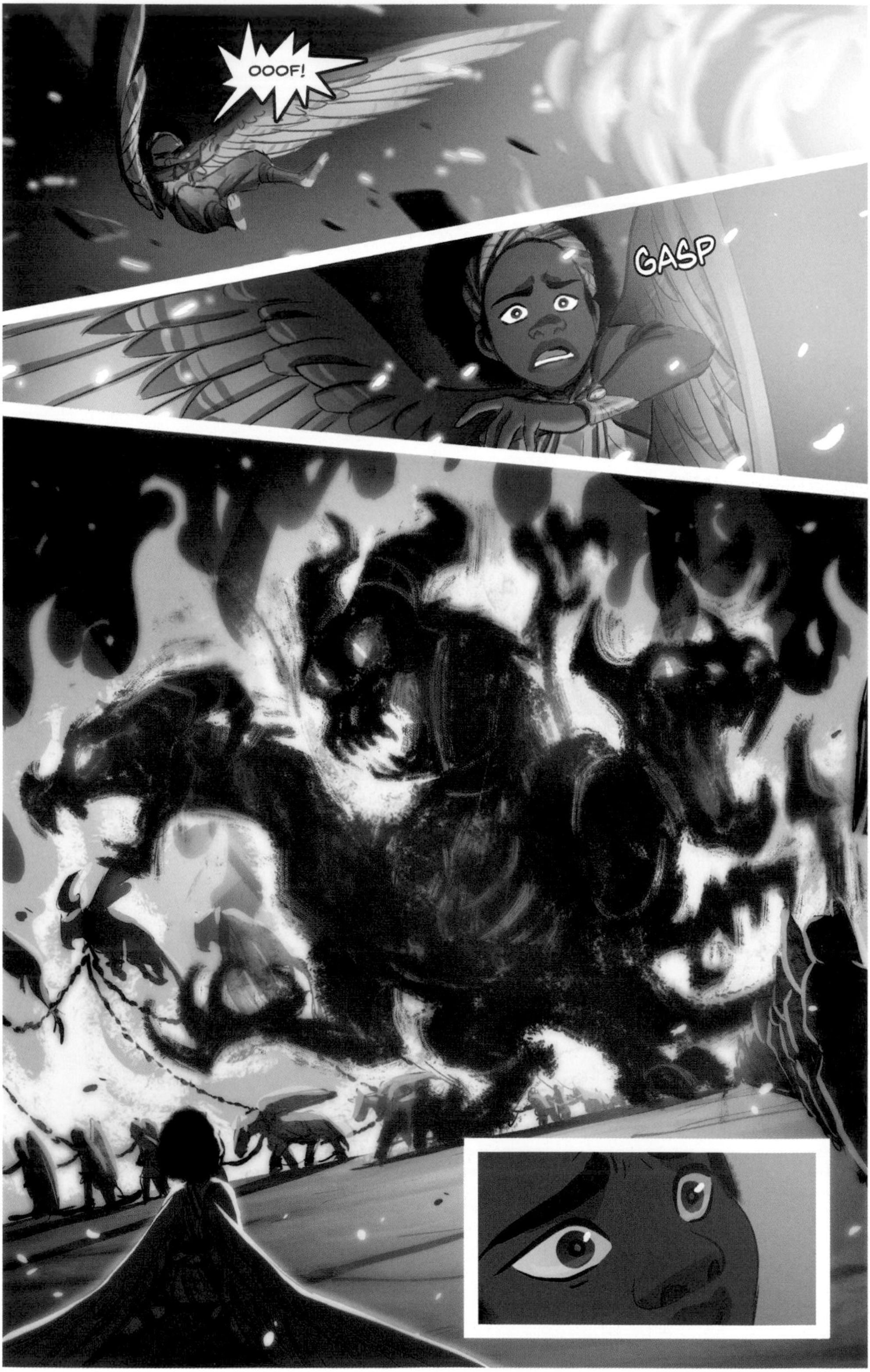
OOOF!
GASP

I HAD TO SEE YOU FOR MYSELF.

EVEN IF IT'S ONLY IN DREAMS.

WHO ARE YOU?

SOME CALL ME A WITCH. OTHERS CALL ME A CONQUERER.

BUT I AM NONE OF THE THINGS PEOPLE IMAGINE ME TO BE.

I AM MERELY...A WOMAN WHO LEARNED TO PLAN.

AND I'VE BEEN WAITING FOR YOU, ZULI.

TOGETHER WE CAN MAKE AT LEAST ONE THING RIGHT.

BUT MAYBE ALL OF IT.

WHAT --

THEY SHOULD NEVER HAVE THROWN ANY OF US AWAY. IT WASN'T OUR FAULT. WE WERE BABIES.

AND THEY STILL HAVEN'T LEARNED THEIR LESSON.

"WE'LL MEET AGAIN."

"SOON."

AAAH!

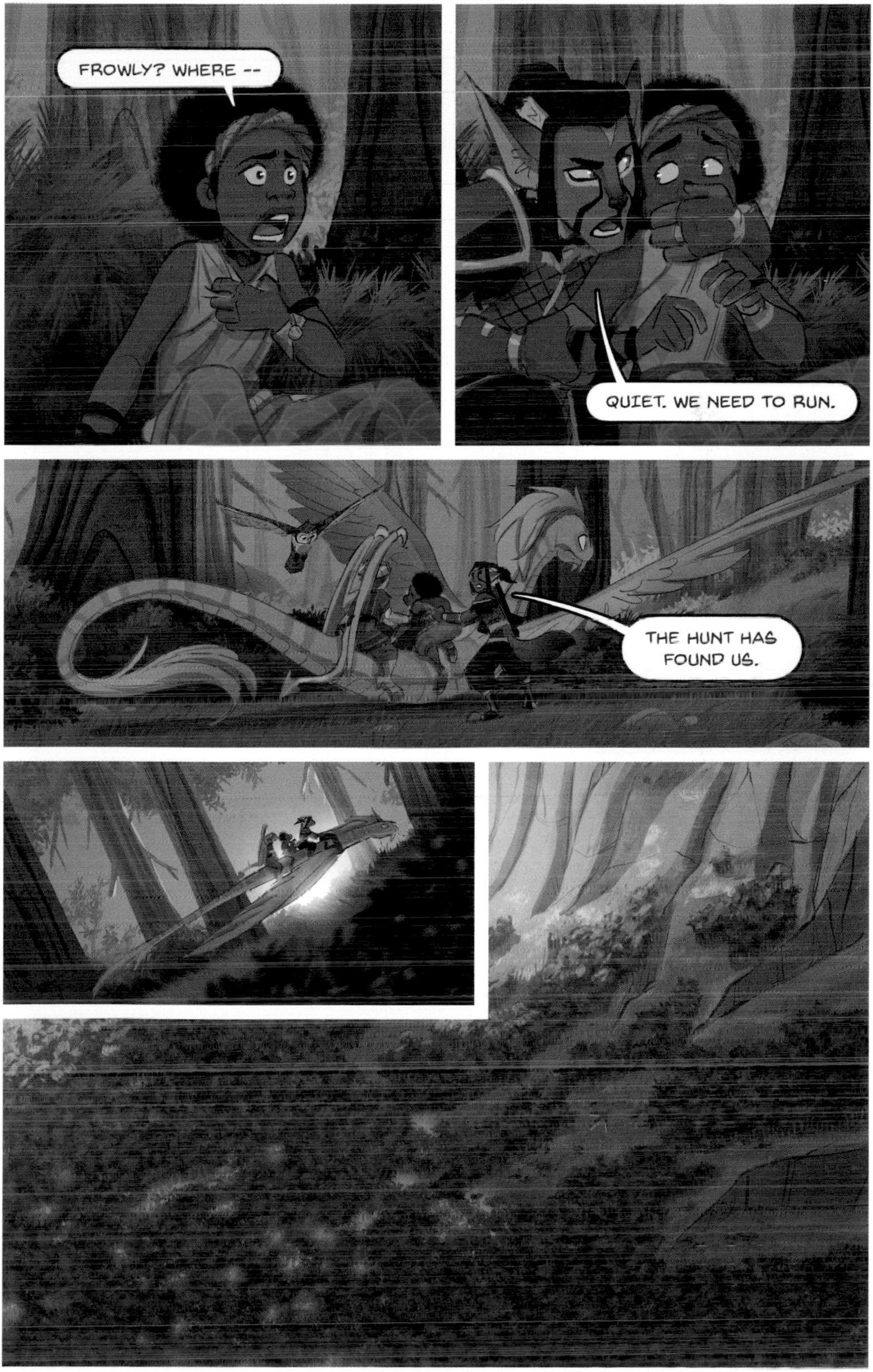
FROWLY? WHERE --
QUIET. WE NEED TO RUN.
THE HUNT HAS FOUND US.

125

126

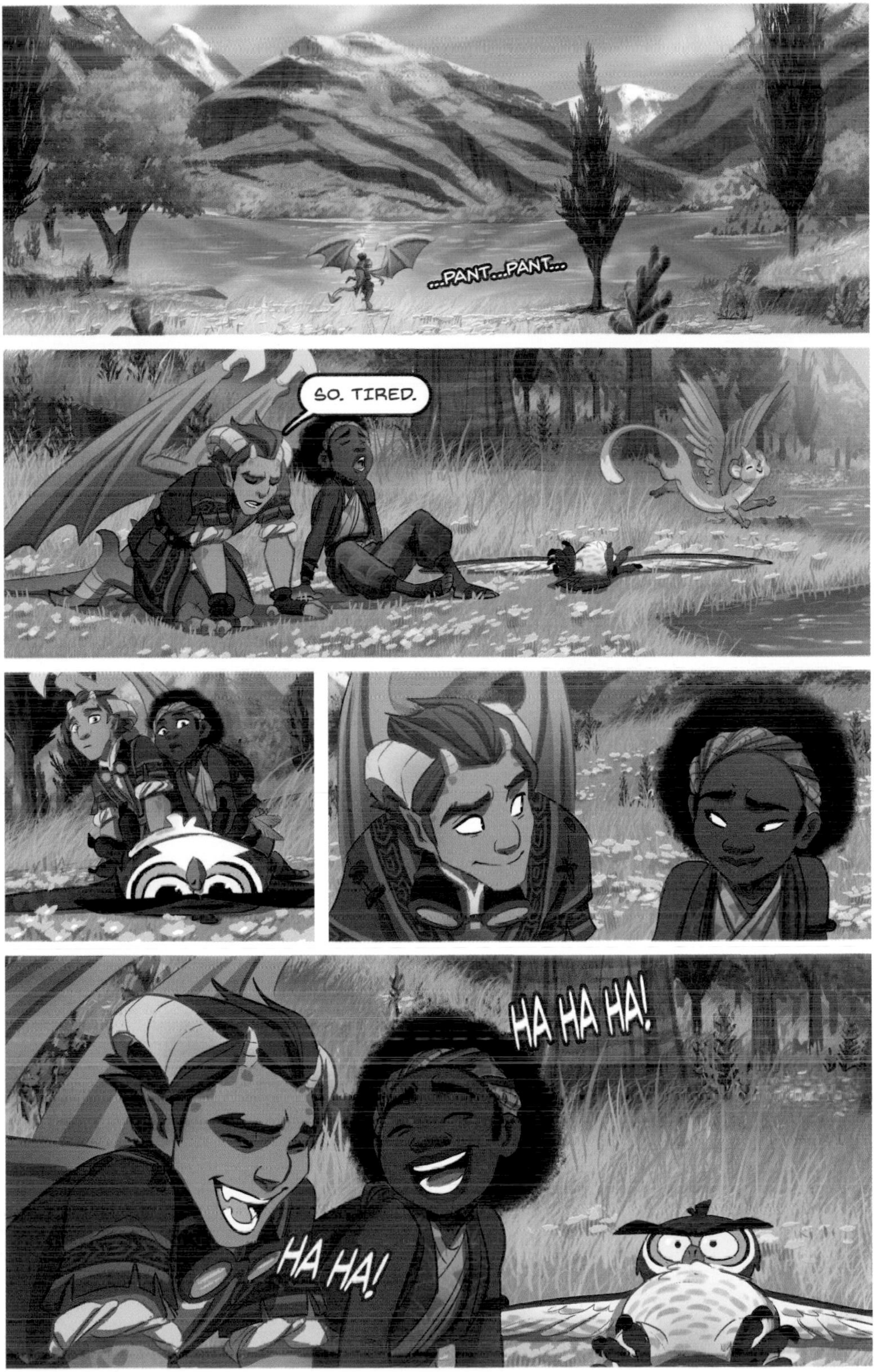
...PANT...PANT...
SO. TIRED.
HA HA HA!
HA HA!

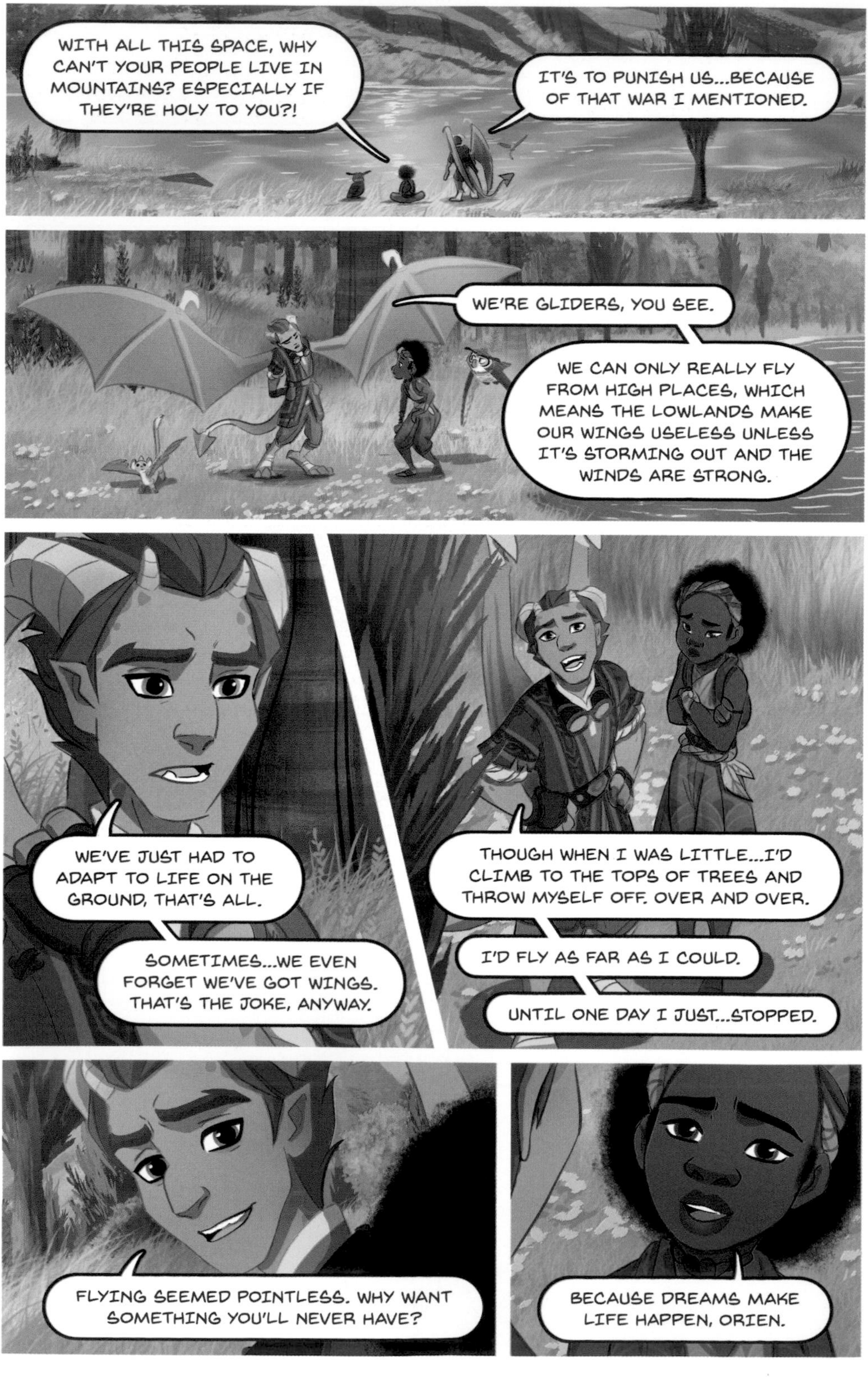
WITH ALL THIS SPACE, WHY CAN'T YOUR PEOPLE LIVE IN MOUNTAINS? ESPECIALLY IF THEY'RE HOLY TO YOU?!
IT'S TO PUNISH US...BECAUSE OF THAT WAR I MENTIONED.
WE'RE GLIDERS, YOU SEE.
WE CAN ONLY REALLY FLY FROM HIGH PLACES, WHICH MEANS THE LOWLANDS MAKE OUR WINGS USELESS UNLESS IT'S STORMING OUT AND THE WINDS ARE STRONG.
WE'VE JUST HAD TO ADAPT TO LIFE ON THE GROUND, THAT'S ALL.
SOMETIMES...WE EVEN FORGET WE'VE GOT WINGS. THAT'S THE JOKE, ANYWAY.
THOUGH WHEN I WAS LITTLE...I'D CLIMB TO THE TOPS OF TREES AND THROW MYSELF OFF. OVER AND OVER.
I'D FLY AS FAR AS I COULD.
UNTIL ONE DAY I JUST...STOPPED.
FLYING SEEMED POINTLESS. WHY WANT SOMETHING YOU'LL NEVER HAVE?
BECAUSE DREAMS MAKE LIFE HAPPEN, ORIEN.

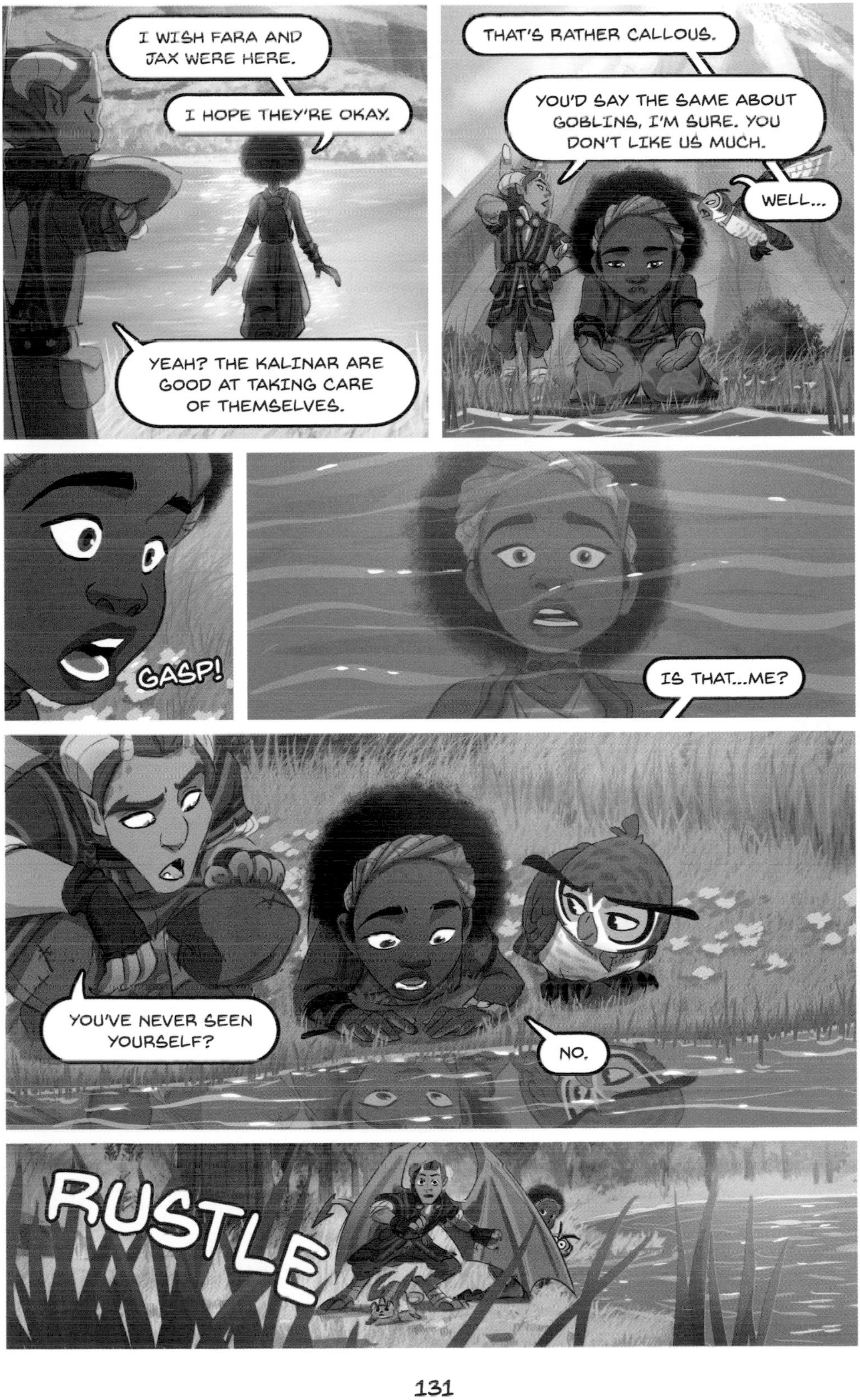
I WISH FARA AND JAX WERE HERE.
I HOPE THEY'RE OKAY.
YEAH? THE KALINAR ARE GOOD AT TAKING CARE OF THEMSELVES.
THAT'S RATHER CALLOUS.
YOU'D SAY THE SAME ABOUT GOBLINS, I'M SURE. YOU DON'T LIKE US MUCH.
WELL...
GASP!
IS THAT...ME?
YOU'VE NEVER SEEN YOURSELF?
NO.
RUSTLE

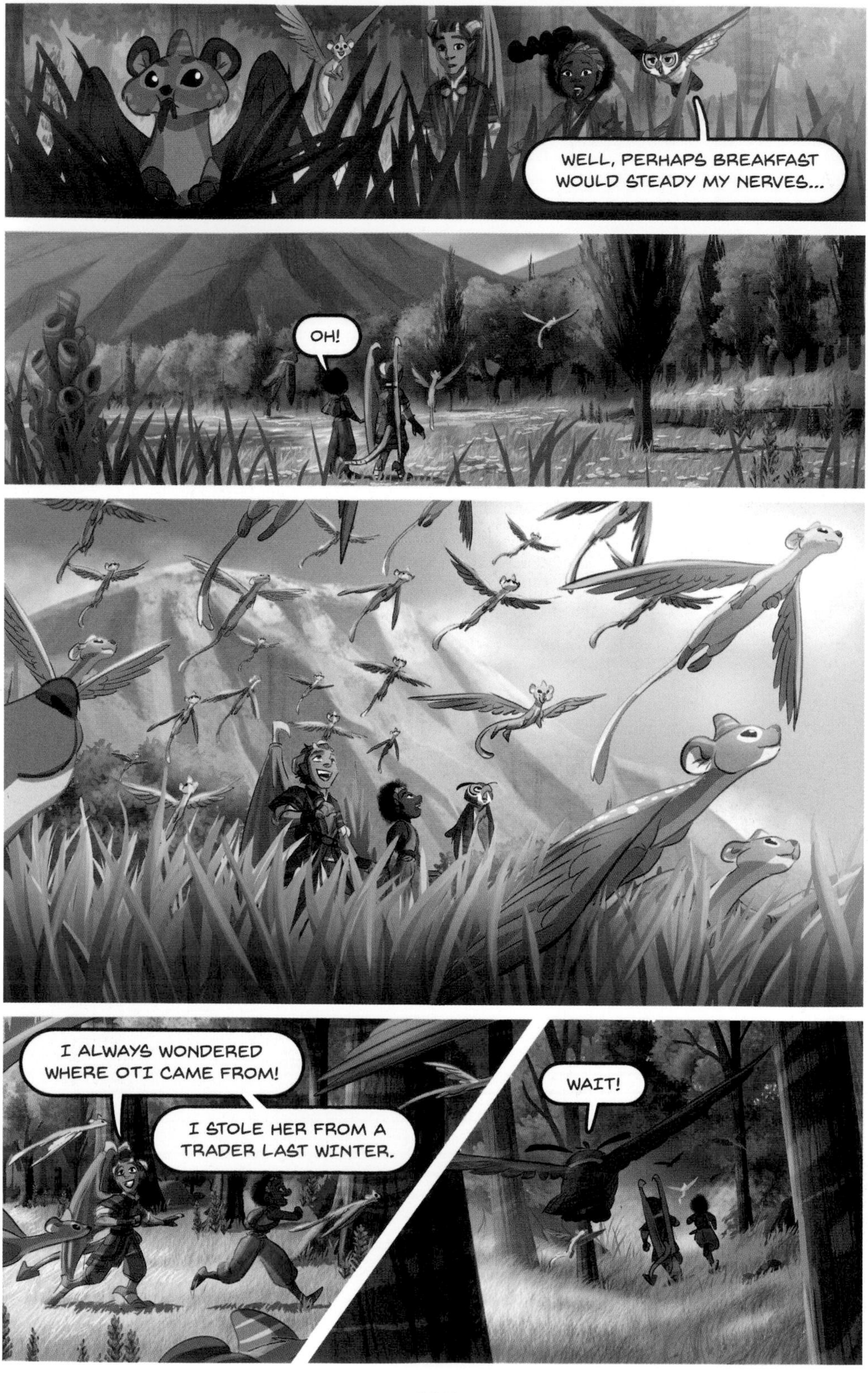
WELL, PERHAPS BREAKFAST WOULD STEADY MY NERVES...
OH!
I ALWAYS WONDERED WHERE OTI CAME FROM!
I STOLE HER FROM A TRADER LAST WINTER.
WAIT!

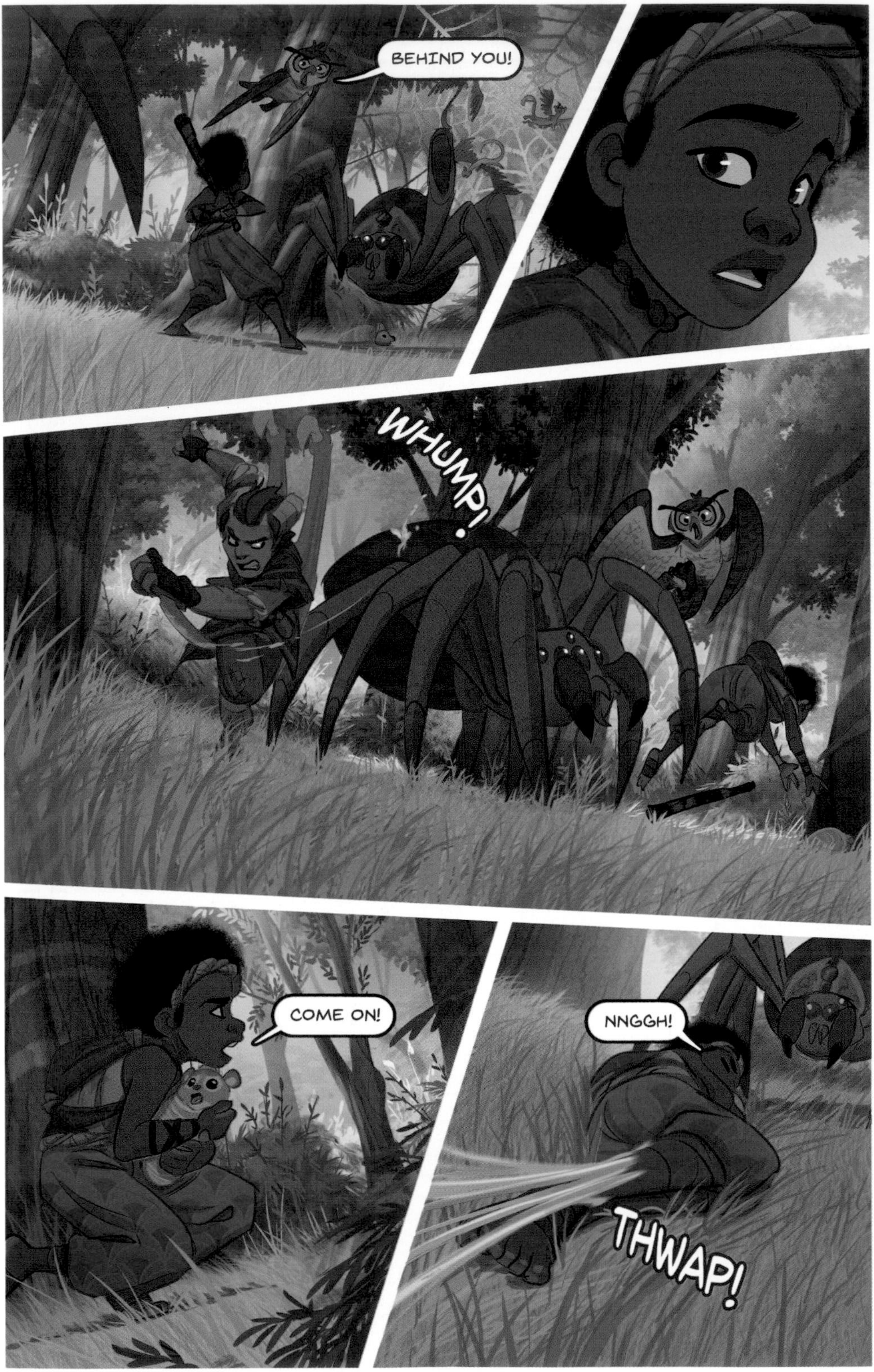
BEHIND YOU!
WHUMP!
COME ON!
NNGGH!
THWAP!

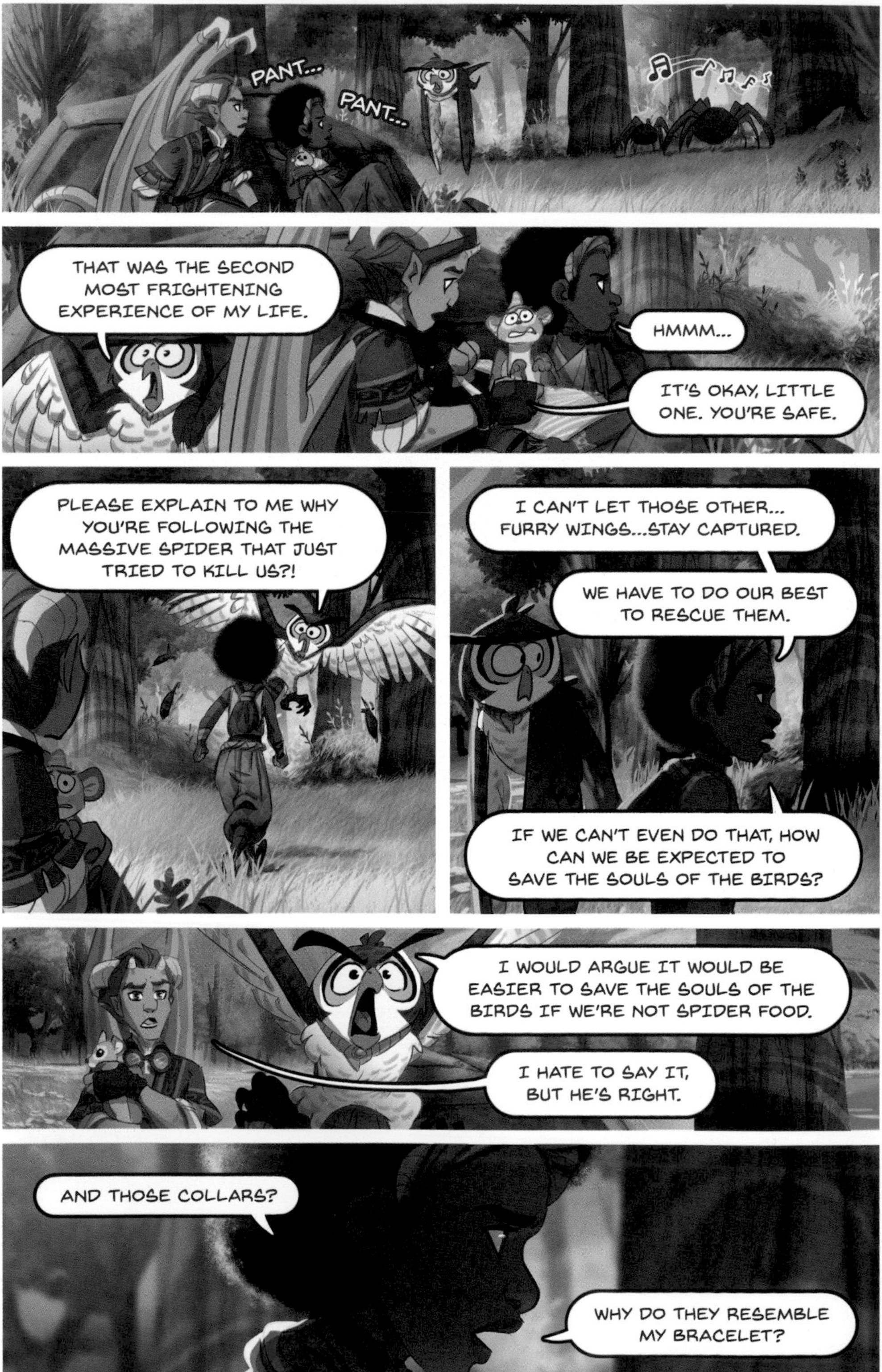
PANT...
PANT...
THAT WAS THE SECOND MOST FRIGHTENING EXPERIENCE OF MY LIFE.
HMMM...
IT'S OKAY, LITTLE ONE. YOU'RE SAFE.
PLEASE EXPLAIN TO ME WHY YOU'RE FOLLOWING THE MASSIVE SPIDER THAT JUST TRIED TO KILL US?!
I CAN'T LET THOSE OTHER... FURRY WINGS...STAY CAPTURED.
WE HAVE TO DO OUR BEST TO RESCUE THEM.
IF WE CAN'T EVEN DO THAT, HOW CAN WE BE EXPECTED TO SAVE THE SOULS OF THE BIRDS?
I WOULD ARGUE IT WOULD BE EASIER TO SAVE THE SOULS OF THE BIRDS IF WE'RE NOT SPIDER FOOD.
I HATE TO SAY IT, BUT HE'S RIGHT.
AND THOSE COLLARS?
WHY DO THEY RESEMBLE MY BRACELET?

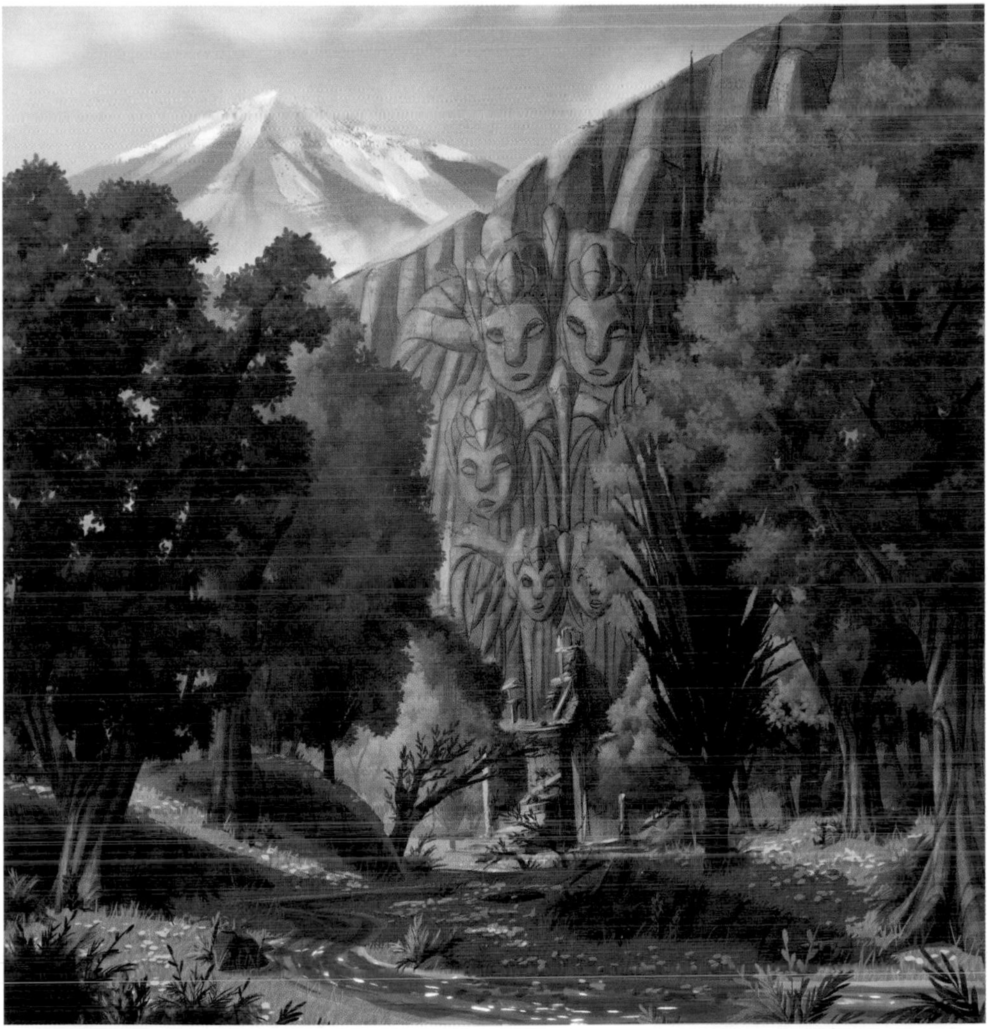

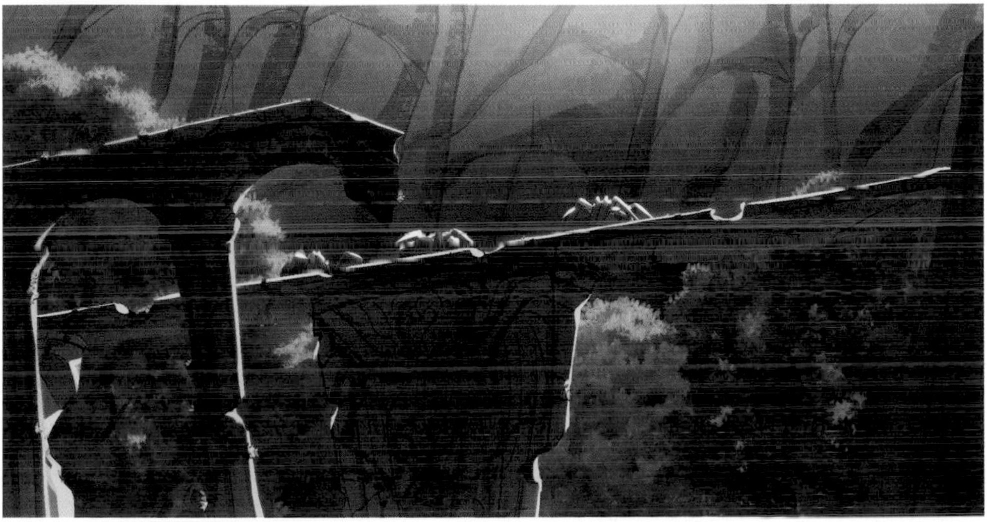

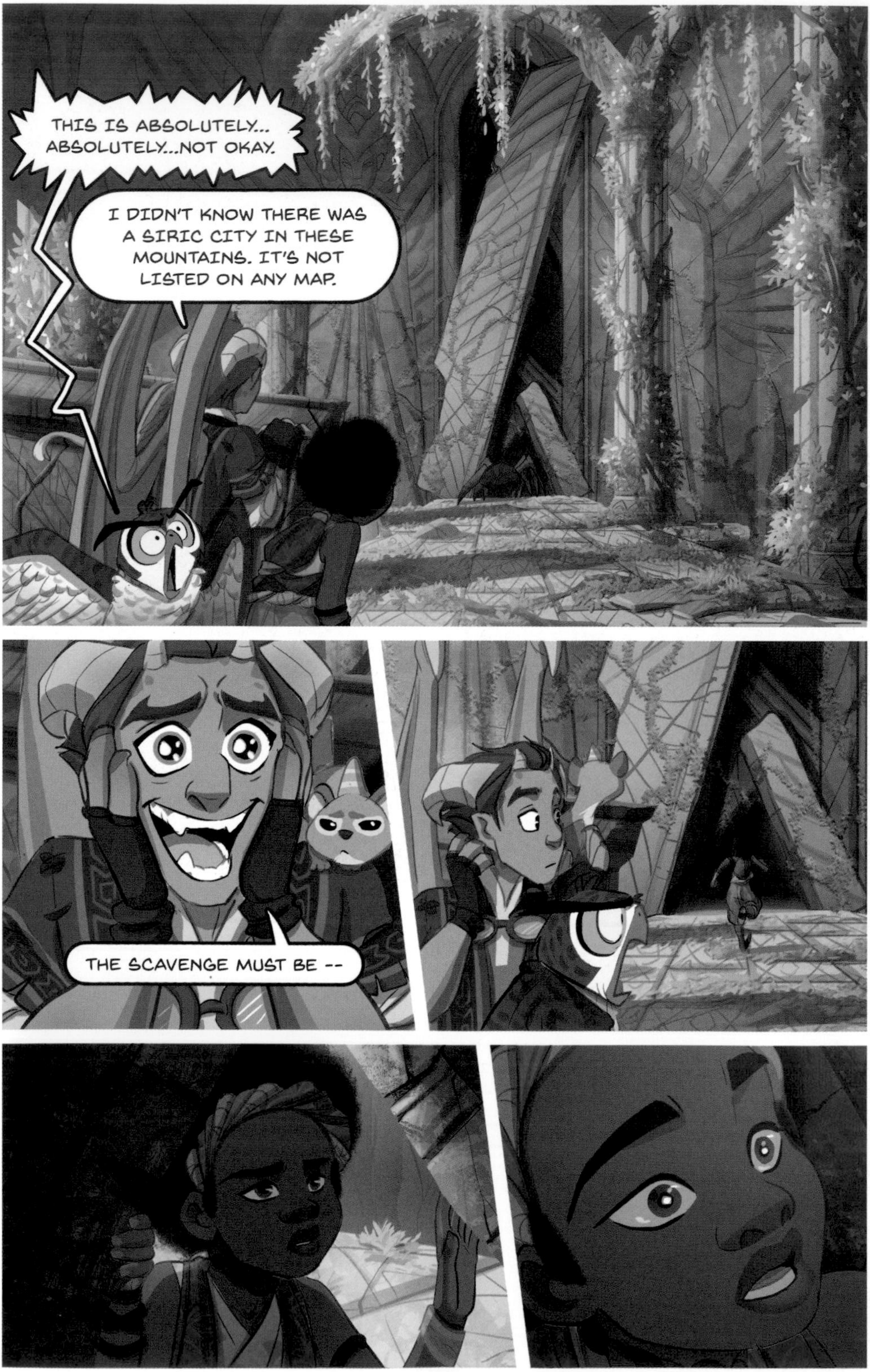
THIS IS ABSOLUTELY... ABSOLUTELY...NOT OKAY.
I DIDN'T KNOW THERE WAS A SIRIC CITY IN THESE MOUNTAINS. IT'S NOT LISTED ON ANY MAP.
THE SCAVENGE MUST BE --

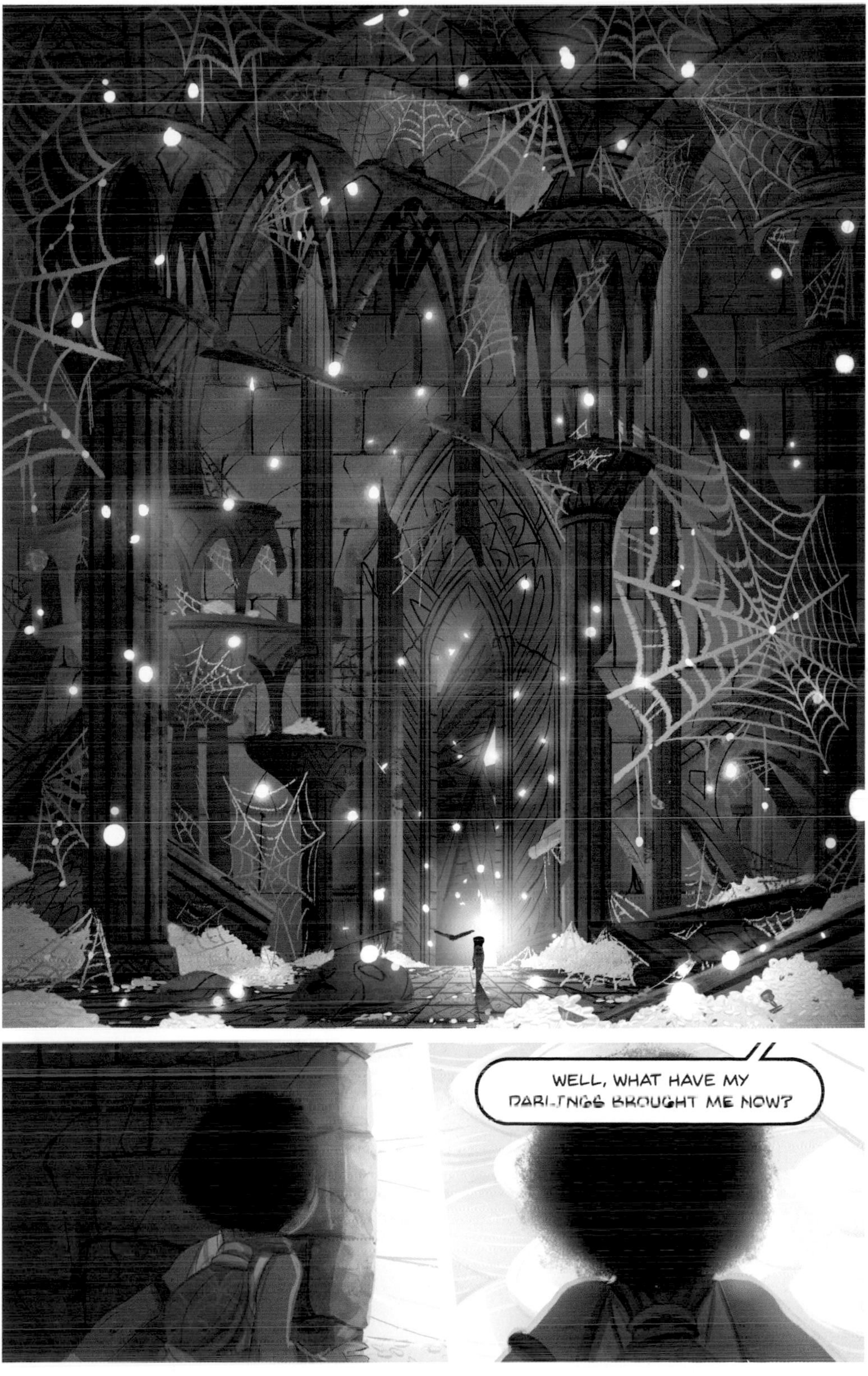
WELL, WHAT HAVE MY
DARLINGS BROUGHT ME NOW?

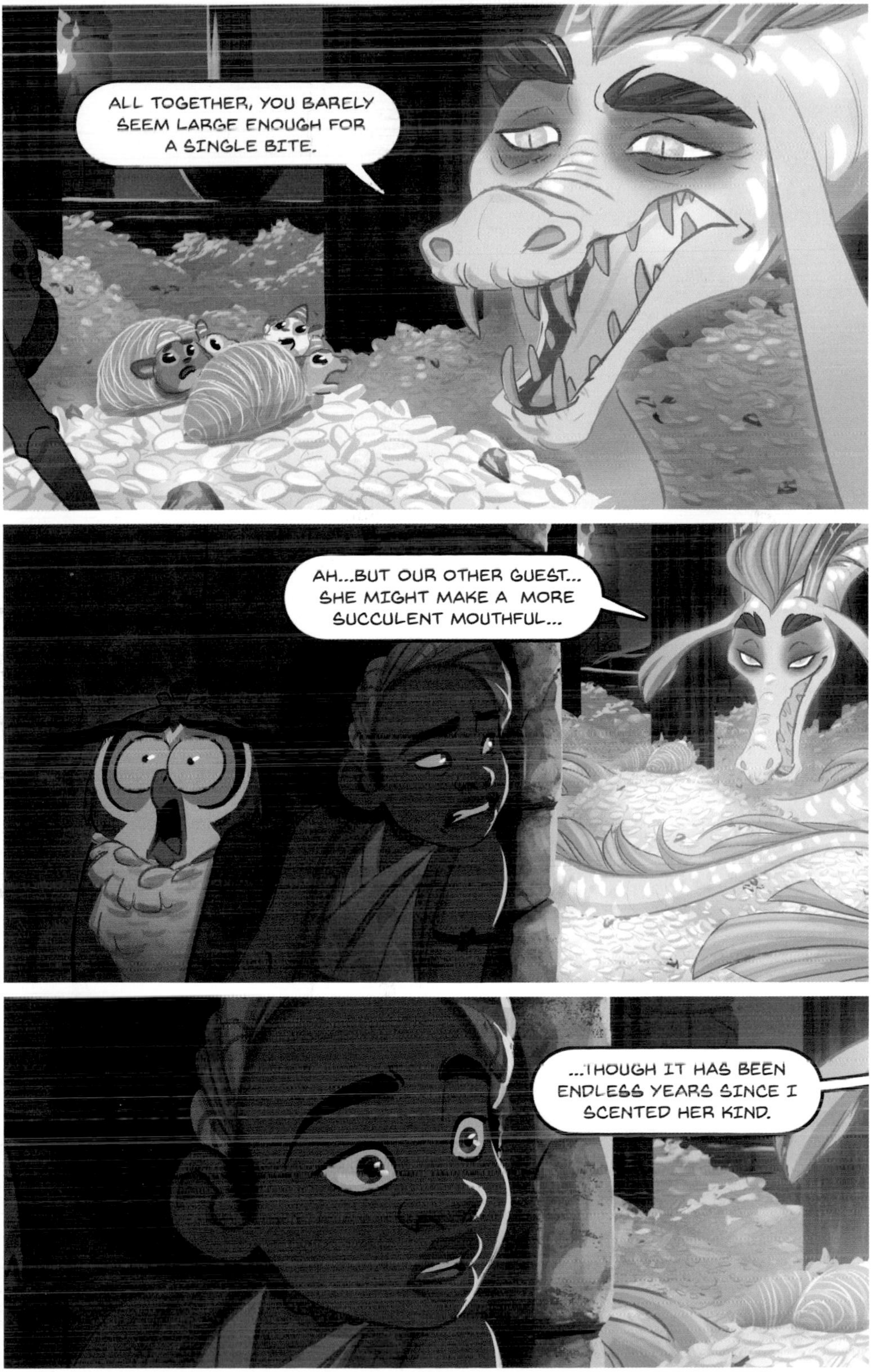
ALL TOGETHER, YOU BARELY SEEM LARGE ENOUGH FOR A SINGLE BITE.
AH...BUT OUR OTHER GUEST... SHE MIGHT MAKE A MORE SUCCULENT MOUTHFUL...
...THOUGH IT HAS BEEN ENDLESS YEARS SINCE I SCENTED HER KIND.

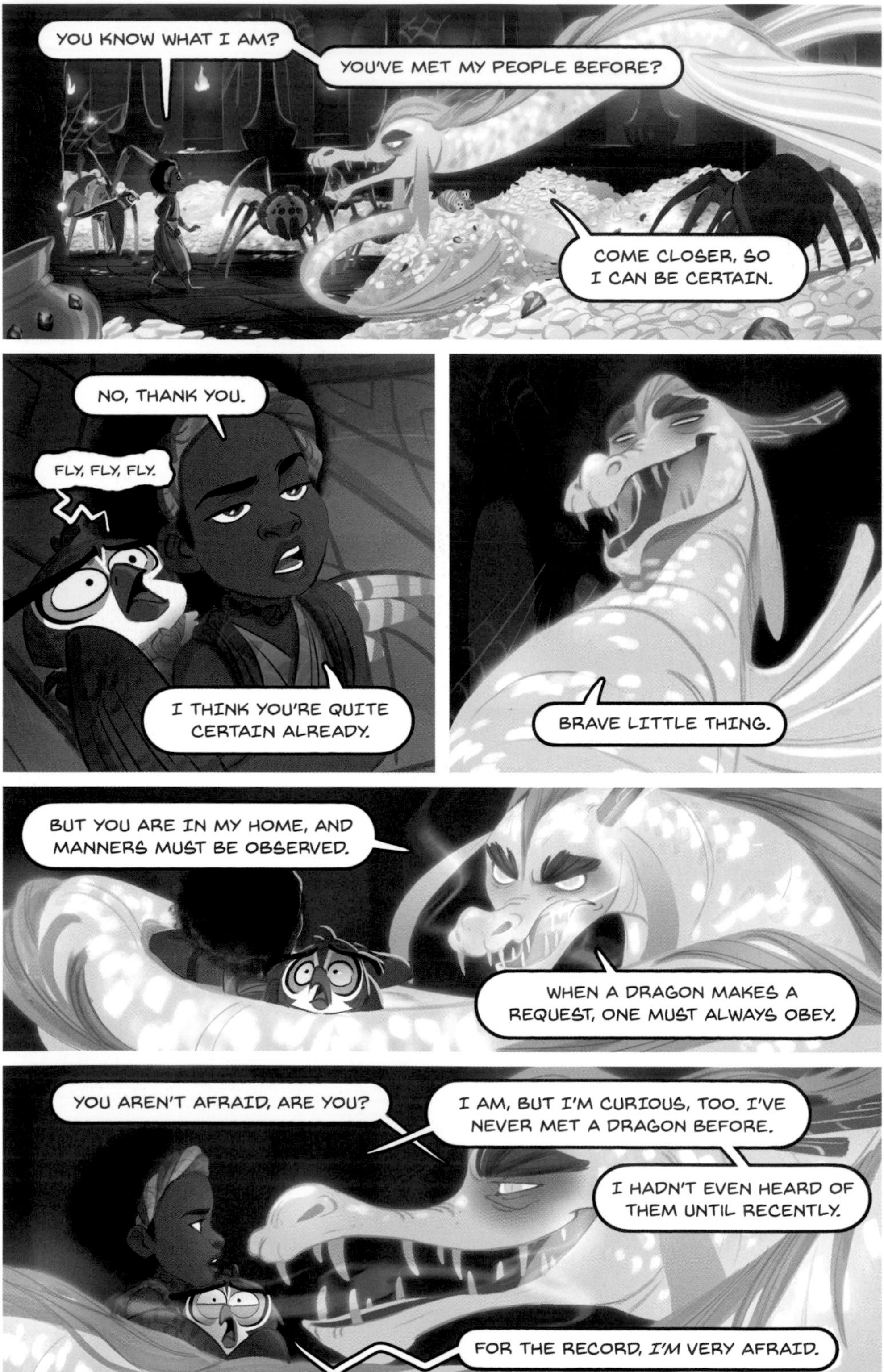
YOU KNOW WHAT I AM?
YOU'VE MET MY PEOPLE BEFORE?
COME CLOSER, SO I CAN BE CERTAIN.
NO, THANK YOU.
FLY, FLY, FLY.
I THINK YOU'RE QUITE CERTAIN ALREADY.
BRAVE LITTLE THING.
BUT YOU ARE IN MY HOME, AND MANNERS MUST BE OBSERVED.
WHEN A DRAGON MAKES A REQUEST, ONE MUST ALWAYS OBEY.
YOU AREN'T AFRAID, ARE YOU?
I AM, BUT I'M CURIOUS, TOO. I'VE NEVER MET A DRAGON BEFORE.
I HADN'T EVEN HEARD OF THEM UNTIL RECENTLY.
FOR THE RECORD, *I'M* VERY AFRAID.

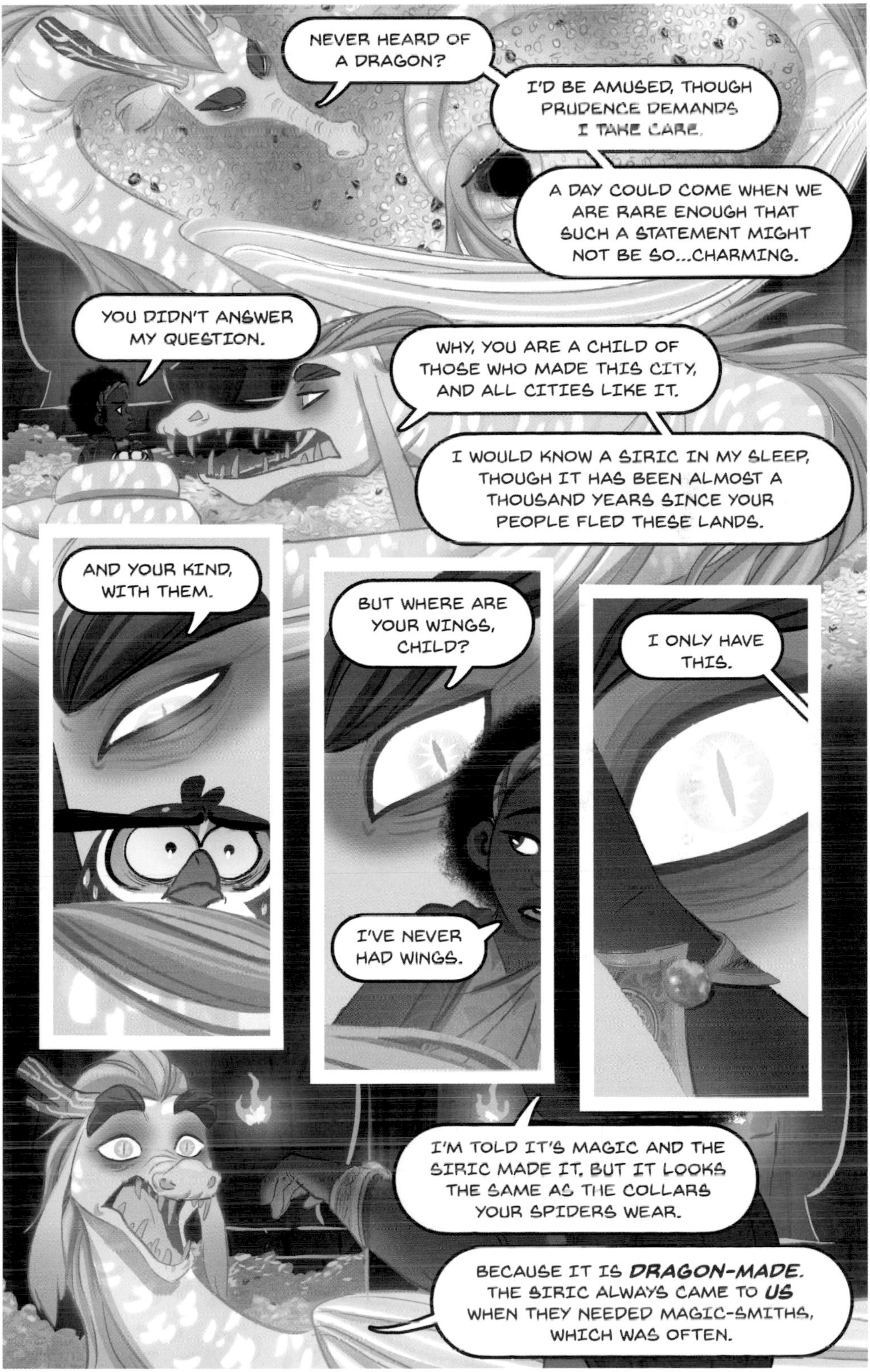
NEVER HEARD OF A DRAGON?
I'D BE AMUSED, THOUGH PRUDENCE DEMANDS I TAKE CARE.
A DAY COULD COME WHEN WE ARE RARE ENOUGH THAT SUCH A STATEMENT MIGHT NOT BE SO...CHARMING.
YOU DIDN'T ANSWER MY QUESTION.
WHY, YOU ARE A CHILD OF THOSE WHO MADE THIS CITY, AND ALL CITIES LIKE IT.
I WOULD KNOW A SIRIC IN MY SLEEP, THOUGH IT HAS BEEN ALMOST A THOUSAND YEARS SINCE YOUR PEOPLE FLED THESE LANDS.
AND YOUR KIND, WITH THEM.
BUT WHERE ARE YOUR WINGS, CHILD?
I'VE NEVER HAD WINGS.
I ONLY HAVE THIS.
I'M TOLD IT'S MAGIC AND THE SIRIC MADE IT. BUT IT LOOKS THE SAME AS THE COLLARS YOUR SPIDERS WEAR.
BECAUSE IT IS ***DRAGON-MADE***. THE SIRIC ALWAYS CAME TO ***US*** WHEN THEY NEEDED MAGIC-SMITHS, WHICH WAS OFTEN.

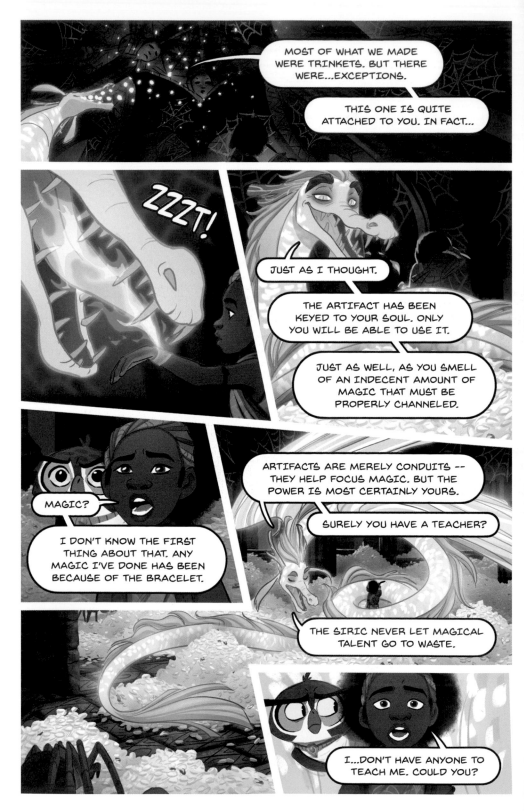

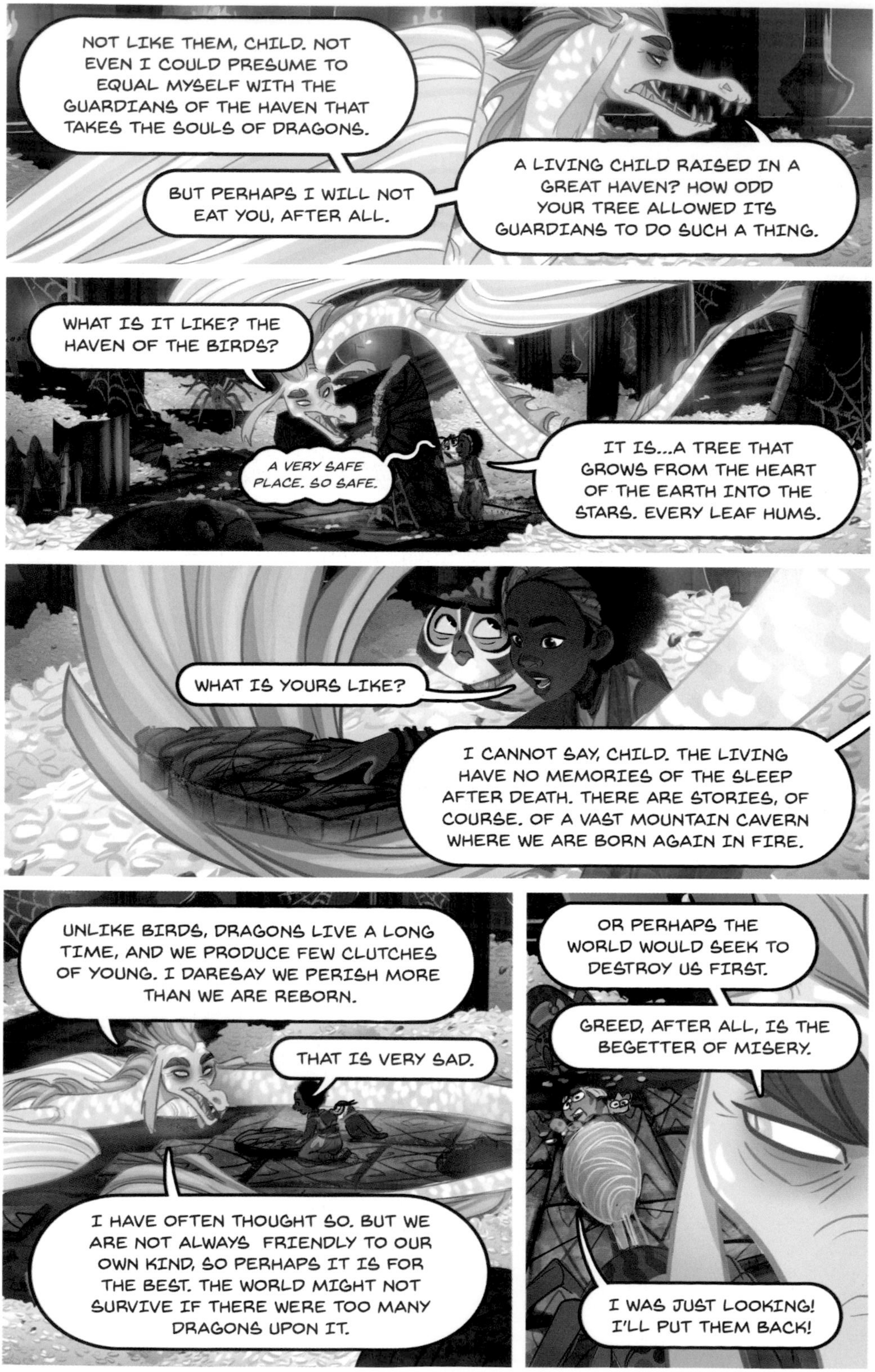
NOT LIKE THEM, CHILD. NOT EVEN I COULD PRESUME TO EQUAL MYSELF WITH THE GUARDIANS OF THE HAVEN THAT TAKES THE SOULS OF DRAGONS.
BUT PERHAPS I WILL NOT EAT YOU, AFTER ALL.
A LIVING CHILD RAISED IN A GREAT HAVEN? HOW ODD YOUR TREE ALLOWED ITS GUARDIANS TO DO SUCH A THING.
WHAT IS IT LIKE? THE HAVEN OF THE BIRDS?
A VERY SAFE PLACE. SO SAFE.
IT IS...A TREE THAT GROWS FROM THE HEART OF THE EARTH INTO THE STARS. EVERY LEAF HUMS.
WHAT IS YOURS LIKE?
I CANNOT SAY, CHILD. THE LIVING HAVE NO MEMORIES OF THE SLEEP AFTER DEATH. THERE ARE STORIES, OF COURSE. OF A VAST MOUNTAIN CAVERN WHERE WE ARE BORN AGAIN IN FIRE.
UNLIKE BIRDS, DRAGONS LIVE A LONG TIME, AND WE PRODUCE FEW CLUTCHES OF YOUNG. I DARESAY WE PERISH MORE THAN WE ARE REBORN.
THAT IS VERY SAD.
I HAVE OFTEN THOUGHT SO. BUT WE ARE NOT ALWAYS FRIENDLY TO OUR OWN KIND, SO PERHAPS IT IS FOR THE BEST. THE WORLD MIGHT NOT SURVIVE IF THERE WERE TOO MANY DRAGONS UPON IT.
OR PERHAPS THE WORLD WOULD SEEK TO DESTROY US FIRST.
GREED, AFTER ALL, IS THE BEGETTER OF MISERY.
I WAS JUST LOOKING! I'LL PUT THEM BACK!

WE SHOULD GO.

EVERY MOMENT MEANS ANOTHER BIRD LOST TO THE WORLD.

THE RAVENS TOLD ME THERE'S A PLACE NORTH OF THE LAST MOUNTAIN, ACROSS WATER THAT LOOKS LIKE SKY. IT'S A PLACE WHERE BLUE FIRE CAN BE FOUND.

I NEED TO GO THERE. DO YOU KNOW WHERE IT MIGHT BE?

BEYOND THESE MOUNTAINS IS THE SEA. AND THE ISLAND BEYOND THE SEA IS PART OF A VOLCANO THAT HAS GONE SO COLD EVEN DRAGONS DO NOT CALL IT HOME.

THE SEA, THE ISLAND, ARE ALL PART OF THE ABYSSAL CHAIN. VERY FEW REMEMBER THAT PART OF THE WORLD, EVEN THOUGH IT WAS ONCE THRIVING AND GREEN.

BUT THERE'S ONLY ONE THING BLUE FIRE COULD BE, AND THAT IS MAGIC.

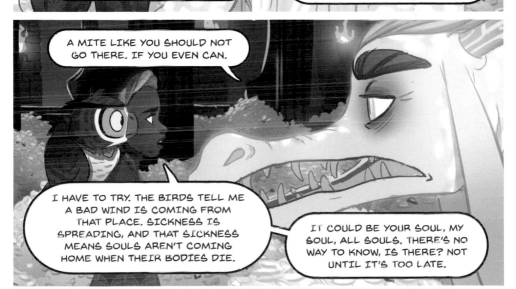

A MITE LIKE YOU SHOULD NOT GO THERE. IF YOU EVEN CAN.

I HAVE TO TRY. THE BIRDS TELL ME A BAD WIND IS COMING FROM THAT PLACE. SICKNESS IS SPREADING, AND THAT SICKNESS MEANS SOULS AREN'T COMING HOME WHEN THEIR BODIES DIE.

IT COULD BE YOUR SOUL, MY SOUL, ALL SOULS. THERE'S NO WAY TO KNOW, IS THERE? NOT UNTIL IT'S TOO LATE.

149

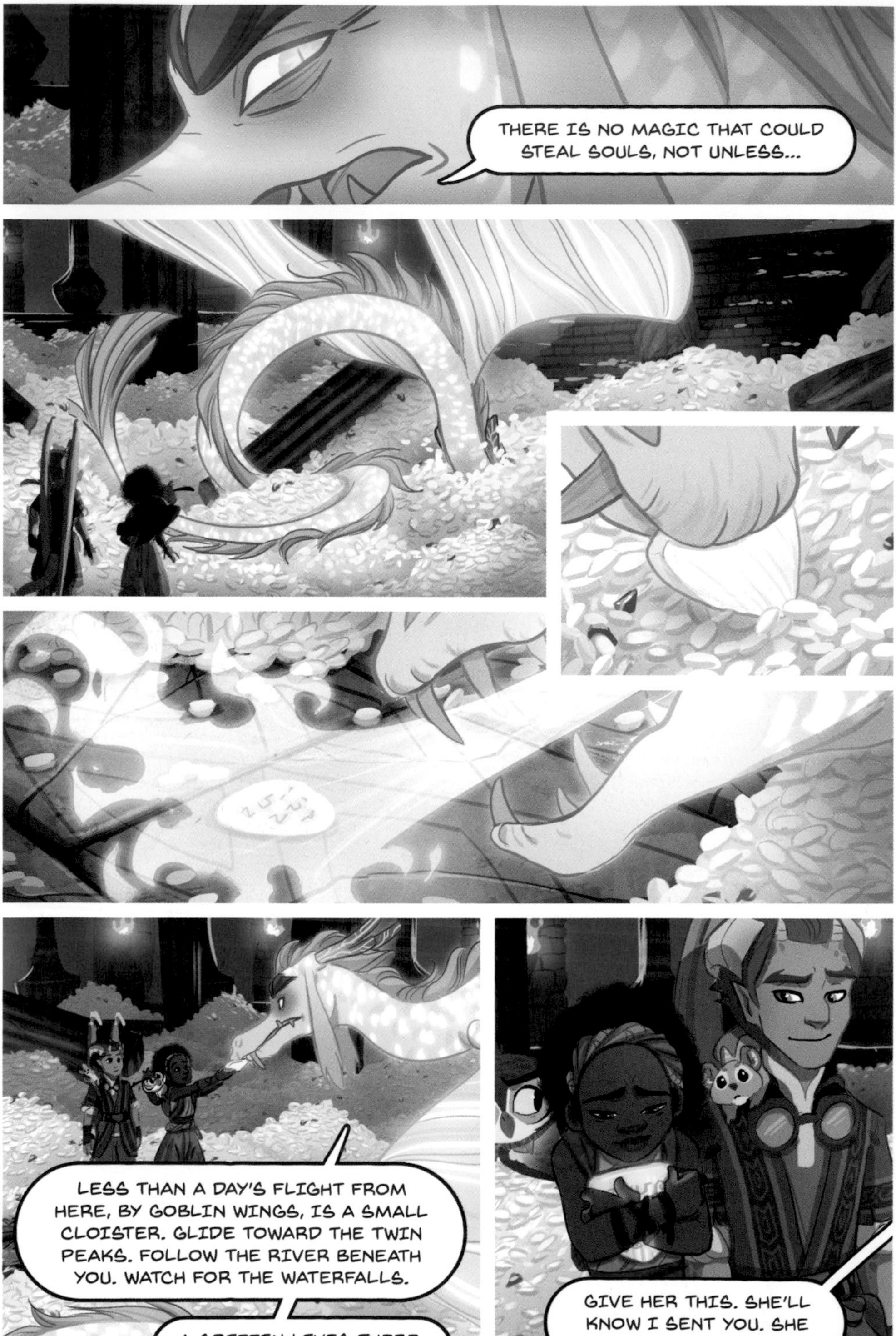
THERE IS NO MAGIC THAT COULD STEAL SOULS, NOT UNLESS...
LESS THAN A DAY'S FLIGHT FROM HERE, BY GOBLIN WINGS, IS A SMALL CLOISTER. GLIDE TOWARD THE TWIN PEAKS. FOLLOW THE RIVER BENEATH YOU. WATCH FOR THE WATERFALLS.
A GRIFFIN LIVES THERE. HER NAME IS HIERAN.
GIVE HER THIS. SHE'LL KNOW I SENT YOU. SHE MIGHT HAVE ANSWERS.

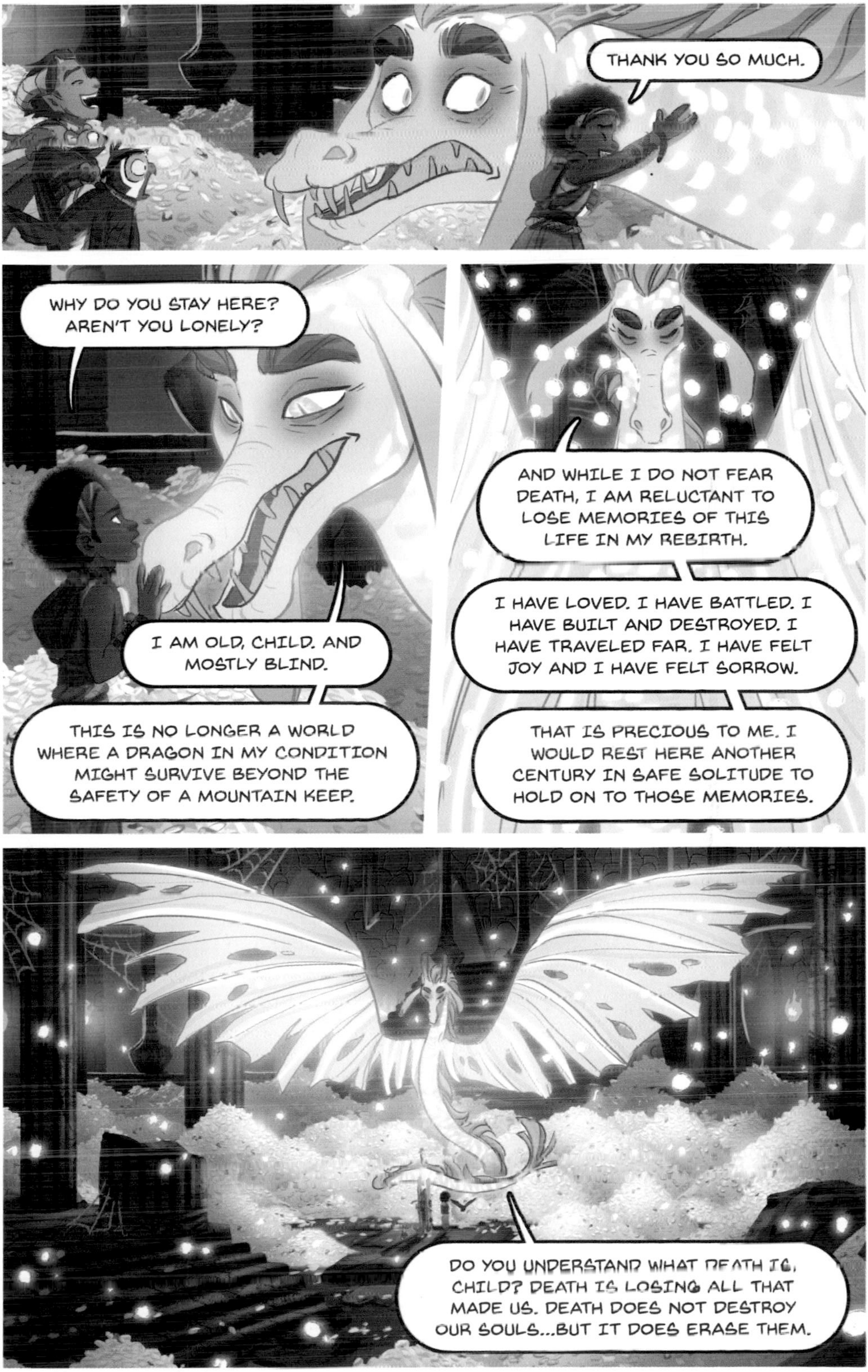
THANK YOU SO MUCH.
WHY DO YOU STAY HERE? AREN'T YOU LONELY?
I AM OLD, CHILD. AND MOSTLY BLIND.
THIS IS NO LONGER A WORLD WHERE A DRAGON IN MY CONDITION MIGHT SURVIVE BEYOND THE SAFETY OF A MOUNTAIN KEEP.
AND WHILE I DO NOT FEAR DEATH, I AM RELUCTANT TO LOSE MEMORIES OF THIS LIFE IN MY REBIRTH.
I HAVE LOVED. I HAVE BATTLED. I HAVE BUILT AND DESTROYED. I HAVE TRAVELED FAR. I HAVE FELT JOY AND I HAVE FELT SORROW.
THAT IS PRECIOUS TO ME. I WOULD REST HERE ANOTHER CENTURY IN SAFE SOLITUDE TO HOLD ON TO THOSE MEMORIES.
DO YOU UNDERSTAND WHAT DEATH IS, CHILD? DEATH IS LOSING ALL THAT MADE US. DEATH DOES NOT DESTROY OUR SOULS...BUT IT DOES ERASE THEM.

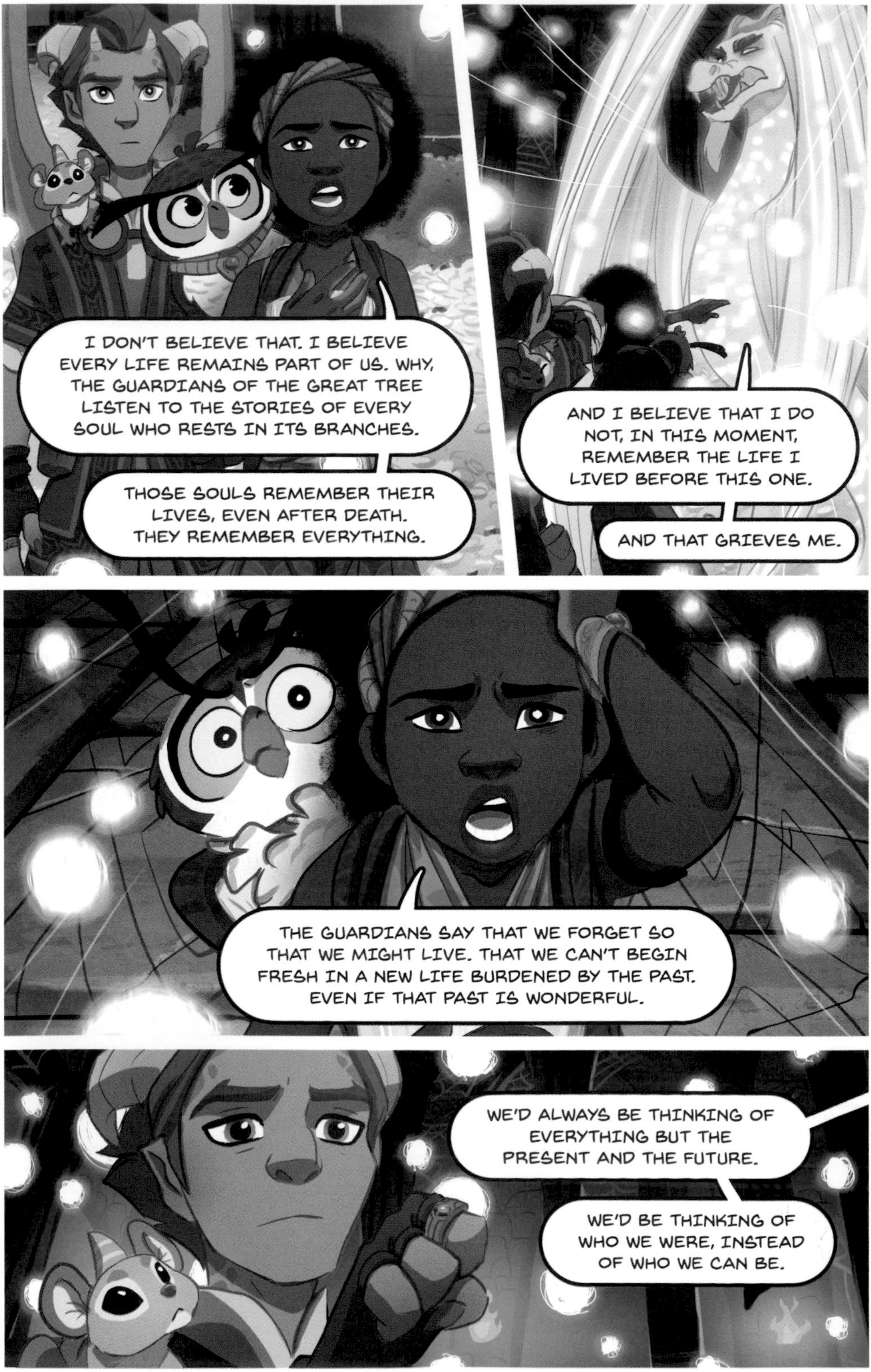
I DON'T BELIEVE THAT. I BELIEVE EVERY LIFE REMAINS PART OF US. WHY, THE GUARDIANS OF THE GREAT TREE LISTEN TO THE STORIES OF EVERY SOUL WHO RESTS IN ITS BRANCHES.
THOSE SOULS REMEMBER THEIR LIVES, EVEN AFTER DEATH. THEY REMEMBER EVERYTHING.
AND I BELIEVE THAT I DO NOT, IN THIS MOMENT, REMEMBER THE LIFE I LIVED BEFORE THIS ONE.
AND THAT GRIEVES ME.
THE GUARDIANS SAY THAT WE FORGET SO THAT WE MIGHT LIVE. THAT WE CAN'T BEGIN FRESH IN A NEW LIFE BURDENED BY THE PAST. EVEN IF THAT PAST IS WONDERFUL.
WE'D ALWAYS BE THINKING OF EVERYTHING BUT THE PRESENT AND THE FUTURE.
WE'D BE THINKING OF WHO WE WERE, INSTEAD OF WHO WE CAN BE.

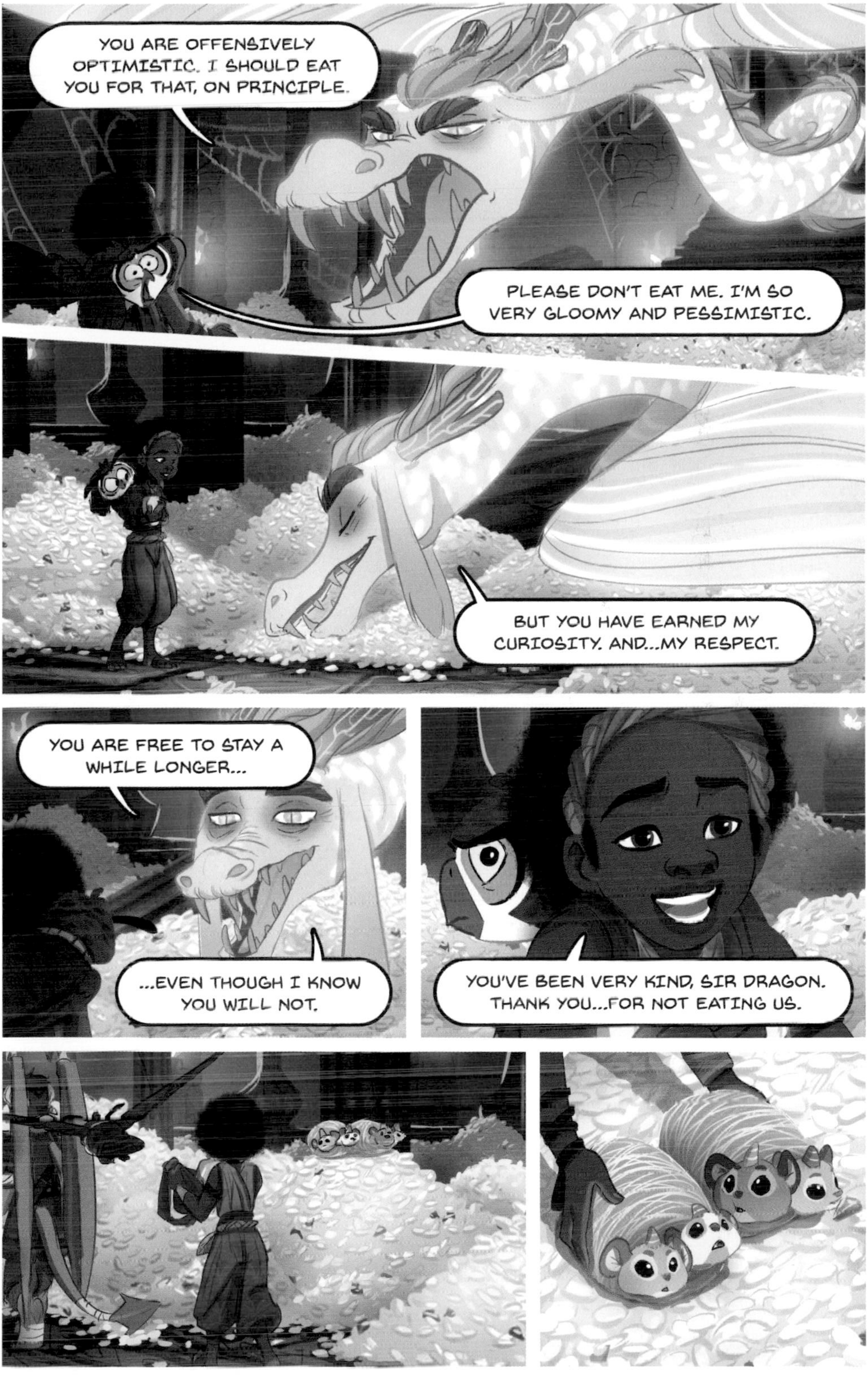
YOU ARE OFFENSIVELY OPTIMISTIC. I SHOULD EAT YOU FOR THAT, ON PRINCIPLE.
PLEASE DON'T EAT ME. I'M SO VERY GLOOMY AND PESSIMISTIC.
BUT YOU HAVE EARNED MY CURIOSITY. AND...MY RESPECT.
YOU ARE FREE TO STAY A WHILE LONGER...
...EVEN THOUGH I KNOW YOU WILL NOT.
YOU'VE BEEN VERY KIND, SIR DRAGON. THANK YOU...FOR NOT EATING US.

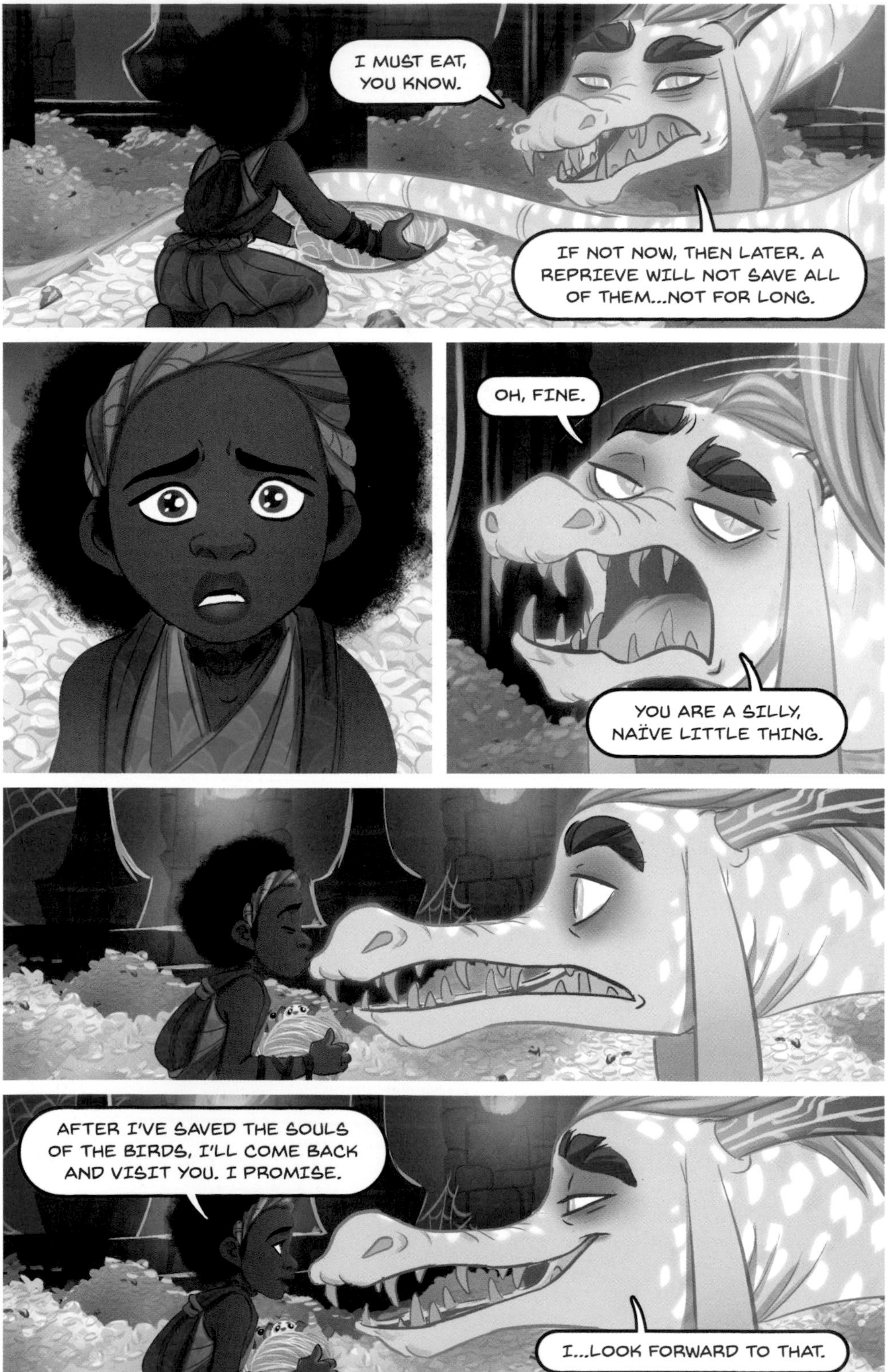
I MUST EAT, YOU KNOW.
IF NOT NOW, THEN LATER. A REPRIEVE WILL NOT SAVE ALL OF THEM...NOT FOR LONG.
OH, FINE.
YOU ARE A SILLY, NAÏVE LITTLE THING.
AFTER I'VE SAVED THE SOULS OF THE BIRDS, I'LL COME BACK AND VISIT YOU. I PROMISE.
I...LOOK FORWARD TO THAT.

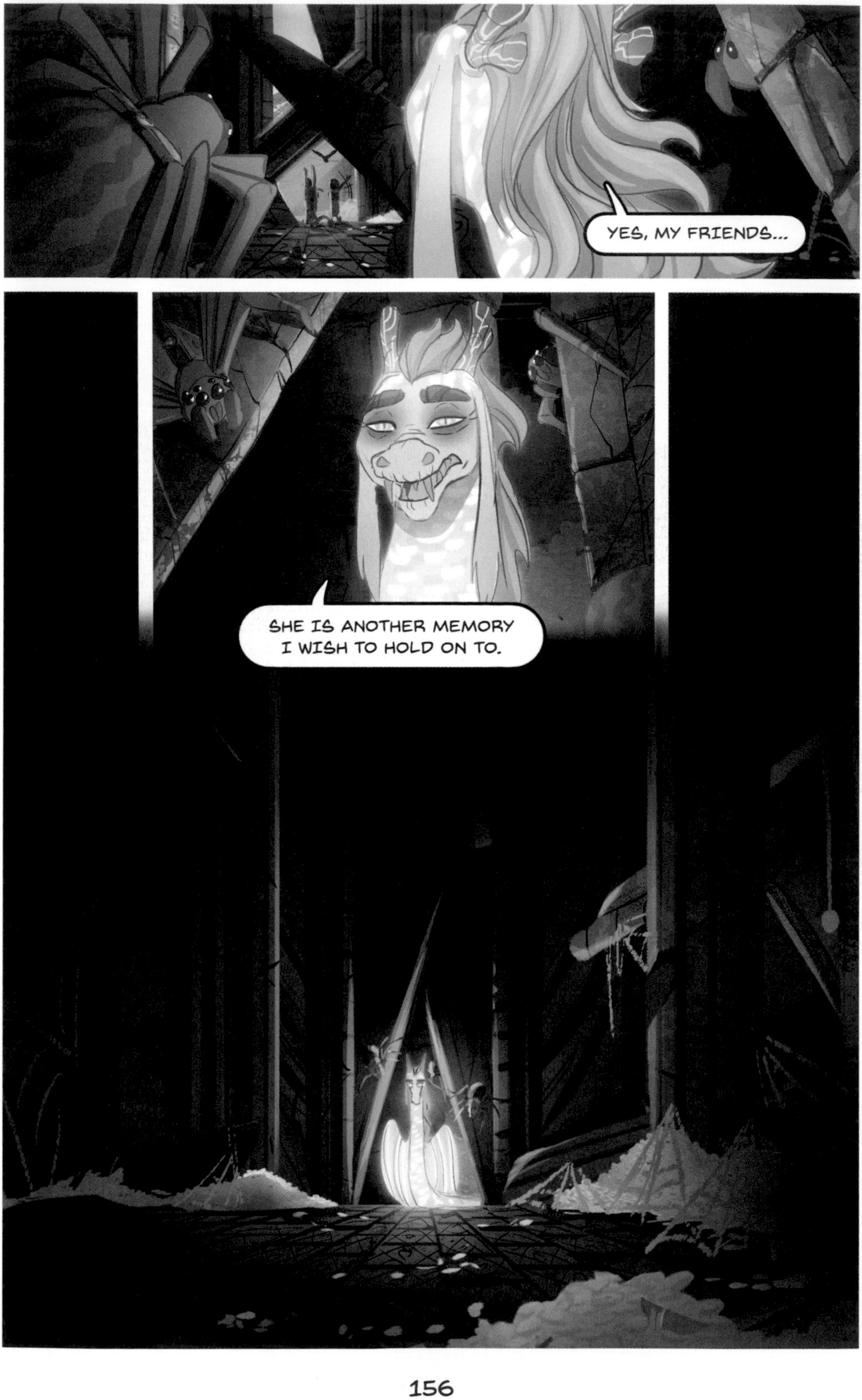
YES, MY FRIENDS...
SHE IS ANOTHER MEMORY I WISH TO HOLD ON TO.

157

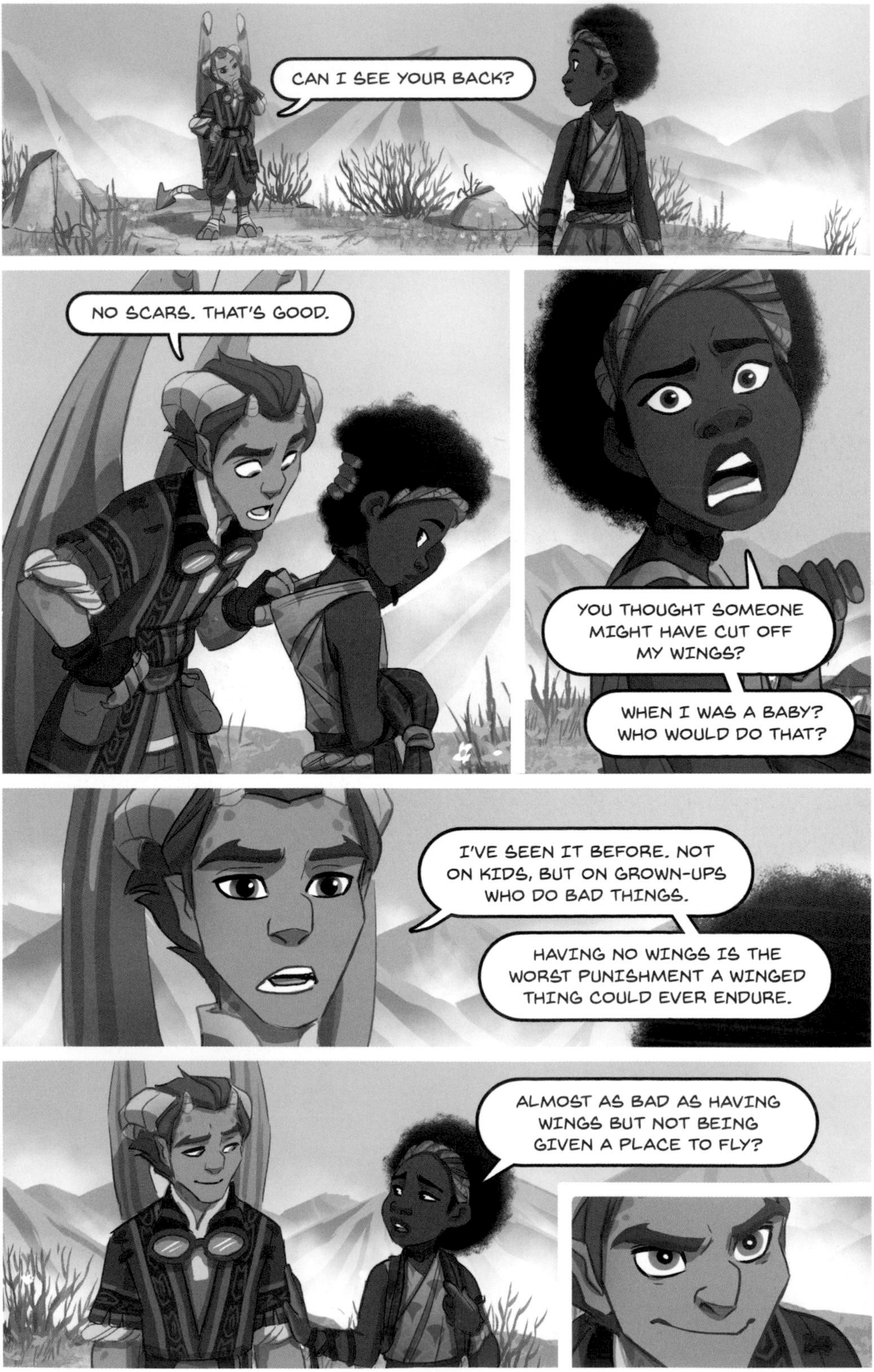
CAN I SEE YOUR BACK?
NO SCARS. THAT'S GOOD.
YOU THOUGHT SOMEONE MIGHT HAVE CUT OFF MY WINGS?
WHEN I WAS A BABY? WHO WOULD DO THAT?
I'VE SEEN IT BEFORE. NOT ON KIDS, BUT ON GROWN-UPS WHO DO BAD THINGS.
HAVING NO WINGS IS THE WORST PUNISHMENT A WINGED THING COULD EVER ENDURE.
ALMOST AS BAD AS HAVING WINGS BUT NOT BEING GIVEN A PLACE TO FLY?

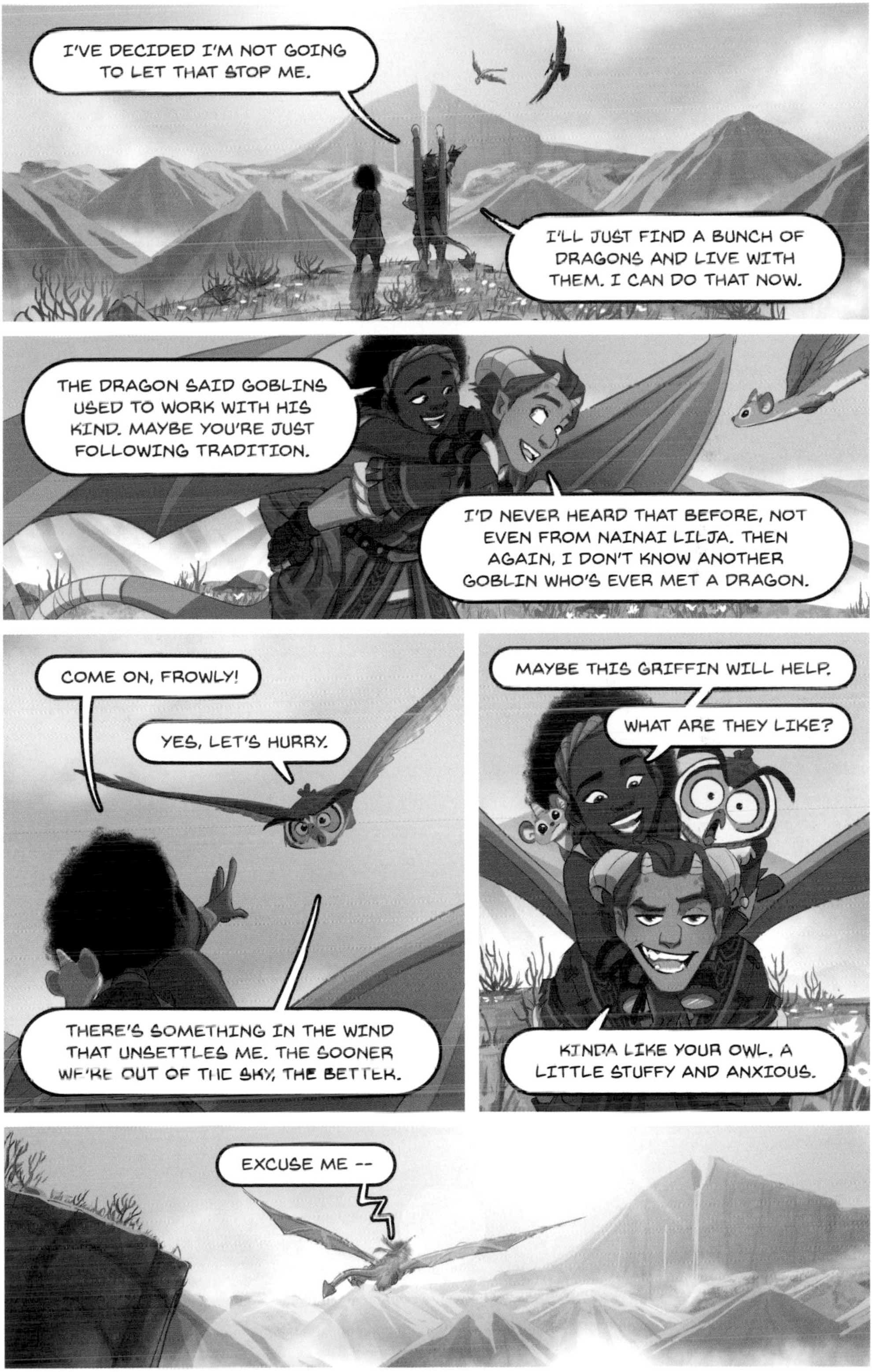
I'VE DECIDED I'M NOT GOING TO LET THAT STOP ME.
I'LL JUST FIND A BUNCH OF DRAGONS AND LIVE WITH THEM. I CAN DO THAT NOW.
THE DRAGON SAID GOBLINS USED TO WORK WITH HIS KIND. MAYBE YOU'RE JUST FOLLOWING TRADITION.
I'D NEVER HEARD THAT BEFORE, NOT EVEN FROM NAINAI LILJA. THEN AGAIN, I DON'T KNOW ANOTHER GOBLIN WHO'S EVER MET A DRAGON.
COME ON, FROWLY!
YES, LET'S HURRY.
THERE'S SOMETHING IN THE WIND THAT UNSETTLES ME. THE SOONER WE'RE OUT OF THE SKY, THE BETTER.
MAYBE THIS GRIFFIN WILL HELP.
WHAT ARE THEY LIKE?
KINDA LIKE YOUR OWL. A LITTLE STUFFY AND ANXIOUS.
EXCUSE ME --

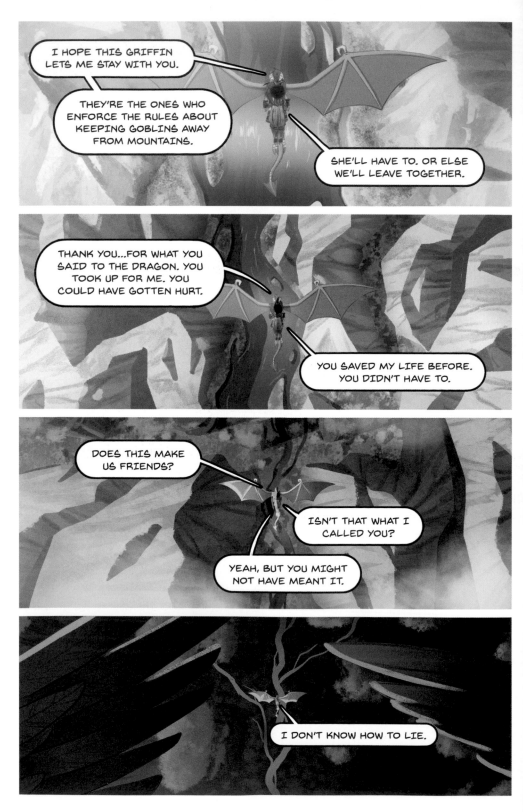

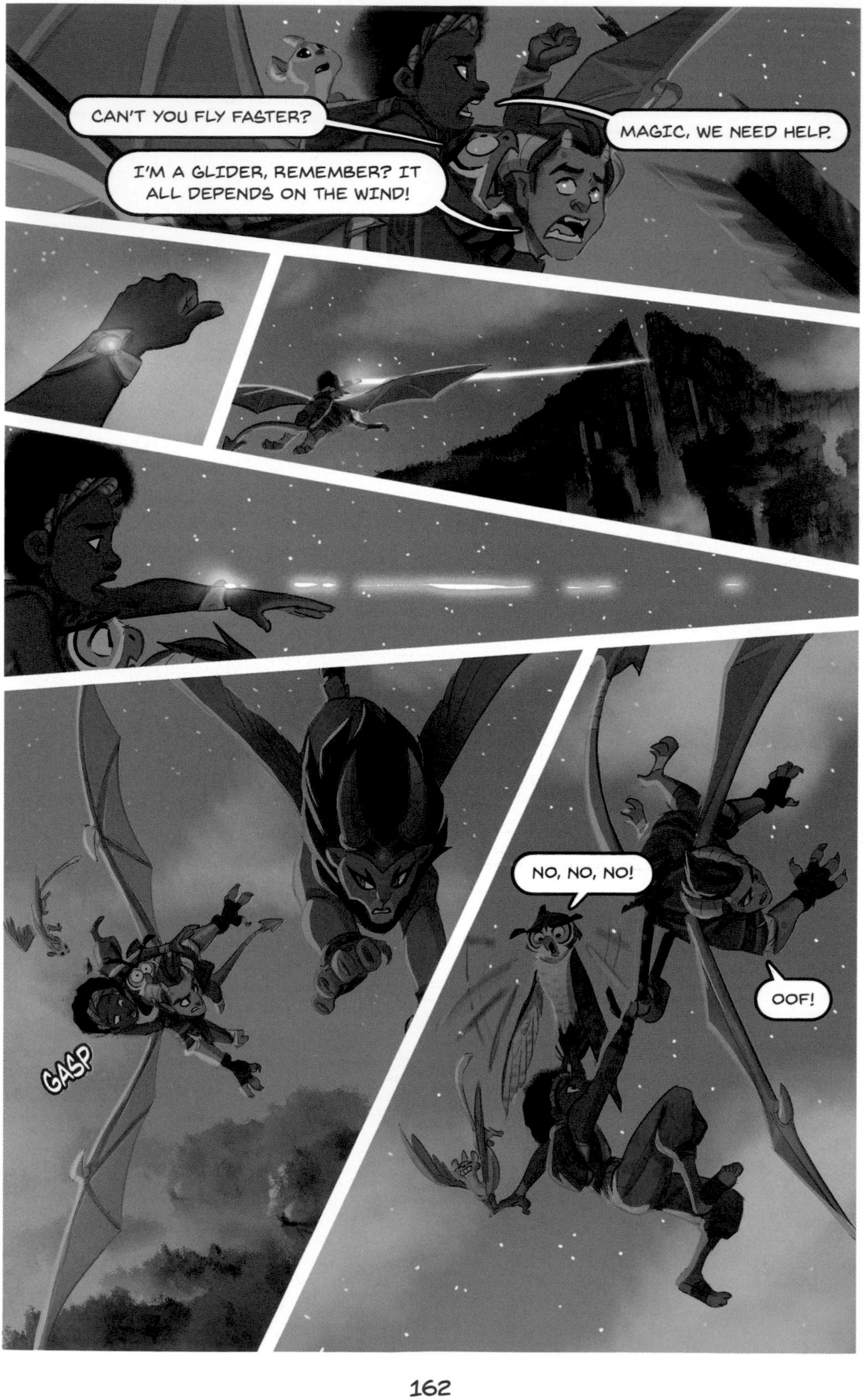
CAN'T YOU FLY FASTER?
MAGIC, WE NEED HELP.
I'M A GLIDER, REMEMBER? IT ALL DEPENDS ON THE WIND!
GASP
NO, NO, NO!
OOF!

167

169

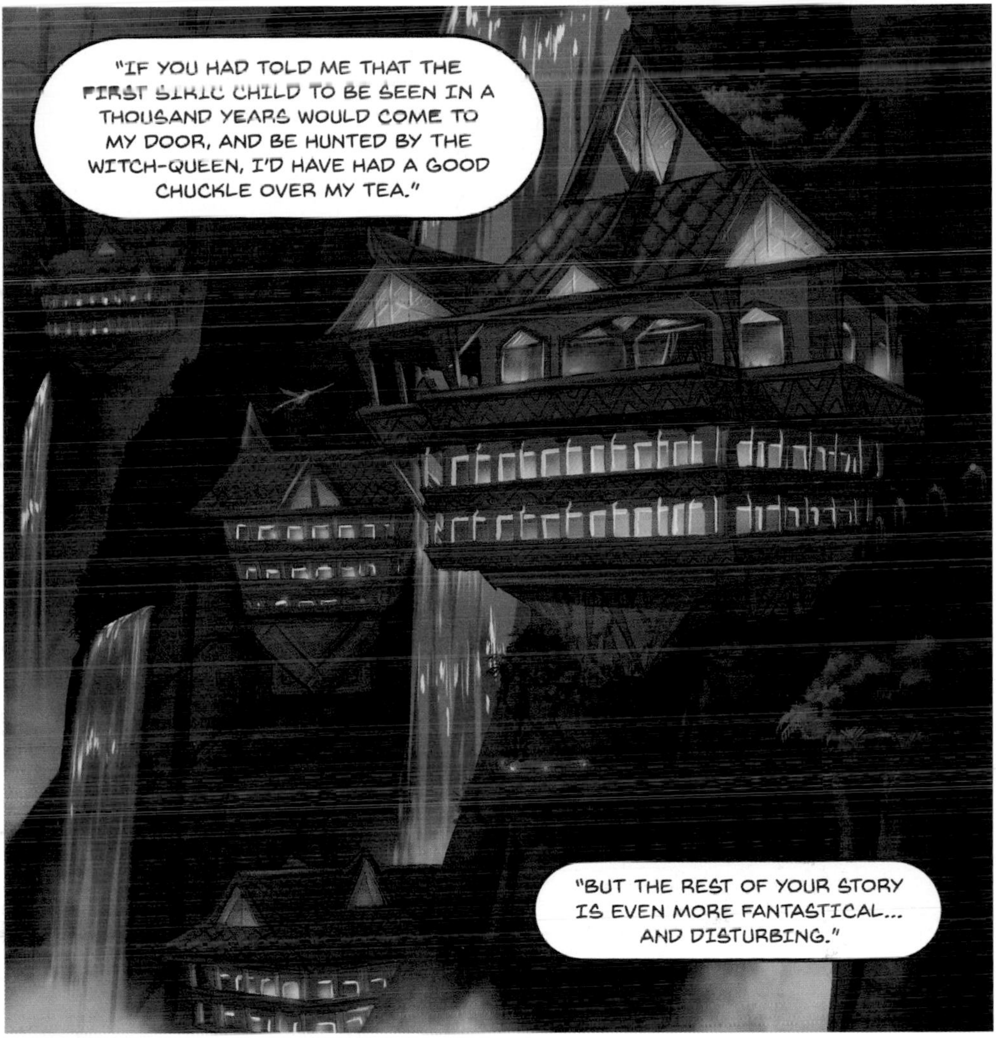
"IF YOU HAD TOLD ME THAT THE FIRST SIRIC CHILD TO BE SEEN IN A THOUSAND YEARS WOULD COME TO MY DOOR, AND BE HUNTED BY THE WITCH-QUEEN, I'D HAVE HAD A GOOD CHUCKLE OVER MY TEA."
"BUT THE REST OF YOUR STORY IS EVEN MORE FANTASTICAL... AND DISTURBING."

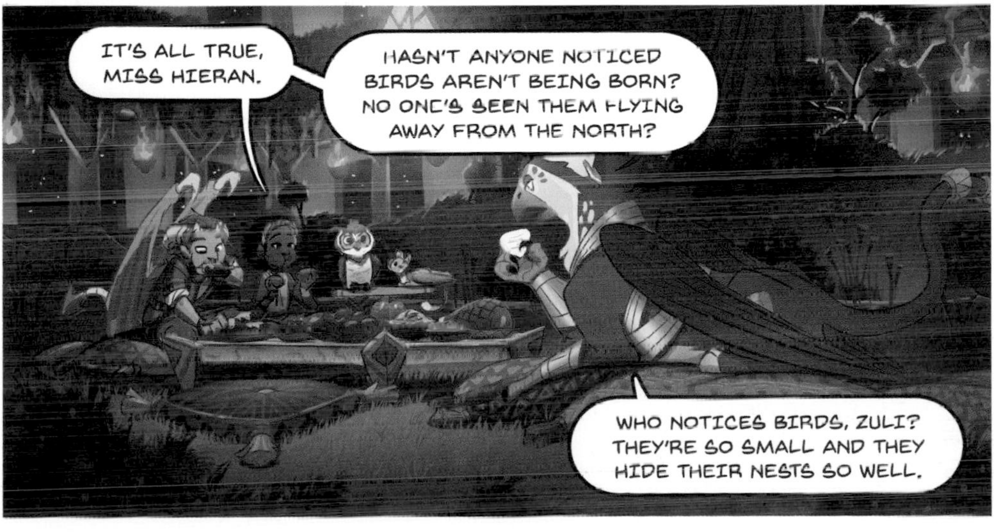
IT'S ALL TRUE, MISS HIERAN.
HASN'T ANYONE NOTICED BIRDS AREN'T BEING BORN? NO ONE'S SEEN THEM FLYING AWAY FROM THE NORTH?
WHO NOTICES BIRDS, ZULI? THEY'RE SO SMALL AND THEY HIDE THEIR NESTS SO WELL.

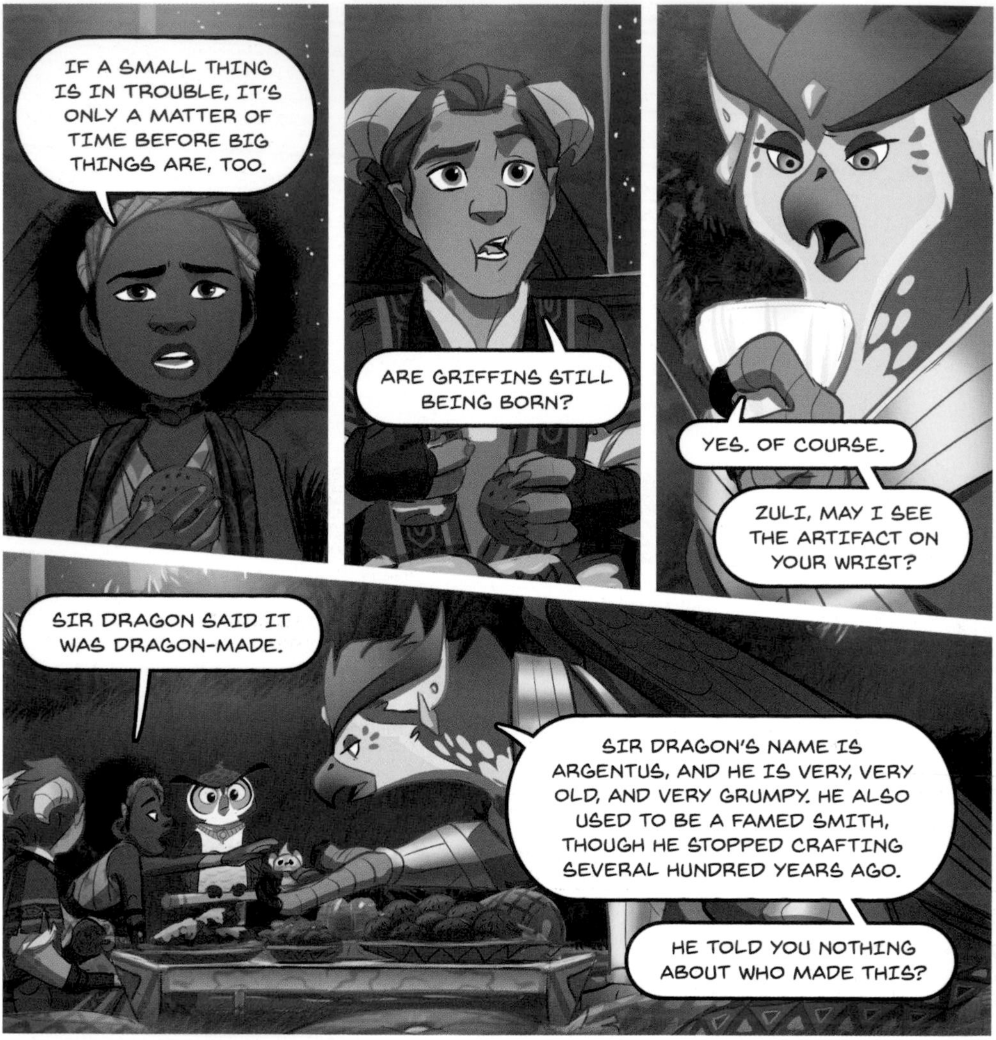
IF A SMALL THING IS IN TROUBLE, IT'S ONLY A MATTER OF TIME BEFORE BIG THINGS ARE, TOO.
ARE GRIFFINS STILL BEING BORN?
YES. OF COURSE.
ZULI, MAY I SEE THE ARTIFACT ON YOUR WRIST?
SIR DRAGON SAID IT WAS DRAGON-MADE.
SIR DRAGON'S NAME IS ARGENTUS, AND HE IS VERY, VERY OLD, AND VERY GRUMPY. HE ALSO USED TO BE A FAMED SMITH, THOUGH HE STOPPED CRAFTING SEVERAL HUNDRED YEARS AGO.
HE TOLD YOU NOTHING ABOUT WHO MADE THIS?
NO. ALL HE SAID WAS IT WOULD HELP ME DO MAGIC...AND THAT I HAVE...A LOT INSIDE ME.
ARGENTUS WAS NOT WRONG ABOUT THAT...
OH...THAT FEELS LIKE...LIKE A RIVER...
OR...OR FLIGHT...

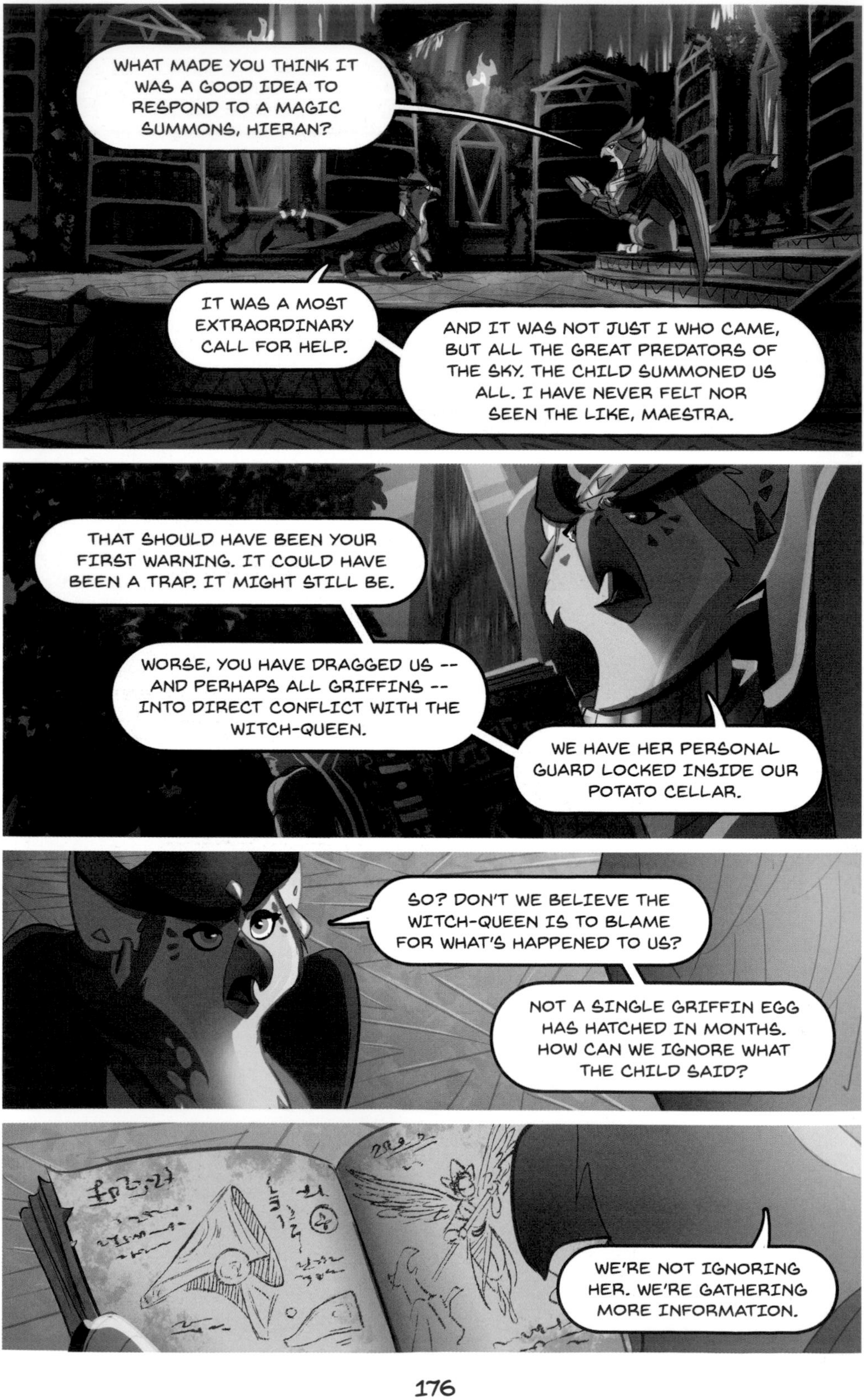
WHAT MADE YOU THINK IT WAS A GOOD IDEA TO RESPOND TO A MAGIC SUMMONS, HIERAN?
IT WAS A MOST EXTRAORDINARY CALL FOR HELP.
AND IT WAS NOT JUST I WHO CAME, BUT ALL THE GREAT PREDATORS OF THE SKY. THE CHILD SUMMONED US ALL. I HAVE NEVER FELT NOR SEEN THE LIKE, MAESTRA.
THAT SHOULD HAVE BEEN YOUR FIRST WARNING. IT COULD HAVE BEEN A TRAP. IT MIGHT STILL BE.
WORSE, YOU HAVE DRAGGED US -- AND PERHAPS ALL GRIFFINS -- INTO DIRECT CONFLICT WITH THE WITCH-QUEEN.
WE HAVE HER PERSONAL GUARD LOCKED INSIDE OUR POTATO CELLAR.
SO? DON'T WE BELIEVE THE WITCH-QUEEN IS TO BLAME FOR WHAT'S HAPPENED TO US?
NOT A SINGLE GRIFFIN EGG HAS HATCHED IN MONTHS. HOW CAN WE IGNORE WHAT THE CHILD SAID?
WE'RE NOT IGNORING HER. WE'RE GATHERING MORE INFORMATION.

WE SHOULD STILL ALERT THE INCANTIC COUNCIL. IF NOTHING ELSE, THEY'LL WANT TO KNOW A SIRIC CHILD HAS BEEN FOUND...

...AND THEY'LL WANT TO KNOW ABOUT THE ARTIFACT THAT'S BONDED TO HER, AND THAT SHE IS ACCOMPANIED BY ONE OF THE LEGENDARIES.

I DARED NOT EVEN LOOK AT HIM.

THE IMPLICATIONS OF THAT ALONE --

SHE HAS NO WINGS, HIERAN. IT'S IMPOSSIBLE THAT SHE'S A SIRIC.

BESIDES, NOT ONE OF THEM HAS BEEN SEEN IN A THOUSAND YEARS, BUT SUDDENLY A CHILD OF THEIR RACE APPEARS...

...CLAIMING TO BE FROM SOME MYSTICAL TREE WHERE BIRD SOULS GO TO BE REBORN?

BIRDS DON'T EVEN HAVE SOULS. IT'S RIDICULOUS.

MAESTRA...SOME OF WHAT THE CHILD SAID MIGHT SEEM FARFETCHED...

...BUT WHAT SHE TOLD ME ABOUT THE NORTH MIGHT BE THE ANSWER WE'VE BEEN SEARCHING FOR.

IT COULD ALSO BE A RUSE FROM THE WITCH-QUEEN.

NO.

ZULI HAS THE BLESSING OF ARGENTUS. HE EVEN BLESSED THE GOBLIN BOY, AND BONDED HIM TO A DRAGON-SMITHED ARTIFACT.

BESIDES...ARGENTUS IS MY MENTOR, AND A FRIEND. HE WANTS ME TO HELP THE CHILDREN. I CAN'T SIMPLY --

THAT'S AN EXTRAORDINARY HONOR, MAESTRA.

181

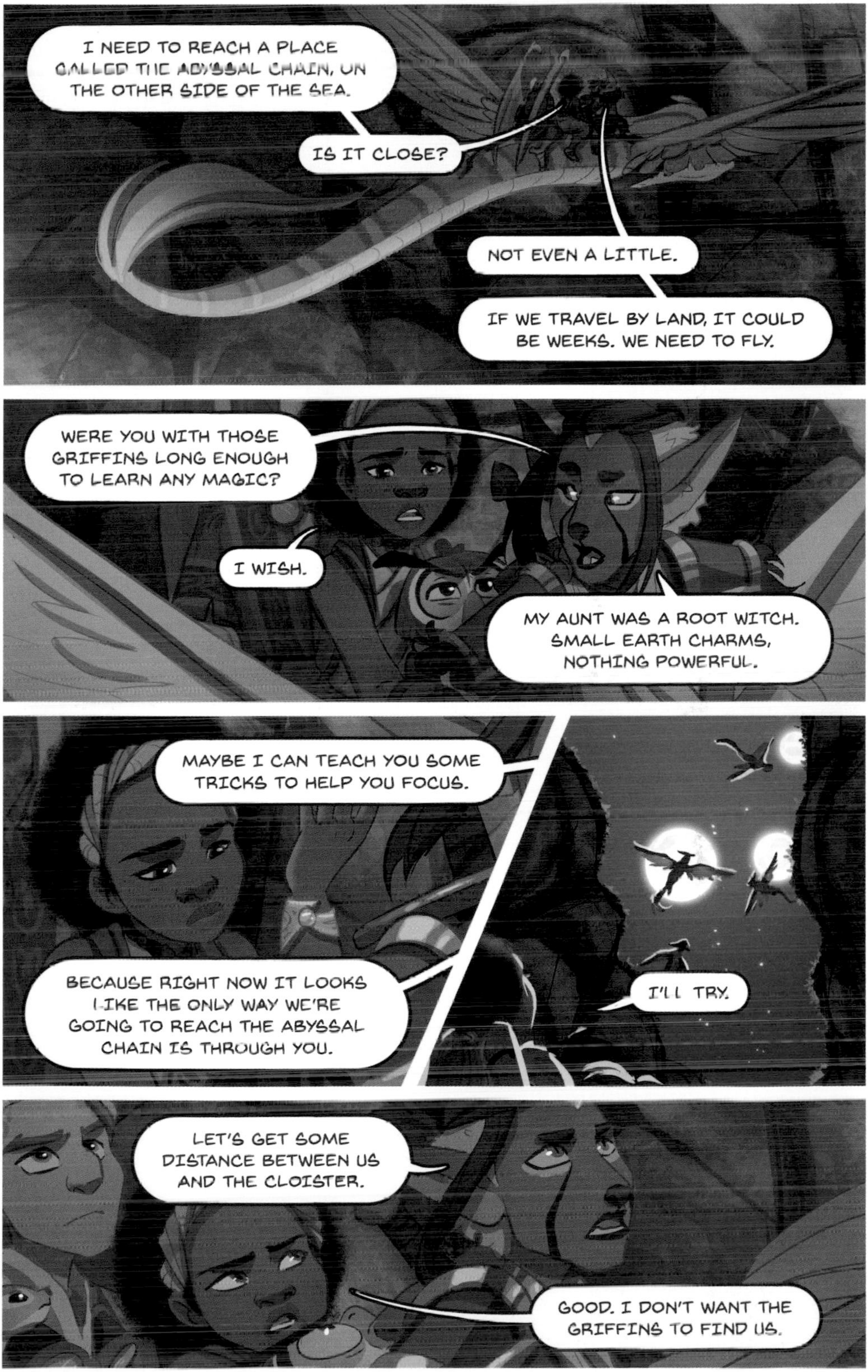

I NEED TO REACH A PLACE CALLED THE ABYSSAL CHAIN, ON THE OTHER SIDE OF THE SEA.
IS IT CLOSE?
NOT EVEN A LITTLE.
IF WE TRAVEL BY LAND, IT COULD BE WEEKS. WE NEED TO FLY.
WERE YOU WITH THOSE GRIFFINS LONG ENOUGH TO LEARN ANY MAGIC?
I WISH.
MY AUNT WAS A ROOT WITCH. SMALL EARTH CHARMS, NOTHING POWERFUL.
MAYBE I CAN TEACH YOU SOME TRICKS TO HELP YOU FOCUS.
BECAUSE RIGHT NOW IT LOOKS LIKE THE ONLY WAY WE'RE GOING TO REACH THE ABYSSAL CHAIN IS THROUGH YOU.
I'LL TRY.
LET'S GET SOME DISTANCE BETWEEN US AND THE CLOISTER.
GOOD. I DON'T WANT THE GRIFFINS TO FIND US.

MEDITATION IS SOMETHING WE'RE TAUGHT AS SOLDIERS.

HOW TO STILL THE MIND IN THE MIDST OF CHAOS.

IT'S PERHAPS THE HARDEST LESSON TO LEARN.

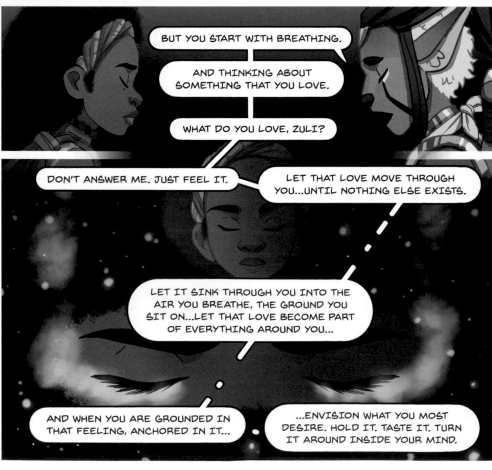

BUT YOU START WITH BREATHING.

AND THINKING ABOUT SOMETHING THAT YOU LOVE.

WHAT DO YOU LOVE, ZULI?

DON'T ANSWER ME. JUST FEEL IT.

LET THAT LOVE MOVE THROUGH YOU...UNTIL NOTHING ELSE EXISTS.

LET IT SINK THROUGH YOU INTO THE AIR YOU BREATHE, THE GROUND YOU SIT ON...LET THAT LOVE BECOME PART OF EVERYTHING AROUND YOU...

AND WHEN YOU ARE GROUNDED IN THAT FEELING, ANCHORED IN IT...

...ENVISION WHAT YOU MOST DESIRE. HOLD IT. TASTE IT. TURN IT AROUND INSIDE YOUR MIND.

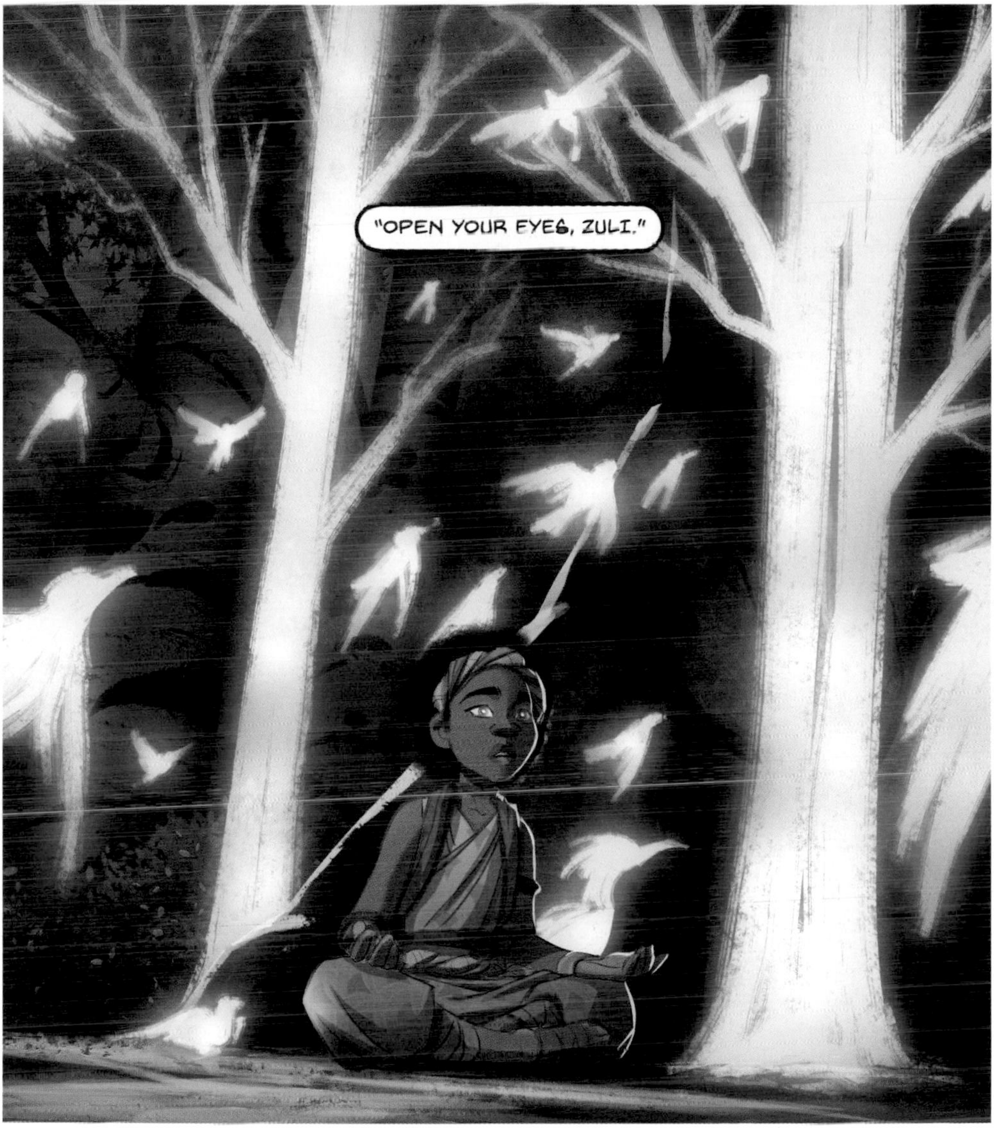
"OPEN YOUR EYES, ZULI."
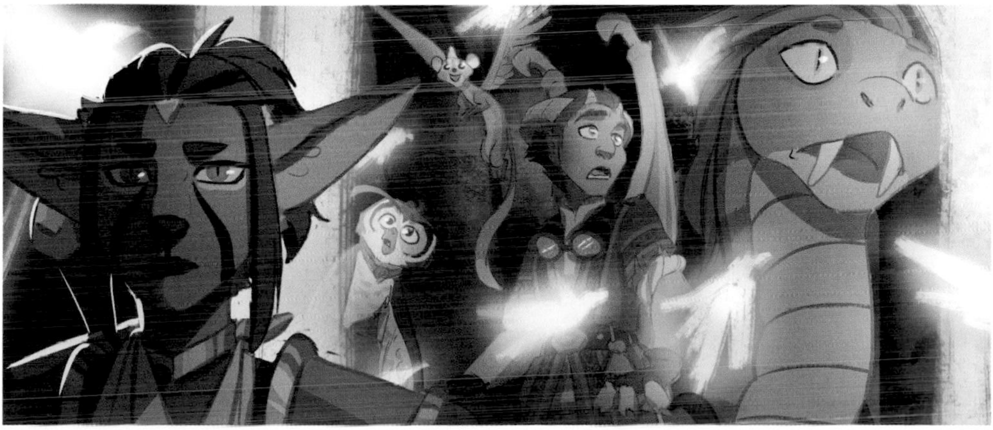

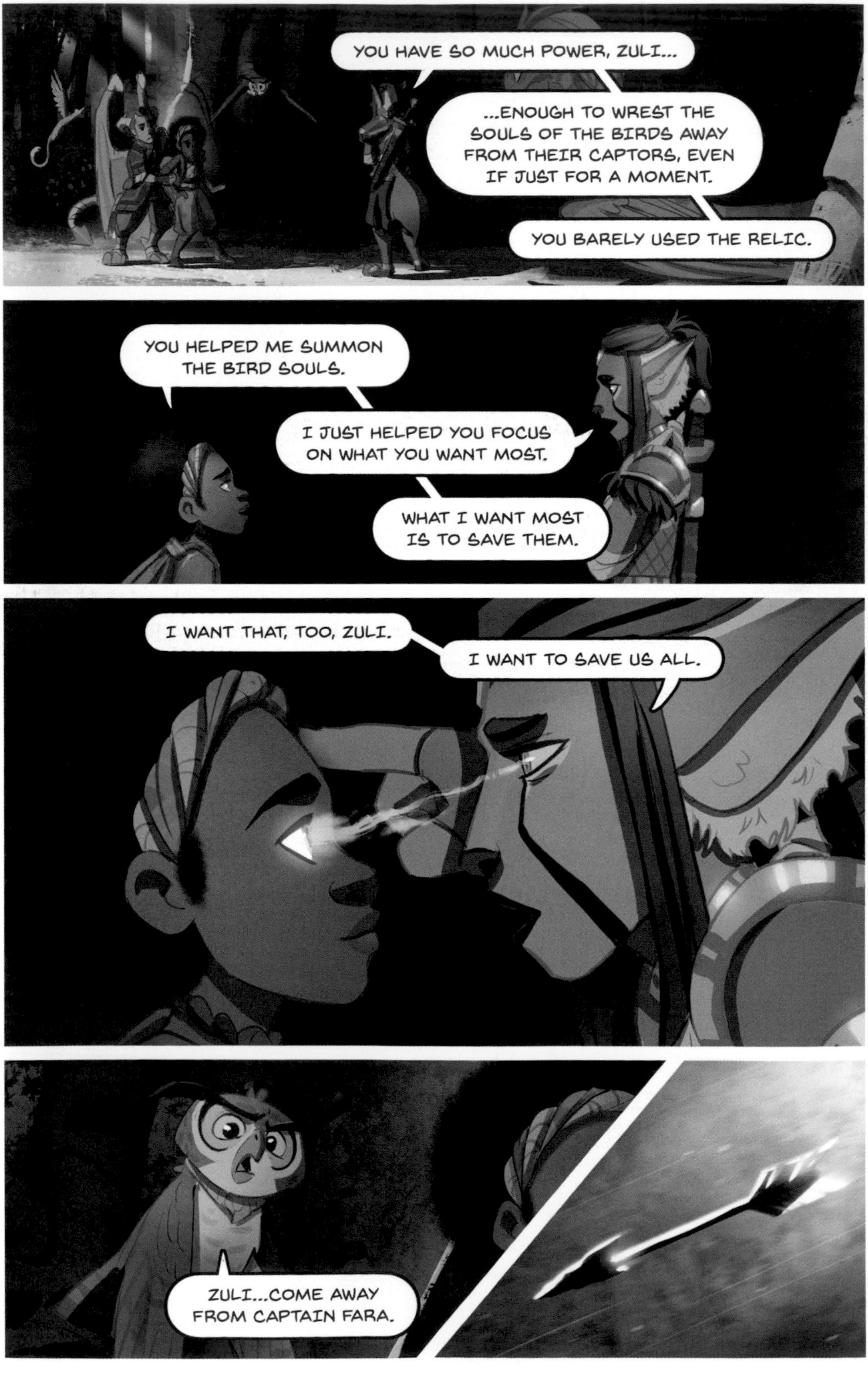
YOU HAVE SO MUCH POWER, ZULI...
...ENOUGH TO WREST THE SOULS OF THE BIRDS AWAY FROM THEIR CAPTORS, EVEN IF JUST FOR A MOMENT.
YOU BARELY USED THE RELIC.
YOU HELPED ME SUMMON THE BIRD SOULS.
I JUST HELPED YOU FOCUS ON WHAT YOU WANT MOST.
WHAT I WANT MOST IS TO SAVE THEM.
I WANT THAT, TOO, ZULI.
I WANT TO SAVE US ALL.
ZULI...COME AWAY FROM CAPTAIN FARA.

NNGH!
GASP
FARA!
HARPY!
I'M GOING TO TEAR YOU APART!
W-WHAT DO WE DO?
D-DON'T PULL OUT THE BOLT. N-NOT YET. TH-THAT'S ALL I KN-KNOW.
ZULI...HELP ME...

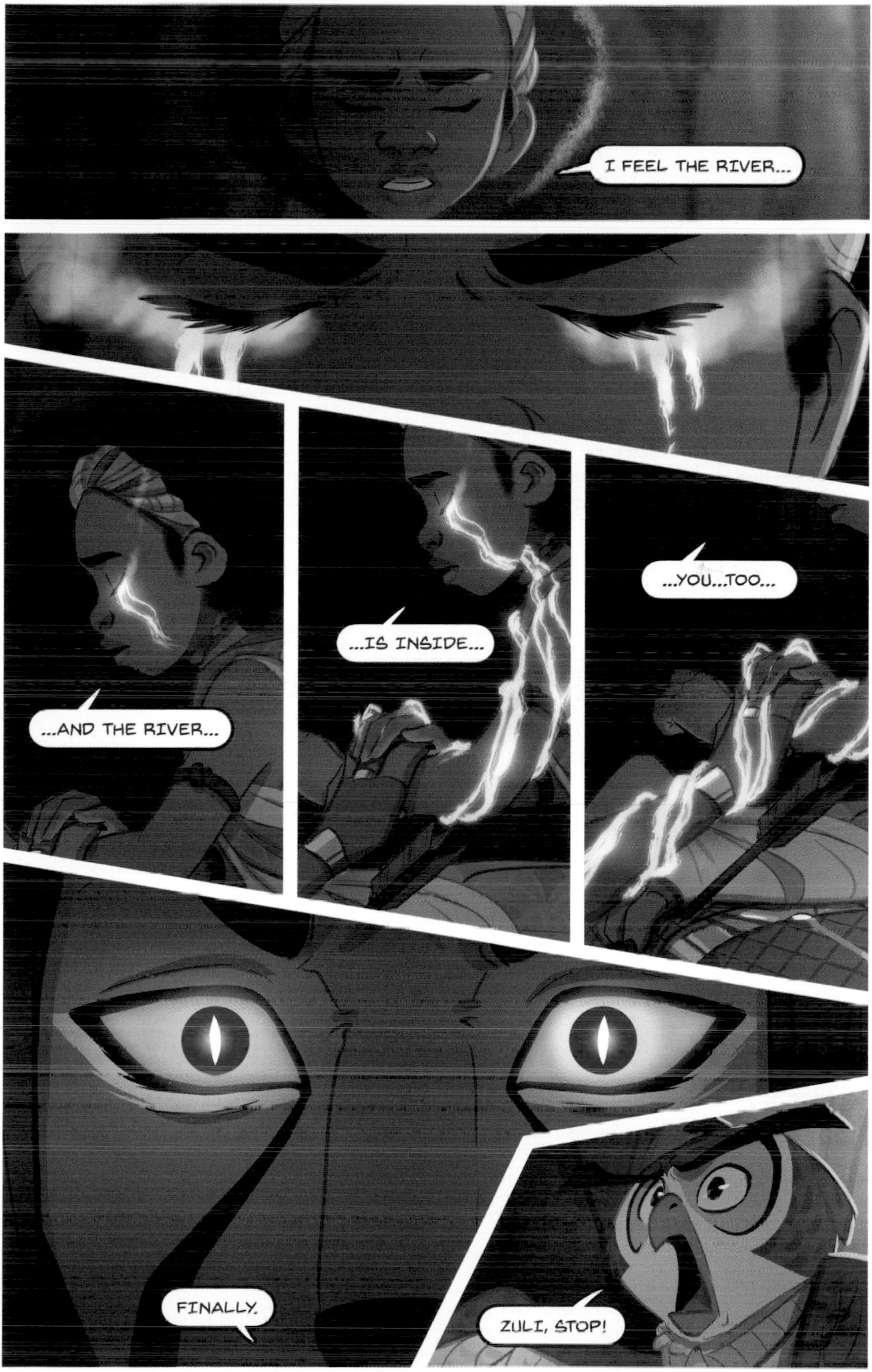
I FEEL THE RIVER...
...AND THE RIVER...
...IS INSIDE...
...YOU...TOO...
FINALLY.
ZULI, STOP!

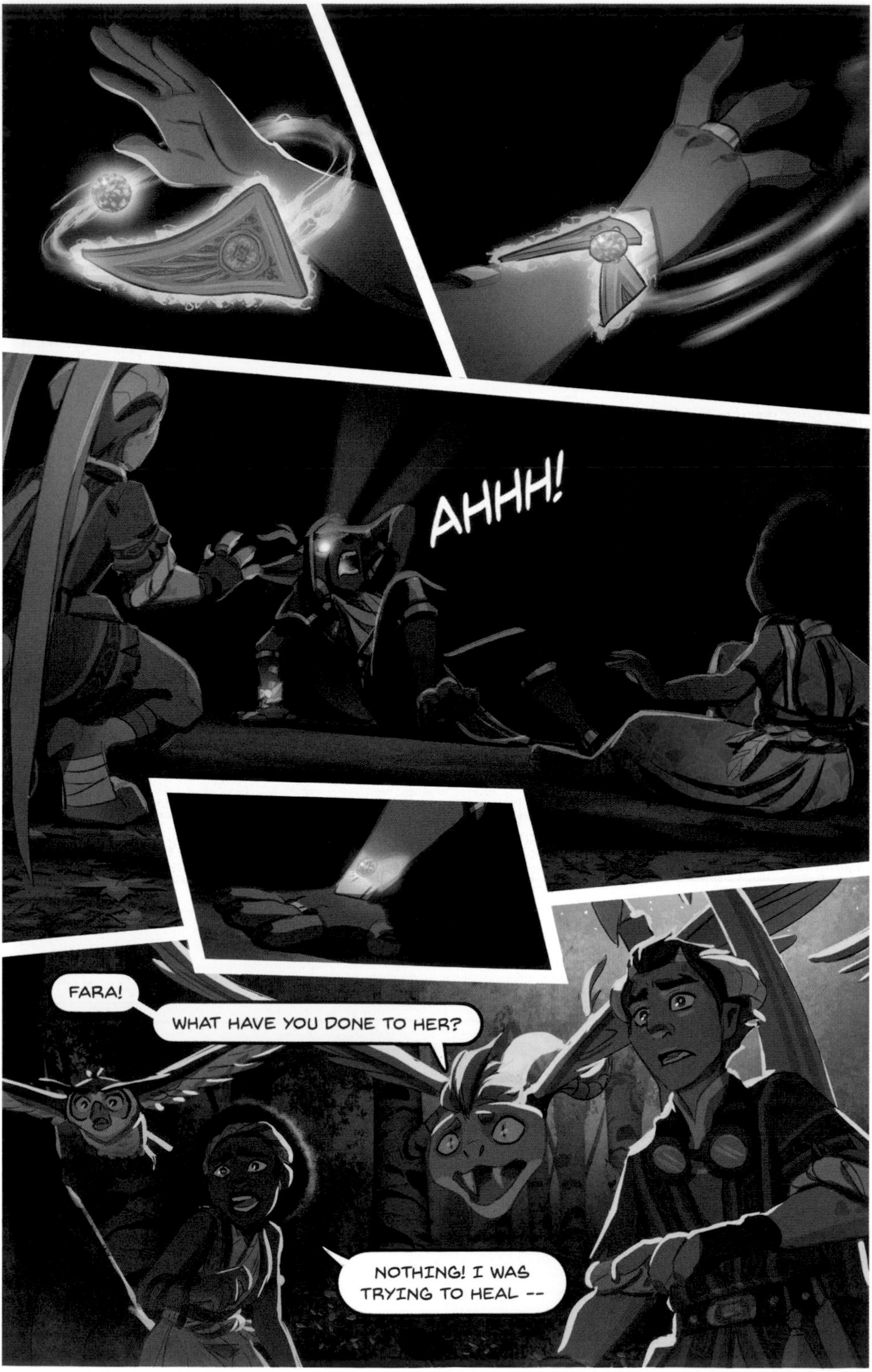
AHHH!
FARA!
WHAT HAVE YOU DONE TO HER?
NOTHING! I WAS TRYING TO HEAL --

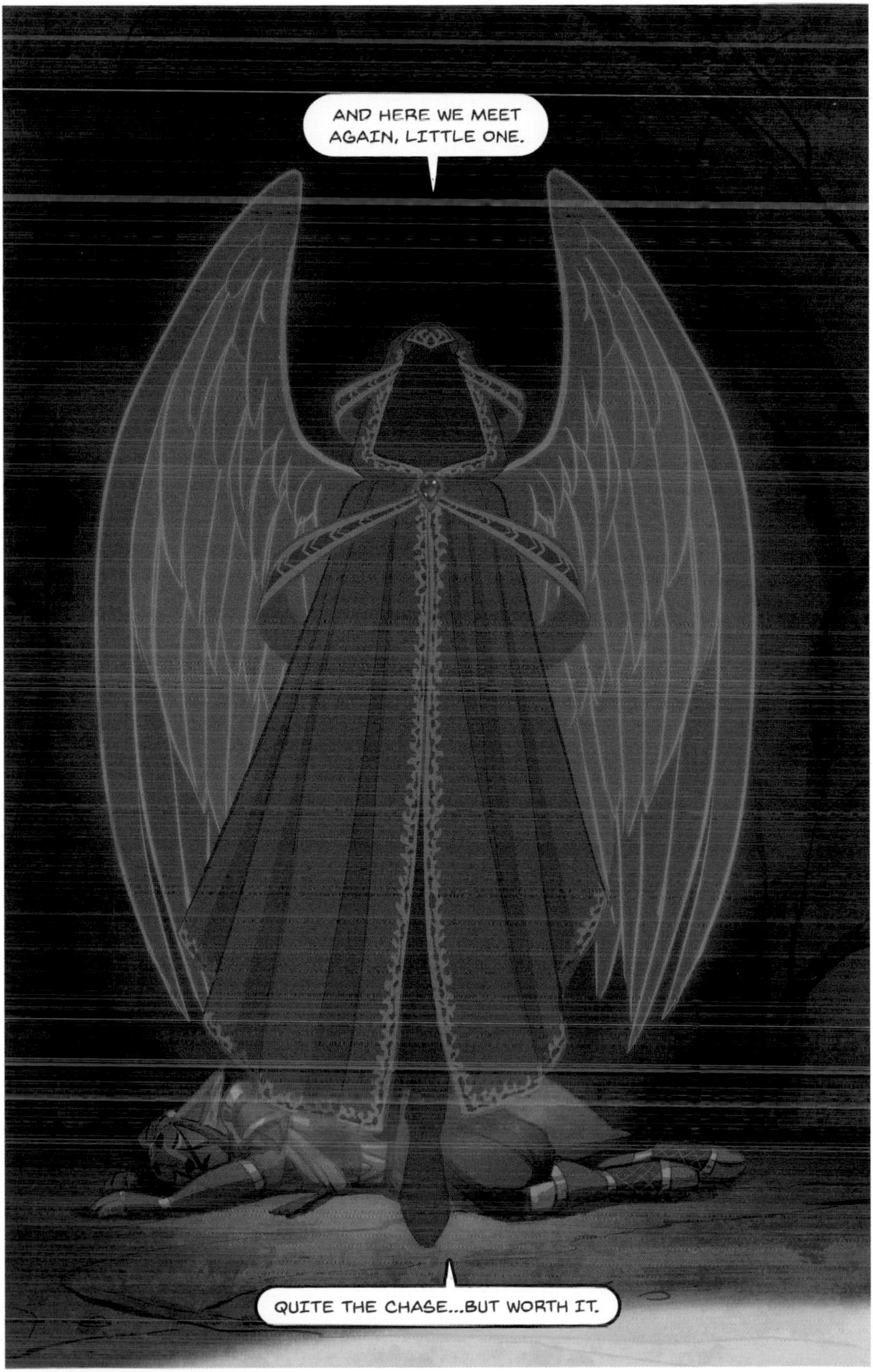
AND HERE WE MEET AGAIN, LITTLE ONE.
QUITE THE CHASE...BUT WORTH IT.

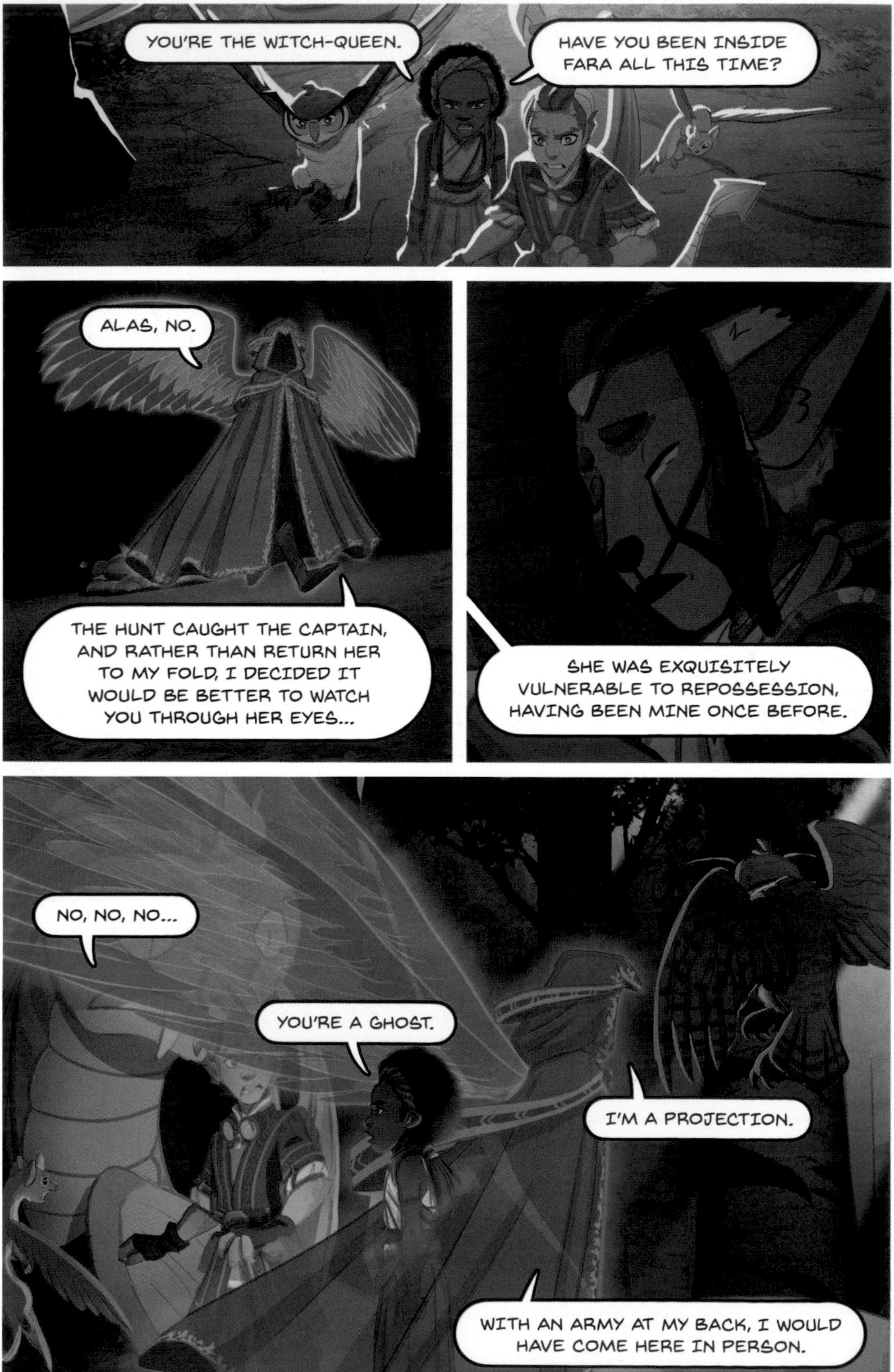
YOU'RE THE WITCH-QUEEN.
HAVE YOU BEEN INSIDE FARA ALL THIS TIME?
ALAS, NO.
THE HUNT CAUGHT THE CAPTAIN, AND RATHER THAN RETURN HER TO MY FOLD, I DECIDED IT WOULD BE BETTER TO WATCH YOU THROUGH HER EYES...
SHE WAS EXQUISITELY VULNERABLE TO REPOSSESSION, HAVING BEEN MINE ONCE BEFORE.
NO, NO, NO...
YOU'RE A GHOST.
I'M A PROJECTION.
WITH AN ARMY AT MY BACK, I WOULD HAVE COME HERE IN PERSON.

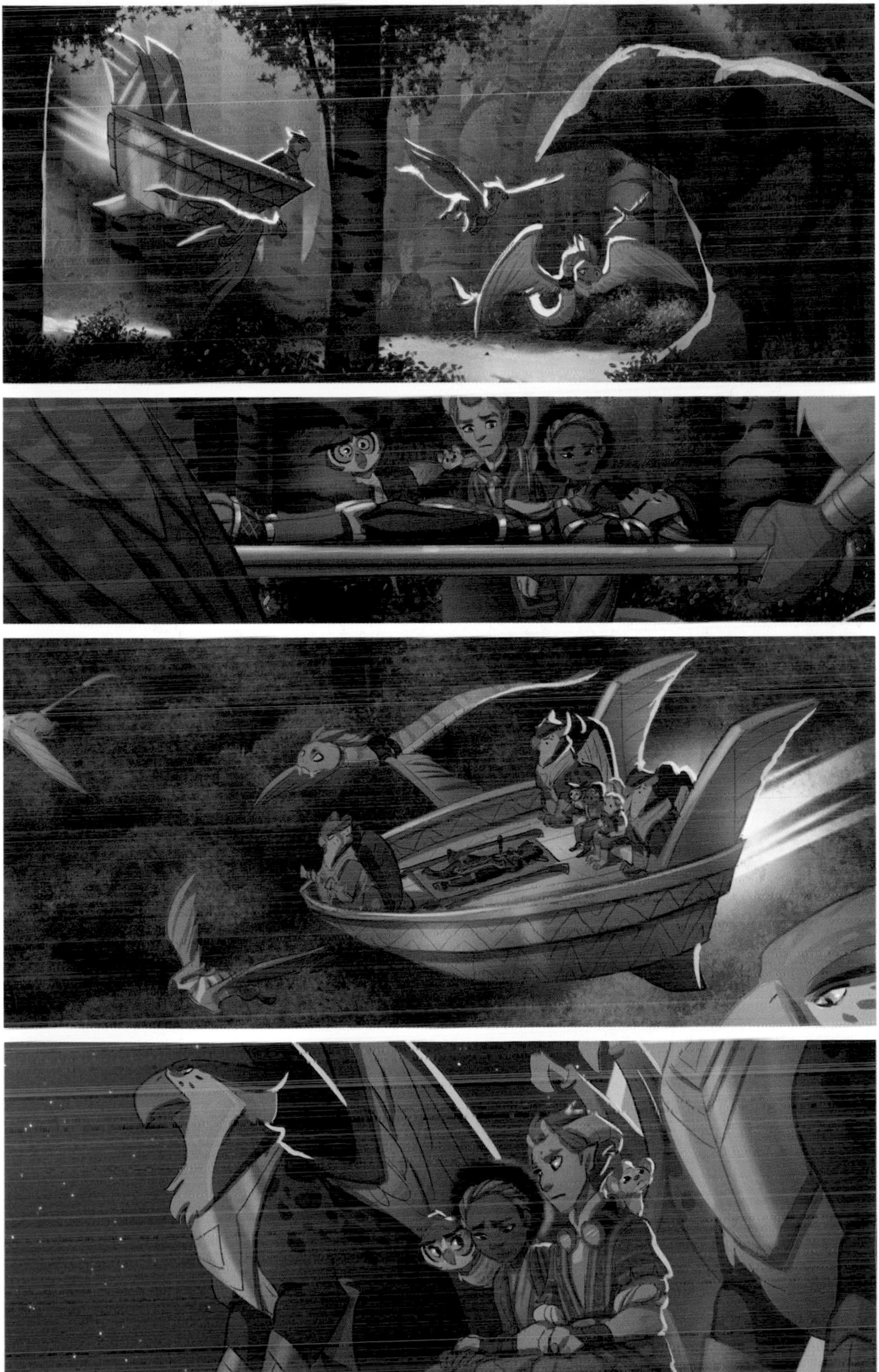

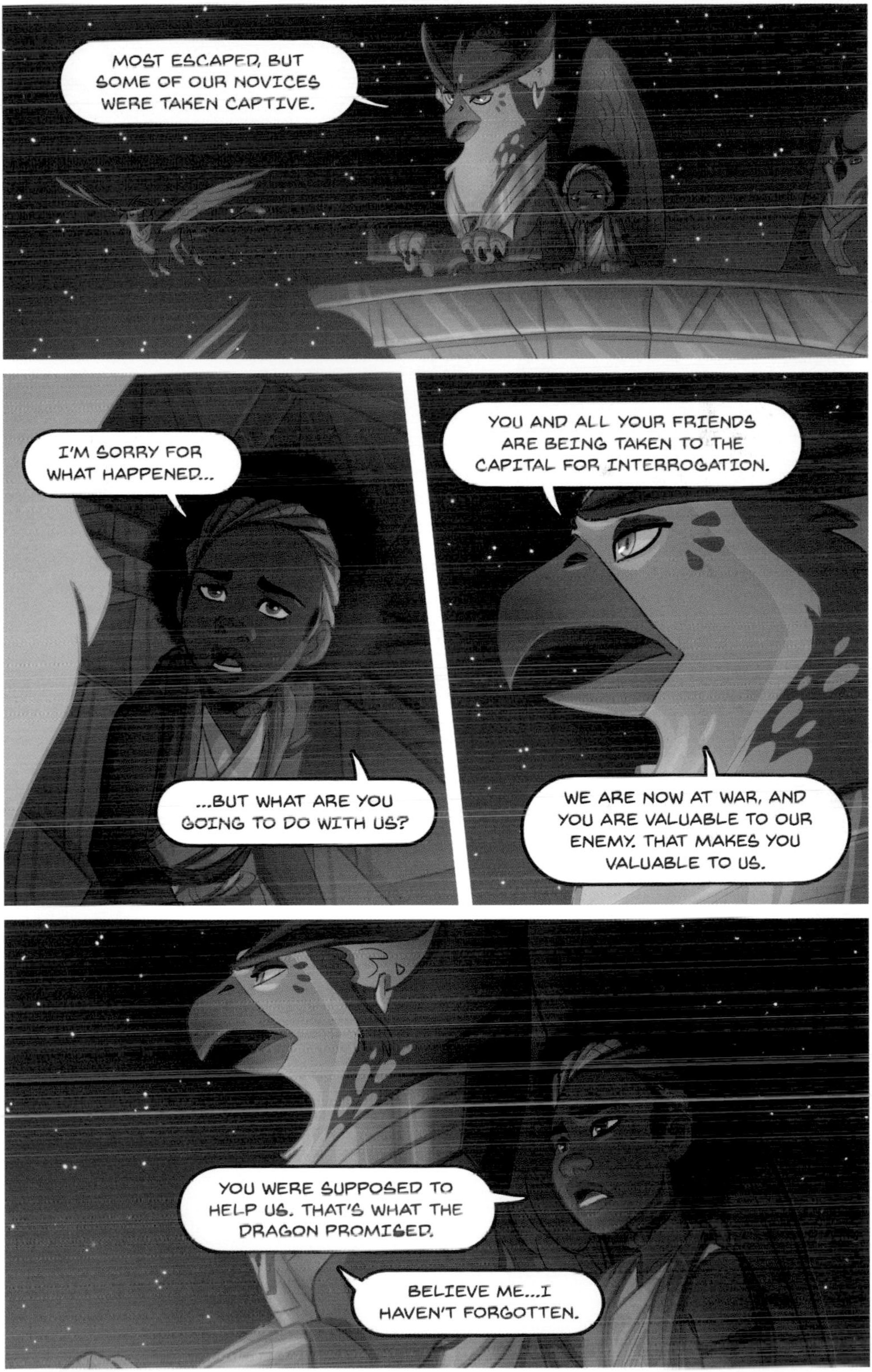
MOST ESCAPED, BUT SOME OF OUR NOVICES WERE TAKEN CAPTIVE.
I'M SORRY FOR WHAT HAPPENED...
...BUT WHAT ARE YOU GOING TO DO WITH US?
YOU AND ALL YOUR FRIENDS ARE BEING TAKEN TO THE CAPITAL FOR INTERROGATION.
WE ARE NOW AT WAR, AND YOU ARE VALUABLE TO OUR ENEMY. THAT MAKES YOU VALUABLE TO US.
YOU WERE SUPPOSED TO HELP US. THAT'S WHAT THE DRAGON PROMISED.
BELIEVE ME...I HAVEN'T FORGOTTEN.

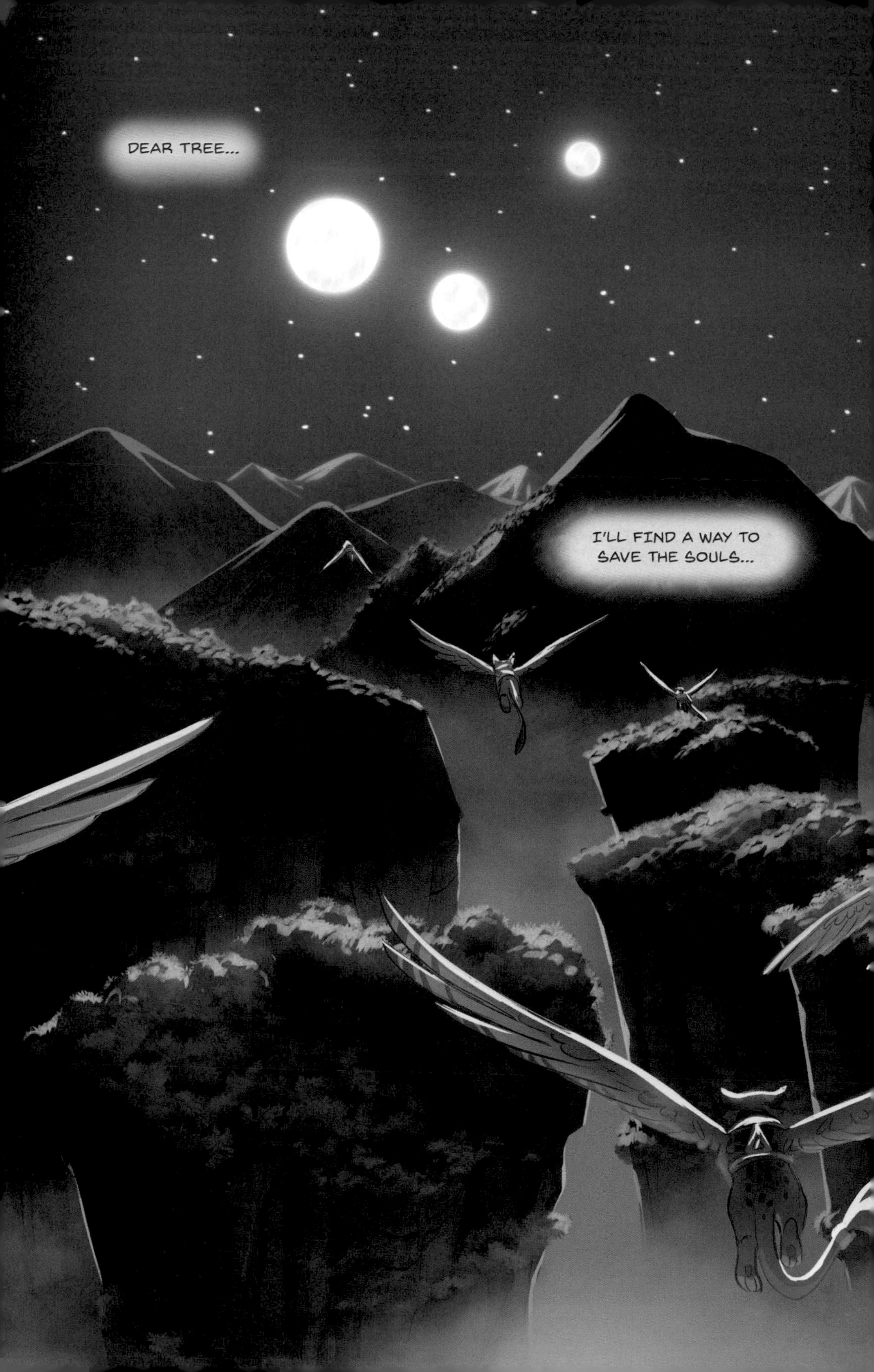
DEAR TREE...
I'LL FIND A WAY TO SAVE THE SOULS...

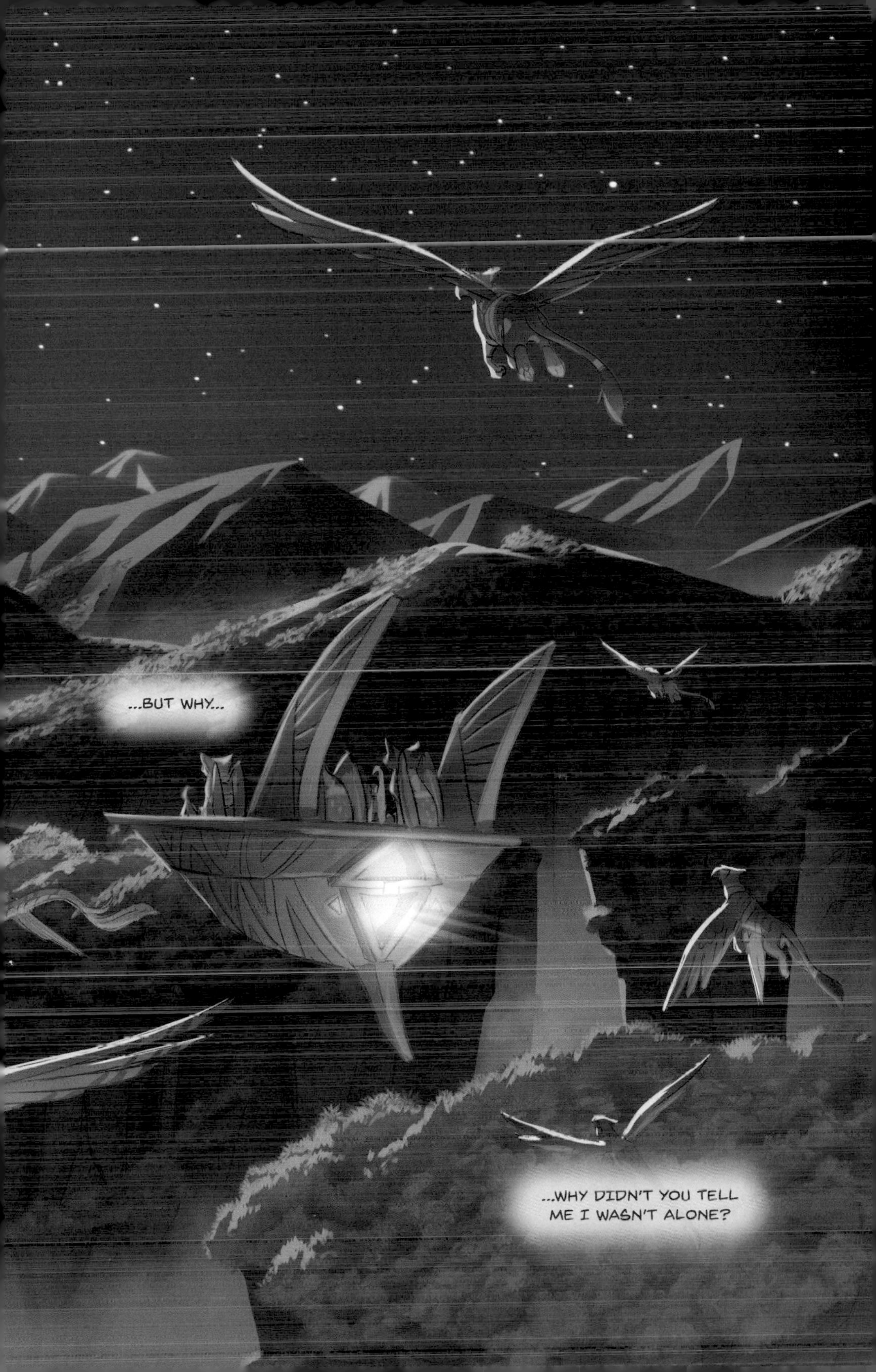
...BUT WHY...
...WHY DIDN'T YOU TELL ME I WASN'T ALONE?

ACKNOWLEDGMENTS

MARJORIE: First, for my cousin Maya. Many years ago, we would run into the woods surrounding our grandmother's house and search for fairies. We'd adventure for hours, climbing trees, living in other worlds. Now she's all grown-up, but those other worlds still exist—and I think we both still visit them. So, thank you, Maya—for being you, for all the wonderful days of being family together. Love you always.

And for my goddaughter India, as well—who asked for a book about a girl just like herself: brave and kind, who never gives up. I hope you see yourself in Zuli—and no, I haven't forgotten about the blue-haired pirate queen!

Finally, my deep gratitude and appreciation for Teny, who joined me on this journey into a new world, and brought it to life with tremendous vision and love.

TENY: The deepest of heartfelt thanks to the incomparable team at HarperCollins Publishers, whose incredible work, uplifting enthusiasm, collaborative spirit, saintly patience, and human compassion made the completion of this book a possibility. Andrew Eliopulos, Alexandra Cooper, Allison Weintraub, Erin Fitzsimmons, and David Curtis, you are nothing short of saints. An equally huge thank-you to Marjorie Liu, an absolute gem, for trusting me to bring her beautiful story to life and allowing me this opportunity to fall in love with this world. Thank you for your contagious enthusiasm, passion, kindness, compassion, collaboration, and beautiful spirit.

A million thanks to my beloved family. To my darling parents, Hilda and Nejdeh, thank you for your encouragement, optimism, and unshakable love and support. Thanks, Shawnt, bro, for your support and for asking me if I was finished every few weeks (ha!). Matt, my love, thank you for believing in me and reminding me that I could do it. Lana and Shogher, thank you for your emotional support through the darkest of days.

A monumental thank-you to my dearest friends—my Tenydo Studios crew—who have supported me in every way humanly possible throughout this challenging project. Your love and emotional support, especially through the hardest of days, kept my soul together and my spirit alive. Thank you for the daily video chat company, spontaneous food deliveries, jajangmyeon reserve, face masks, muscle creams, etc. You are the definition of true, unwavering friendship, my dazzling, award-winning, multidisciplinary Tenydo Studios: Susey Chang, Estella Tse, Grace Kum, Celine Kim, Jennifer Shang, Kellye Perdue, Kat Park, and Sylvia Lee.

And a shout-out to my entire awesome Armenian family, who are probably going to buy a copy of this graphic novel in support! Hello, Gretta morkoor, Sato, Silva, Lillian, Varand, Vahik, and everyone else! I love you all! Getseh Hye joghovoort!